D0997042

SHADOWS ON THE MOOR

When Amy Appleton starts working for Ben, a gloomy farmer with a tragic past, she tries desperately to cheer him up – but the cattle plague is raging, and his sheep are stolen. Meanwhile, the cheery, carefree Patrick falls in love with Amy but, as always, love's path never runs smooth. Now dark forces on the moor cast long shadows over their lives. Amy, Patrick and Ben all face death, unless the lurking evil can be overcome...

SHADOWS ON THE MOOR

SHADOWS ON THE MOOR

by

Ann Cliff

Magna Large Print Books
Long Preston, North Yorkshire,
BD23 4ND, England.

British Library Cataloguing in Publication Data.

Cliff, Ann
    Shadows on the moor.

    A catalogue record of this book is
    available from the British Library

    ISBN   978-0-7505-3529-8

First published in Great Britain 2010 by Robert Hale Limited

Copyright © Ann Cliff 2010

Cover illustration by arrangement with Robert Hale Ltd.

The right of Ann Cliff to be identified as the author of this work
has been asserted by her in accordance with the Copyright,
Designs and Patents Act, 1988

Published in Large Print 2012 by arrangement with
Robert Hale Limited

Magna Large Print is an imprint of Library Magna Books Ltd.

Printed and bound in Great Britain by
T.J. (International) Ltd., Cornwall, PL28 8RW

ONE

Masham, 1867

'What are you doing here? You're trespassing!' The harsh voice cut through the evening. A velvet, golden sunset light lay over the little fields and the landscape was at peace. Amy had hoped that the farmer would be indoors and busy with his evening meal, but here he was, glaring at her over a hedge. She looked round, but the bluebell wood was too far away for her to disappear into the bushes. There was no escape.

'I'm Amy Appleton, I just wanted to see whether the bluebells are out yet,' Amy explained, feeling embarrassed. 'I used to live here, you see.' Before her father died they had farmed this land, the familiar fields that she was now trespassing upon. She had thought of the farm as belonging to the Appletons. 'I thought you wouldn't mind if I walk this way sometimes?' Walkers had always been welcome at Banks Farm in her father's day, provided they kept to the paths and shut gates behind them; her father had said the river path was an ancient right of way. The land lay beside the River Ure and the Masham folks loved to walk there on a warm evening. She tried not to look at the man's gun, which was pointing in her direction. No doubt he was after rabbits, but he shouldn't hold it like that. He ought to know about gun safety.

'Bluebells? Well, they're not flowering and you can forget about them. It's not easy here, you know, what with losing sheep and the cattle plague. I won't have people running wild over this land, spreading disease, leaving gates open and lord knows what else. So you can go home, right now.' The man was tall, with dark hair and a very dark frown.

Nobody seemed to know where the new tenant had come from, but he didn't sound like a local lad. They had been told that he was a young man and Amy had hoped he would be pleasant, somebody you could talk to. If he had a wife she might turn out to be a friend and then Amy would be able to visit sometimes. This man was a disappointment, so grim he looked quite old. He wore well-cut riding breeches and carried himself well, but the set of his wide shoulders was somehow unfriendly.

Amy stood still and the man waved his gun again in her direction, but she didn't flinch. Of course he wouldn't shoot, unless he was mad. 'And you can tell that to anybody else that thinks of coming down here. Tell them that I've a gun and can use it, I'm sick of losing sheep because some idiot leaves a gate open.' The deep voice was almost a growl.

'Some idiot leaves a gate open? Masham folks didn't ever do that when I lived here.' Amy waited but there was no response from the scowling figure with the gun.

It was time to go home. The sun was slowly dropping out of sight behind the moors to the west, the familiar sweep of high land that Amy loved. All the colour was draining from the fields and woods on each side of the river; the valley was now a place of long shadows. Did the man really mean what he said? Amy shivered in a sudden breeze off the river. 'But I'm one of your new neighbours.' She looked up at him. 'It's hard at the start for you ... but I know farming, I won't do any harm, Mr – er...' The man shook his head impatiently. 'Surely you could let me in? The rinderpest has died down now, anyway. The danger's over, they say.' Maybe she could talk him round.

The man lowered the shotgun at last and glared at Amy. 'You know nothing about it. Last November we thought so, but this month it's back in Yorkshire again and it's heading this way. Now, get off this land before I march you off.' The voice was quiet but harsh and the looming face as he came nearer was even harsher. The new tenant was strong and muscular and could have picked her up easily. 'I don't care if you lived here. Your day is over now, and don't you forget it.'

Amy stood up very straight and faced him squarely for one last try. 'I can help you with the lambs, I used to save most of them when we–'

'Get out!' the farmer shouted and the gun came up again. This man would make no friends in Masham. Deliberately Amy turned and walked slowly back along the river path until she reached the stone bridge that crossed the public road. Once on the road she was safe. She looked back and saw the man was staring after her. What had the agent been thinking of, to let Banks Farm to such a misery?

Leaving the farm had been terrible; Amy had lived there all her life and she had not yet recovered from the shock. There had been no alternative. Her mother had no heart for taking the tenancy once her husband died and His Lordship much preferred a male tenant, although he was said to be kind to widows and orphans. The land was still there, it was just the same as always; bats flitted through the dusk and from the wood came the sleepy twitter of birds going to roost. It was time to go back to her grandmother's house in the town. There was nowhere to call home as yet.

A horse was clopping along the road,

moving at a brisk walk In the twilight Amy could see that it was the estate agent, Mr Russell on his big bay. To her surprise the agent dismounted and walked beside Amy. 'That's better! I've ridden all the way from Pateley, I could do with a walk. Now, Amy, how goes it with you, lass? It will be hard to settle down... I'm still looking out for an estate cottage for you and your mother, but nothing has come up as yet. Except the old bakery. That's been empty for years, but it's not in very good repair. I dare say your ma wouldn't want the place.' His big red face beamed with goodwill. Mr Russell had been very kind to them since Father died. He was a Masham lad and understood the local ways.

'The new man – I don't know his name – he told me to leave and not to go back, I can't walk by the river any more. He pointed a gun at me.' Amy was still indignant.

Russell shook his heavy head. 'Ben Yardley will be a good tenant, I think, but he has a lot of worries just now. They call him a recluse already, but there's the plague about, you see, and it seems likely that disease can be carried by people ... maybe on their boots. I'm not sure whether I believe in these new-fangled germs myself, you can't see them, but that's what they say and young Benjamin believes it.' He paused. 'And Ben should know better than to go after rabbits with a

11

gun, without landlord's permission. It's too easy to go from rabbits to His Lordship's pheasants, and that would put cat among the pigeons!' The agent laughed heartily. 'I happen to know his family ... he's not the poaching type, they're very respectable. But he needs to set a good example.'

'I think he may be right, though,' Amy said reluctantly. 'Last time the plague was here, Mr Fryer from Bedale told us what to do, and it worked. The cows were all healthy right through. We used a lot of carbolic, kept everything very clean. But we didn't stop folks from the town walking by the river... Maybe we should have thought of it. The cows were not down there at that time.' Mr Yardley had been very unpleasant, but he had right on his side.

'Mr Fryer's reckoned to be a good veterinary, he'd give you the right advice.'

Amy nodded; Mr Fryer was a local hero. 'Where did Mr Yardley come from, do you know?' Amy had never seen him before and she knew most of the local people.

'He had a smaller place, down near York. He kept a few sheep ... and did other things.' He looked uncomfortable for a moment. 'He'll need to learn about our kind of farming, won't he? Well, I'd better be getting home to Maisie.' The agent climbed into the saddle. Amy watched him clatter off down the street and then turned with a sigh into the lane leading to her grandmother's house. Ben Yardley evidently had a lot to learn, if he came from the rich land on the Vale of York. This was a different world and a different climate. Strangely enough, the folks at Masham didn't like to be threatened with a gun. Somebody should tell Mr Yardley that fact.

Coming in from the cool evening, the little house in town seemed overheated and stuffy. Amy's mother Molly was knitting by the lamp and her grandmother was nodding in her chair next to the fire. She woke when she heard the door close. 'You've been raking about again? Should be ashamed, it's not ladylike to go out at this time of night. If you're looking for a lad, that's not the way to go about it.'

'I went out earlier ... I needed a walk,' Amy said wearily. 'I finished my stockings before I went. I've met the new man at Banks Farm, Gran.'

The old lady looked up, eager for information. 'And what's he like, then? Is he a decent God-fearing body?'

At least they were off the subject of Amy's shortcomings. 'Tall, dark and nasty. He's horrible.' She glanced at her mother, but the rather stern face was closed.

'Must finish another pair tonight, carrier'll be here tomorrow with more wool,' was all she said. Molly Appleton was trying to earn

13

their living, or part of it, from knitting stockings and Amy was knitting her share. Molly evidently did not want to think about the farm.

'Do you need to work so hard, Mother? We had a good sale, the farm money isn't all gone yet.' Farm prices had been good for the last few years.

Molly and Gran looked at each other and Amy sensed that between them hung an unspoken question. Would the restless girl be married soon and off their hands? Or would she buckle down and go into service? Molly put down her knitting. 'Not yet, lass, but brass will soon be gone if we don't earn some more. Your father always said we should never spend capital, and he was right. Now, if you was to ask the housekeeper at the Park, you might be lucky. They might take you on to train and you'd learn a lot about service.' Molly looked knowing; she must have been talking to someone at the Park.

'I learned a lot about farming...' Amy began, taking off her shawl and trying to smooth down her curly fair hair. Domestic service would be like prison.

'It looks very like as you're running after a farm lad. Nay, you'd best forget about farming, unless you're going to wed a farmer and even then, he might not like a forward lass who'll give him advice about crops and stock.' Gran was on her favourite theme

14

again. 'Aye, it was a pity you had to work with your dad, with no lad in the family, but it's no job for a decent lass, that it isn't. Why, you dress like a gypsy, just look at you! All farmers I know would seek a biddable lass that could cook and clean, not one as wears big boots and strides about land. Forget about farming I say, it's over with now.' Gran sat back, happy to have proved her point. She was a small woman with an iron will and firm opinions on everything. Amy tried to be dutiful, but Gran was hard to love. The old lass had hated farming and was sorry that her daughter had married a farmer. Her husband, Mothers' dad, Ernie Lowther, had been a blacksmith. Amy smiled to herself as she wondered what they would have said if she'd wanted to follow in Ernie's footsteps, instead of her father's side of the family. The Appletons had always been farmers, until Dad died.

Forget about farming! Might as well tell her not to breathe. It was a strange feeling that drew Amy out of doors to the woods and fields, drew her these days to look long-ingly over the hedges at other people's cows and sheep. She always knew the phase of the moon and the state of the crops ... but she was a girl and often her interest wasn't understood. It was not the first time that someone had said she was meeting a lad because she walked by the river. If only, she thought wistfully, there was a lad in Masham worth meeting.

Amy was lost without the farm and it drew her back, time and again. But surely a woman could run a farm, with her experience and some good labourers – and money, of course. It always came back to money. Gran wouldn't let a penny of their precious capital go into a farm.

Molly looked uncomfortable, but she agreed with Gran. 'It's true, Amy love. A spell at the Park, they entertain royalty, you know, it would set you up for life, I'm sure of it. Smarten you up a bit. Maids all wear the same, neat little black dresses and white caps and aprons...' She turned back to her knitting, realizing that Amy was not listening.

'Smarten you up, and not before time,' Gran put in. 'Look at the hem of your dress, now. A stitch in time saves nine!' She cackled. Another little victory for Gran. Smartening up had no appeal. As long as you were clean and tidy, what did it matter how you dressed?

Amy stood at the back of the room, as far away from the heat of the fire as she could and she hoped her mother couldn't see her expression. Poor Ma, she had tried so hard to dress up her daughter in ribbons and bows, without success. But it was no good arguing. Least said, soonest mended ... she was begin-

16

ning to think in Gran's little sayings. 'I'll go to bed now, goodnight,' she muttered, lit a candle and went up the creaking stairs to the attic under the roof that was all she had to call her own. Of course they were trying to help her, but what could she say? Working at the Park with a gaggle of chattering maids would be hell.

Cool night air flowed in through the open window and Amy leaned gratefully on the sill. Masham was a small town, but even so the town's lights hid the stars. Why was Gran so hard on her only granddaughter? They couldn't have it both ways. If she had been chasing the lads, surely she wouldn't have gone out looking like a gypsy?

Somewhere far away an owl called and beyond, the river would be flowing on in the dark, murmuring over stones and hurrying down to Ripon on its long journey to the sea. Then the moon would rise; she had loved to watch the moon rise over the river when they lived at Banks Farm. What could a girl do with her life? If she had been born Arthur instead of Amy – she knew that was what they had hoped for – she could have taken the tenancy of their farm or gone off to find work. But a 'decent' young woman, Gran kept telling her, must stick to home and housekeeping. It wasn't fair.

The beamed attic ceiling seemed to press down on Amy as she turned from the window. It was time to take charge of her life, as much as any lass could manage it. After her father died there had been months of organizing, arranging a sale of stock and equipment, sorting out what they could keep – there had been no time to think about the future. Her mother had been exhausted by grief and seemed quite happy to settle down with Gran, but it was no life for Amy and only now did she realize that she faced an empty future, unless she could make something happen.

Working with Father, buying and selling, Amy had learned the simple rules of good business. You made sure that you knew the current value of everything you bought and sold, so that you got and paid a fair price. You didn't start a new venture until you had worked out the costs and returns, although with farming, you could never be sure. A bad harvest would ruin all your careful sums in a couple of weeks of bad weather, or the cattle plague... Best not think about it.

She hopped into the little narrow bed and felt the lumpy mattress sag under her weight. People always put their old beds in the attic. Amy was quite small and slim, but the bed protested every time she got into it. Lying with eyes closed, far from sleepy, her thoughts raced on. So yes, she knew a lot about cattle and sheep and a little about business. Farming was out of the question, but what else could a young woman do? Knitting socks was not well paid; it was all her mother had been able to think of. The carriers brought the wool in bundles known as 'bumps' and they dealt with families in the Dales because folks nearer the big towns could earn better money elsewhere. Men, women and children knitted in Masham, often as they walked along the road. The only time some of them stopped was for church, because Vicar didn't like the clicking of needles.

A servant's life was almost the only choice for Amy. Perhaps she could find a job in a dairy where they wanted help with butter and cheese making? There was a dairy here in Masham, but it was run by a family with plenty of children to help with the work. Then there was a small bakery on the way out of town, but nobody liked their stuff, it was made on the cheap with poor quality flour and few eggs... Wait a minute: a bakery. Mr Russell had mentioned the old bakery in Silver Street that had been empty and neglected for – well, for as long as Amy could remember. She'd walked past it for years without thinking of it.

Now, could she and Ma start a bakery? They would be competing with the other one, of course, but Masham was full of country folks on market days and a lot of farm women might welcome the chance to buy good fresh bread and cakes as a change from making everything themselves. Then there were summer visitors to the Yorkshire Dales, hearty hikers with big appetites who would buy pies and scones. And there were folks who hired a cottage for the summer, artists and writers. Amy smiled in the dark; this was an idea.

Well, just suppose Mr Russell agreed to let them rent the old bakery, what sort of a deal could they arrange? I could ask for a year's free rent in return for cleaning the place up, she told herself. Amy was an expert with a whitewash brush and had even carried out simple building repairs at the old farm, taught by her father, who had never spared her because she was a girl.

At the end of an hour Amy had the business up and running in her head and went to sleep happier than she had been since they had come to live with Gran.

Morning brought early mist and Amy went out as soon as she could, saying she would collect the milk from the dairy. By the old bakery she lingered and tried to peer through grime-encrusted windows and festoons of spiders' webs across the tiny panes of the shopfront. The place must have been empty for at least ten years; she could hardly remember a bakery here. Glancing up, she saw that the slate roof seemed to be sound. A thought occurred to her; there would be a back entrance somewhere. There was no one about as she slipped down a narrow alley and walked along until she judged she was level with the bakery.

Masham was built in stone, some of it mellow sandstone, but this street was ancient and built of a dark grey gritstone that made it look forbidding. Shivering a little in the foggy air, Amy pushed gently at an old wooden yard door and it yielded; the latch had rusted away. This must be the bakery. Now this really was trespassing, she thought guiltily. Why had the estate let it fall into this neglect? She went cautiously into the yard. An old lilac bush had grown out into the space and from under it a black cat jumped out with a yell, making her catch her breath. But there was a clear way to the back door after all, and strangely, the door opened when she turned the knob and swung inwards easily. Too easily; there was something going on here. Instead of the damp and musty smell she expected, the air was warm and in fact there was a hint of wood smoke. The windows at this side of the building were clean.

Amy trod carefully across a scullery and noted that the floor was swept. The next room would be a kitchen ... and there was a pleasant fire on the hearth. The room was freshly whitewashed and there was a crusty loaf of bread on the table. Crouched by the

21

fire was a slim figure, holding a slice of bread impaled on a toasting fork. Amy held her breath and stood quite still.

Looking over his shoulder the young man said cheerfully, 'Have you breakfasted yet? You might like a piece of toast. Cut another slice of bread, please.' He turned back to his task.

TWO

'But I've invaded ... why don't you throw me out?' Amy looked at his back. His hair was a coppery colour and rather long, but he looked young and quite clean, not like one of those men who tramped the road looking for work. Was he an escaped prisoner, evading capture? But no, prisoners had their hair cut short. She decided to stay, to find out more about this mysterious person. 'I thought the place was empty and I just wanted a look at the bakery.'

'Everybody thinks it's empty, Miss.' The lad looked at her cheerfully as though he didn't mind being discovered. The toast was brown and he put it on a plate, then turned his attention to the slice that Amy had cut. 'I must say, I haven't had a guest before. Pass the butter, it's on the table.' Her host looked over at her, his blue eyes crinkling in a smile.

'I shouldn't stay, you know. It's not proper.' What would Gran say if she knew? But soon Amy was sitting at the table eating toast and drinking tea, looking round at the room. The window looked over a tiny garden and she could see rows of spring vegetables peeping from the moist earth. From the rafters hung a large ham and through an open door she could see a well stocked pantry. The blue eyes were fixed on her and Amy looked down in confusion. She had wrapped up against the morning fog, but her old brown shawl was damp now and she felt shabby. Perhaps she did need to smarten up, after all. The lad opposite was plainly dressed in country clothes, but he was clean and very neat.

They ate toast in silence and Amy felt she should say something. Did this mean that it was too late to make plans for the bakery? Putting down her teacup, she looked over the table. 'Pardon me for asking, it's none of my business. But if you've rented the building, why don't you clean it all up and use the front as well?'

'Because I like people to think it's empty. I only need a couple of rooms, so I cleaned them up and left the rest. I – I'm lying low for a while.' He smiled mysteriously and Amy noticed he had very white teeth.

'You are lucky, I'd love to do that myself,'

Amy found herself saying. 'My Gran knows what's good for me and tells me every day...' she tailed off, feeling disloyal, but the lad nodded sympathetically.

'Exactly. So does my mother! It must be worse for a girl, of course. But my mother – she's a dear soul but she has set her heart on sending me off to train as a clergyman. Her brother's in the Church ... she thinks it's the thing.' He had an attractive laugh.

'So, your mother doesn't know you're here.' Amy laughed a little herself. He looked quite old enough to be out without his mother, probably in his early twenties, about the same age as Amy.

The lad shook his head. 'She lives in Ripon, she'll soon find out if you tell anyone you've seen me.'

'Of course I won't!' Amy said impulsively. 'I could help you, maybe ... bring things in for you, to save you going out.' Already, she was planning to come here again. Was it forward of her? Gran would heartily disapprove.

'I go out when the town is busy, so they think I'm a visitor. I'm not likely to be noticed, Miss–' he stopped. 'We haven't been introduced,' he said, in such a good mutation of a lady's refined tones that it might have been his mother speaking. 'My name's Patrick Seaton.' He paused. 'My father was the organist at Ripon Cathedral, the whole family is involved with the Church.'

'So they want you to follow on,' Amy nodded. She stood up to go; her own family would be waiting anxiously for her by now. 'And what do you yourself want to do with your life, Patrick? My name's Amy.'

Patrick stood up himself and bowed slightly. 'Very pleased to meet you, Miss Amy. What do I want to do? I want to be a farmer.' He smiled ruefully. 'I planned to come here and find a farmer who would teach me all about it and then try to get hold of some of the family money to buy or rent a farm. It's a long term prospect, I know.'

'That's a sound idea,' Amy reassured him.

'But I'd reckoned without the cattle plague. You can't get onto a farm now, or speak to a farmer. They don't want to see strangers at all.'

'I know,' Amy said wistfully. 'I was seen off a farm myself last night. I used to live on a farm, but my father died. I'd love to be a farmer myself, but you need money and you need to be a man!' She stood up. 'It's time to go, I'm late with the milk.'

'Come again soon, little Amy,' Patrick said softly as she opened the door and Amy felt very warm under her shawl. If only Percy looked at her like that!

'I will. In spite of Gran! I'll see you soon, Patrick. It's an Irish name – are you Irish?' She wanted to know more about him.

'An Irish grandfather. To be sure, it's me

that has the blarney!' Patrick was laughing quietly as they went down the yard. 'Not a word to anyone, mind.'

A butcher's shop was next to the dairy and as she went by, Amy noticed a paper in the window.

WANTED – a dairymaid. Experience necessary. Good wages. Apply within. Guiltily, she picked up the milk and sped down the street with her can, ready for trouble when she reached home. Did she want to be a dairymaid? It depended on whether the job was on a farm. It was probably the dairy here in town that needed help, although why not put the notice in their own window? It was not much of a job, really, sloshing about in water all day. Better forget about it.

'That took a long time, Amy.' Gran looked over her spectacles. 'The early bird catches the worm, you know. We're waiting for the milk.'

'You'll have to smarten up if you want to get a place, I've told you often enough,' was her mother's contribution. The older women were waiting round the table so that Amy could feel how late she was with the milk. After a breakfast of porridge, Molly Appleton went out with her bag of knitted socks to meet the carrier on the square, while Amy dutifully swept and dusted the house, watched by a critical grandmother. She peeled potatoes for dinner, wondering what her mother would bring home; with money from the carrier she would buy the meat.

Molly was back by mid morning. 'Here's some lamb's liver, put it in the pantry. Now Amy, you go straight round to the butcher and ask about that job in the window. And tidy yourself lass, before you go.' Ma had seen the notice too; Amy would not be able to ignore it.

'Yes, Ma.' She had intended to wash and change, but it was irritating to be told to do it. Maybe this was why spinsters were so sour? Living with your older relations, kept in your place and told what to do year after year would take all the joy out of life.

But where was the alternative? The Park, of course, to be kept in your place by the upper servants.

The butcher was slicing ham while talking to a customer when Amy went in. 'Nay, Missus, there's no cattle plague in Masham and none on the meat. All our beasts are home killed and fresh, don't you worry about that.' She had to wait her turn, but she got little information. When she asked about the job, the butcher shrugged. 'Dunno who it is. Woman said she'd be at the King's Head on market day, you're to ask for Mrs Shaw.' Amy didn't know any Mrs Shaw.

Market day in Masham was Wednesday, the following day, so there was not long to wait. Clean and brushed once more, her yellow curly hair strained back severely under a bonnet, Amy wandered through the market, enjoying the bustle and good humour. She waved to Daisy on the vegetable stall and fingered the rolls of dress material on another, trying to put off the interview, but then she thought it would be best to get it over with. She crossed the cobbles to the stone front of the King's Head and stepped rather fearfully into the inn. It was dark after the spring sunshine outside and the passage had many doors. Amy shivered and thought of going home.

A chambermaid went past, carrying a tray. 'Mrs Shaw? She's in there, just knock, love,' she said with an encouraging grin. 'You're the third to go in today.' Heart beating, Amy knocked on the door and after a pause, it opened.

A tall woman went across to stand in the window, straight backed against the light. At first Amy thought she looked like a dragon, but there was the hint of a twinkle in the dark eyes and her low voice was pleasant. 'Come in, don't be shy, girl. Sit down here, and tell me what you can do. I am Katherine Shaw, I'm looking for a dairymaid and I expect you are hoping for a place.'

Amy sat down in the chair indicated and the woman took her place across the table. The face and even the hat were vaguely familiar; where had she seen Mrs Shaw before? Of

28

course, at church, but only for the last few weeks. She must be new to the area. 'I'm Amy Appleton,' she began, sitting up straight with her hands folded in her lap. 'I can make butter and cheese, and milk cows too. We had a farm, before my father died.' I'm not just a farm servant, she wanted to add, I'm a farmer.

Mrs Shaw smiled slightly. 'How old are you, Amy? Twenty-two? Old enough to be married. Have you a sweetheart in mind?'

Amy shook her head. 'No, ma'am.' No use mentioning Percy, her sole admirer because she would rather die than marry stuffy, righteous Percy, although he came to tea often on a Sunday, encouraged by Gran. Maybe the woman wanted to be sure that her new dairymaid wouldn't be flighty, or run off to get married after a few months. 'No one in mind.' There had been few chances of meeting a possible husband when she worked at home on the farm; she would soon be an old maid.

There was a silence and they looked at each other. Mrs Shaw seemed unsure of how to go on and Amy suddenly felt some sympathy; perhaps she should make it easier for her. 'Round here we make small white cheeses, not really hard cheese and we make good butter. Some folks call the cheese Wensleydale. And sometimes I made a cream cheese to sell at Christmas.'

'Tell me about your farm.' Mrs Shaw leaned forward slightly.

Amy told her story without interruption, about how they had kept Shorthorn cattle and various breeds of sheep, a few pigs and several working horses including a Welsh cob to pull the trap. They had a few customers for milk, but most of it was made into dairy products. She tried not to remember the farm sale, when all their animals had been sold off and she had cried hopelessly, walking away so she didn't have to see them go.

Mrs Shaw looked thoughtful. 'What would you say is the most important thing to remember in the dairy?'

Well, that was a hard question. There were so many things to remember and if you got one of them wrong, you could ruin a whole batch of milk. The pigs had not seen very much spoiled milk at Banks Farm. 'Everything's important, Mrs Shaw. My mother taught me to do things the way she'd been shown when she was young, I suppose it's a tradition. But to pick one important thing ... you have to keep the milk clean, right from the start. If there's dirt in the milk, you can't make good butter or cheese.' She looked over the table. 'Is that what you wanted me to say?'

The woman laughed. 'I'll be honest, Amy. I want to set up a dairy, but I don't know the work. So I am looking for someone who knows enough to work on her own, and perhaps to teach me the ... management side of things, selling the produce. Are you the woman for the job? You are rather small and young, I feel.'

Amy looked down at her small self. She had always envied buxom dairymaids who could handle heavy weights. Since they left the farm she had kept healthy by walking for miles, in trouble with Gran for going out too much and 'raking about.' But she wouldn't be put down by this woman who didn't know dairy work. Looking directly across the table she said strongly, 'My Ma won prizes at Leyburn Show with her butter, so I reckon I was taught right.' That seemed to impress, so she went on. 'I can work on my own, of course I can. But–' it was time to ask a few questions herself. 'Are you on a farm, Mrs Shaw, or have you bought a village dairy? You see, I miss the farm, I'd rather a farm dairy if I had the choice.' There, she'd probably lost the job by opening her mouth too often. Amy blushed and looked down at her hands. Town and village dairies bought their milk from farms and operated like little factories. In the bigger towns they kept cows indoors all the year round, the poor sad things never seeing a grass field or sitting in the sun. But why would anyone take on a business that they didn't understand?

31

'I have decided not to reveal the location until I appoint someone,' Mrs Shaw said quietly. 'If you are at church on Sunday, I will tell you of my decision then.' The precise way of speaking reminded Amy of a schoolmistress. Somehow, Mrs Shaw didn't seem to fit in a dairy.

The interview was soon over after that. Amy had to think of two righteous citizens of importance in Masham who might be persuaded to give her a character reference. She suggested the Vicar and Mr Russell the agent; it was a good job her Gran wouldn't be asked to vouch for Amy Appleton's morals. Then she was free to skip over to see Daisy, who had sold most of her vegetables and herbs. 'I've been for an interview. For a dairy place,' she told her friend.

'Well, you was bright enough at school, Amy. I always thought you would do right well,' Daisy said generously. 'Good luck, I hope you get it and that it's not too far from here.' Then she stopped smiling and shook her head sadly. 'But Amy, think on, don't rush into it. She might be from one o' those places over the moor, where you never see nobody from one week to the other. You'd have to live in, you'd be buried up there and how could you meet a decent husband then, I ask you?' Her face was tragic at the thought of such a fate.

Amy considered. 'I've seen the woman at

church, so she must live fairly near – moorland folk have their own church. As for a husband, I'm not too keen on promising to obey anybody. I've had enough ordering about at home.' She laughed. 'Not like you, Daisy, you've got your future all planned and your man picked out – he'll likely have to obey you. Does he know yet?'

Daisy giggled. 'I think he's getting the message,' she admitted as she weighed potatoes for a customer. Amy looked across and saw that it was Patrick, the young man who lived in the bakery.

'Good day, Miss Amy,' the lad said easily and they chatted for a few moments about the weather and the chances of a good harvest later in the year; Patrick sounded like a farmer already.

Daisy looked at him curiously and when he had wandered off with his potatoes, she turned to Amy. 'Friend of yours? You're a dark horse, lass! Now there's a nice looking lad.'

'Er ... I met him the other day.' There wasn't much more she could say about Patrick.

Sunday morning was wet and Amy splashed through puddles on her way to the little church at the far side of the square. Gran had been feeling shivery with cold and so Ma had stayed at home with her for company. They were both very keen to see the young hope of the Appletons well turned out to meet her future employer, but Amy pointed out that she might not get the place. 'Or I might not want it, Ma.'

'What do you mean?' Molly asked sharply. She settled Amy's Sunday coat more becomingly on her shoulders and gave the collar a little shake, with a gesture that was half love and half impatience. Appletons rarely showed any affection.

Gran clucked and tutted. 'You might at least give it a try. Nothing ventured, nothing gained.'

'If it's to board with the family, there won't be as much money for you,' Amy pointed out patiently on her way to the door. 'I'd best take a job where I can come home at night and share my wages. Live-in maids only get paid once or twice a year and as far as I can see, they mostly work for their keep.' And they get shut away on the moor for months at a time, she added to herself. Daisy had been right about that.

As she walked demurely to church, Amy wondered what would become of her. The future to her was as dark as the raggy clouds flying over the church spire.

The vicar's sermon was long and Amy had to resist the temptation to wriggle like a child as she waited for the service to end. Mrs Shaw was there, calm and composed, giving nothing away. At long last the congregation made their way out into the chilly air and suddenly Mrs Shaw was standing in front of her. 'Good morning, Amy. Would you like to walk across the square with me?' They were out of earshot of the rest before she stopped and looked at Amy. 'You seem to be of good character, according to the Vicar. I will offer you the position of dairymaid for three months in the first instance,' she announced formally. 'After that, we will see whether the arrangement suits us both, and also whether there is enough work for you.' She paused. 'Do you accept?'

The next three months would be the busiest in a dairy because most of the cows calved in spring and the fresh grass meant a flush of milk. They might make use of her, learn what she had to teach them and then dismiss her. Should she accept? 'Perhaps you'd tell me where it is?' All this mystery was silly. But the woman waited, her mouth firmly closed. She was not going to say anything until Amy accepted the place. And once she accepted, what tiny bit of freedom she had would be gone. Amy took a deep breath. 'Very well, I accept.' She couldn't help adding, 'But unless you tell me where the dairy is I won't be able to find it.'

Mrs Shaw pursed her lips. She looked sterner today than she had at the interview, but Amy decided to keep a small piece of freedom inside her, the right to say what she thought. 'Not far from here. We are by the river, at Banks Farm.'

Amy didn't know whether to laugh or cry. It was bad enough to think of strangers on 'their' farm, but to see them there every day would be a severe trial. Even worse, the farmer was a misery; she disliked Mr Yardley and it seemed that most of Masham would too, if he stopped them walking on the river path.

'Yes, I know where it is.' Amy was thinking furiously; should she change her mind? *There's many a slip 'twixt cup and lip* ... but the thought of being cooped up in the little house with Gran's incessant proverbs decided her and, of course, the money that would help them all. 'I can start tomorrow, if you like.' The rain was clearing away and there was a patch of blue sky above the river; perhaps it was a good omen.

The rest of the day passed like a dream as Amy tried to get used to her new position. Gran and Ma were quite impressed, although they said she should have asked about the wages; how much, and how often, and did she have a clean and ironed working dress and apron and where were her farm boots?

Percy, sitting with his feet together under the tea table, disagreed. 'In my experience,' he began weightily and Amy sighed inwardly, 'it is better not to mention money until you are established and they know what you can do.'

'What is your experience, Percy?' Amy asked mischievously. As far as she could see he was a lump of a lad with no imagination, whose life had been planned by his mother and involved nothing more adventurous than selling groceries in his father's shop. This year Percy had been promoted from a bicycle to a horse and trap for deliveries, and he seemed to feel far more important since then. Gran and Ma thought Percy Coldbeck would make a good, solid huband for Amy and would curb her wild tendencies. That was also his own opinion, but his mother had grave doubts about Amy's flightiness. One other thing stood in their way: Amy herself, strangely indifferent to his charms. It was Gran's chief complaint against her.

'Now, Amy, you are a tease,' the lump said indulgently and patted her hand in a patronising way. Molly passed him another scone and nothing more was said, but Amy wondered wearily how she could ever discourage a young man who smiled whatever she said to him, without actually hitting him on the head. Perhaps if she worked at the dairy on Sundays, she might avoid these boring meals.

Eight o'clock on Monday morning and a mist was rising from the river. Amy strode down the familiar track, its hedges decked in May blossom above the bright green grass of spring. She noted small differences: a gate widened here, a new fence there. They were improvements no doubt, but they were reminders that time had moved on at Banks Farm since she left it at the end of a bleak autumn. This time, Mr Yardley might be more normal and if he didn't mention that they had met before, Amy decided to forget the episode with the gun.

The farmer was in the yard when she arrived, opening the cowshed door and Mrs Shaw was coming out of the house. When he saw Amy, Yardley stopped dead. 'No!' he said, with a look of disgust on his dark face. 'What were you thinking of, Kate? What did you want to hire her for? She'll be no use at all.'

THREE

'Goodbye, Mr Yardley,' the new dairymaid said frigidly. She turned on her heel, head held high, and walked away. Nobody could be expected to stay after that and she was not going to risk being turned off the farm a second time.

As she passed the cowshed door the milking cows were coming out and even in her anger, Amy cast a professional eye over them. They were well nourished Shorthorns, some roan and some red and they had a familiar look: Foxglove and Violet, Primrose and Tulip, Marigold and Apple, the hard milker, Thistle who kicked... She stopped dead in her tracks: these were her father's cows, swinging out of their shed as they always did and as though the world had not been turned upside down. 'Our cows!' she gasped. Tulip and Marigold, two older cows, walked up to Amy and licked her arm. Amy patted them, tears running down her face. 'I thought I'd never see you again.'

Mrs Shaw walked over to stand by her side. 'You know the animals? They seem to know you! My nephew bought them here at the dispersal sale. He was so worried about the cattle plague, he didn't want to bring in cattle from elsewhere. And apparently the estate agent told him they were healthy and well bred.'

Good old Mr Russell; he had helped Ma quite a lot after Father died and he and Uncle Bill had arranged the sale. Did she say the misery was her nephew? Amy wondered whether the woman lived at the farm and why she had to put up with him. 'I hardly knew who bought our stock at the sale. I'd no idea they were still here!' On the day of the sale Amy had kept herself busy making tea and scones for the hard faced buyers, men like vultures descending on the farm for any bargain they could find. Farm dispersal sales were often sad, the end of a dream, and when your father had died, it was the final blow. She had not wanted to meet the new tenant, the man who would take over her beloved farm and so Mr Russell had dealt with him.

The farmer had been watching closely and now he came up to stand at the other side of Amy. He rubbed Tulip's head between the horns, and his face seemed less hostile. 'So,' he said. His normal voice was deep and quite pleasant. 'You must have worked for the tenant that was here before me, forget his name...'

'His name was Jon Appleton,' Amy said severely; how could he forget? He must take no interest in people. 'I'm his daughter, we lived here all my life. I hope you're taking good care of these cows,' she added and then she realized that he liked the cows almost as much as she did and they seemed to like him. They formed a group in the yard, in no hurry to go out to pasture, almost as if they were joining in the conversation.

Mrs Shaw smiled. 'Well, Benjamin, if the cows want Amy to work here, who are you to object?'

Amy expected an outburst of temper, but Yardley merely agreed curtly. 'Very well. I have work to do,' and he let his dog off the chain.

'Bess!' Amy went down on her knees to greet the collie, who bounded straight across to her. 'You took our dog, too!' She looked up at Yardley. He turned away, muttering. 'You look very well, Bess,' Amy told the dog, stroking the glossy coat.

'Benjamin likes the dog,' Mrs Shaw agreed. 'He took Bess when the agent said she would be shot, as she hadn't been sold... He's a kinder man than people realize. And of course, she's good at rounding up both cattle and sheep. His own dog died, just before he came here.'

'Father and I taught her, she knows all the signals.' Amy sighed. They should never have abandoned the faithful collie, but that was Gran's fault. She had refused to have a dog at her house, in spite of Amy's pleading for Bess to be kept and it had been the first of many differences of opinion between them. Amy had never dared to ask what happened to Bess and Molly hadn't mentioned the farm since they left; it upset her too much. In any case, Gran didn't like farm talk.

'Of course he took the farm cats as well, everyone does that, do they not? Cats go with the farm. He's even kind to cats.'

'Really?' She must be trying to put him in a better light than he could manage for himself. But the kind farmer was also rude.

41

However, the farm itself was now much more attractive, with so many of Amy's animals here. 'They are a bit like friends,' she said aloud. 'When you work with animals for years, you get to know each other.'

'So you like to work with animals?' Mrs Shaw looked at her closely. 'Well, you'd better come and help me to feed the calves.' They crossed the paved yard to the calf pens, set up in a big stone barn. About ten calves were wailing mournfully, but they soon stopped when their little heads were buried in pails of warm milk. Amy forgot her employer and concentrated on the work. When the calves were fed and bedded with clean straw, perhaps they would get to the dairy.

It was a while before she realized that there was no dairy. Mrs Shaw took the empty calf pails into the room for washing and Amy was shocked to see there was no butter churn and worker, no cream setting pans and not a sign of cheese making equipment. The place had a damp, sour smell. 'My nephew did not intend to set up a dairy,' the older woman said regretfully. 'But as soon as I got here, I told him that was what he should do.' She paused. 'I came here to help him through his first year on the farm, you see.'

'And did he agree to the dairy?' Amy wanted to know. Operating in the teeth of that dark disapproval would be hard enough and if the Misery didn't want a dairy in the first place, it would be hell. (Sorry for swearing, Gran.)

'He will,' Mrs Shaw said firmly, 'when he sees what we can do. I'd like to see the dairy established before I go back to York. I'm alone now, since my husband died some years ago, and so I shut up the house and came here to help.'

Amy felt she had to say something. 'That was kind of you, Mrs Shaw.' So Amy only had a job if Mrs Shaw could persuade the Misery that she was needed.

'I fancied a change of air, and although I'm not used to farming, I think we shall get on very well.' She was willing him to succeed. 'Dear Benjamin – my nephew has been unfortunate. He's had a sad time and now he expects the worst. Until he recovers his spirits, I am determined to help him.' Standing there in her boots, she certainly looked determined.

In Amy experience most farmers expected the worst and it usually happened, but she'd better not say so just now. Butter and cheese were all very well, but how could they improve dear Benjamin's temper? She would say as little as possible, but she had many questions. Was there a wife, a Mrs Yardley who had to put up with the Misery? There was no evidence of one. Without Mrs Shaw, he would have been all on his own.

Next they tackled the cowshed, although Amy did most of the work of shovelling the manure into a barrow, swilling down the floor and putting down fresh straw while Mrs Shaw watched and talked. 'I was successful in business, you see, with my husband in York. So I feel that a proper business approach will help Benjamin to establish himself. He has tried to find a market for his milk, but all the dairies in this area are fully supplied, for the summer at least. The answer will be to make butter and cheese from our milk and sell them – how did you sell them, Amy?'

The aunt seemed to have her feet on the ground. 'We took butter to Masham market as a rule, every Wednesday. Cheese we made when we could, and every few months, a factor came to collect it. Our local cheese is lovely, it's laced up into calico – some folks call it Colsterdale, or Wensleydale.' Amy stopped sweeping as she thought back to happier days. 'Of course you get competition from the other dairy stalls. Folks like to buy from farms they know, so you've got to build a good reputation.' Better not to mention that in the hot weather it was easy to lose your reputation and your money; rancid cheese or melted butter could not be sold. It was one thing to follow in Ma's footsteps, but to start again from scratch was a big job. 'It's a lot of work every week, just selling the butter and a few eggs.' Dare she ask a question? 'Mrs Shaw, what kind of business did you run in York?'

The woman smiled, as though at a pleasant memory. 'Timber, we had a big timber yard,' she explained. 'Wood for building, mainly.'

'If you don't sell the timber, you can store it for years if needed?' Of course you could. 'Well, that's one of the problems in farming; your produce won't keep. You have to sell dairy products quickly and even fat cattle and lambs need to go when they're ready. That means you take whatever price you can get and if all the other farmers are selling at the same time, the price can go down. But Mr Yardley will know all this.' Amy was used to this kind of conversation with her father, but Mrs Shaw looked surprised.

'You're not just a dairymaid, are you? It seems you have a grasp of the business side. Well, dear Benjamin lived on the Vale of York, a small acreage with a few sheep and the bees. He had a profession, other income, so he was not always at the mercy of markets. I think–' Mrs Shaw broke off, as a shout made them turn to see Yardley running into the yard.

'Sheep are out,' he panted. 'I don't know where they've gone. You'd better come now, no not you, Kate, you can't run, your heart won't stand it. The girl can help me.' He didn't look at Amy, but rushed off down the drive. Amy whistled to Bess and they followed him, catching him up easily.

'I might know where they got out. Shall we try to get them back the same way?'

Amy drew alongside and looked at her employer sideways. There was a spot under an oak tree where sheep sometimes made holes in the hedge and escaped to freedom. It had happened before, and no doubt it would happen again.

Yardley shot Amy a look of pure dislike, but he followed her. After pointing out the gap in the hedge, Amy and the dog ran straight down the track to the road. Carefully they managed to work round the bunch of ewes and lambs, who were out on the public road and heading for trouble. They were nibbling the forbidden grass as they went, but their aim was obviously a day out in Masham. Thinking of what they might do to town gardens, Amy shuddered. Gradually, with the help of the dog Amy edged them back to the oak tree and the sheep skipped through the gap before Yardley had time to do anything. A couple of lambs went the wrong way and Bess brought them back with great skill and patience.

That's how it's done, dear Benjamin, Amy thought as she rejoined her employer. Aloud she said blithely, 'There's your next job. You'll need a few posts and some rails to mend the fence.' He should have been pleased to receive this advice. He could have thanked her for getting them back, but he just grunted. The dark frown was much in evidence and Amy wondered how much of him she could stand. Her father had been a fair, sunny-tempered man with quiet grey eyes in a sunburned face. Yardley was the opposite. He didn't seem to like taking advice, either.

The mist was quickly vanishing in the sun, a skylark was singing and if you looked round, away from the miserable farmer, the world was a beautiful place. Bess, with her tail wagging and a grin on her face, thought so too. The sheep seemed almost to shrug when they found themselves cheated and settled down to eat the home grass as if nothing had happened.

It was probably wise to keep silent, but Amy wasn't always wise. 'You could have left them out for a while,' she suggested demurely. 'People round here usually do that, so they get a free feed. You can head them off from the gardens, but you'll need to go round the boundary soon, to check on holes in the hedges.'

'When I want your advice, woman, I'll ask for it,' Yardley growled, but his heart obviously wasn't in the fight; he was too depressed. 'You are the most irritating girl I've ever met.'

'So you won't be employing me, then. Good. Because I don't want to work for you either, dear Benjamin.' Amy felt herself flushing as she gave her job away. She would have to go home and tell Ma and Gran that she had failed on her first day, but she had spoken the truth.

To her surprise, the tall man laughed. 'So now we understand each other, Miss Knowall. Let's keep trying for a while and see how we get on.' He paused. 'Katherine's right, I do need help on the farm. If you are all she can get, I'll try to put up with you. The other local women are probably just as bad.'

'Much worse, I believe. We say what we think, round here.' There was a silence and Amy thought for a moment. Her instinct was to walk away right now and go home, leave him to it. But... Bess pressed gently against her leg as though she understood, and Amy decided to stay. 'I'll try it for a month or so,' she agreed. 'But if I'm doing farm work I want a proper wage and I would appreciate some manners, Mr Yardley. It costs nothing to be polite. Manners maketh the man, as my Gran says.' She bent down to pat the dog and when she straightened, Yardley was smiling. He looked completely different when he smiled.

When the man caught her eye he scowled instead. 'And I will appreciate it if you know your place and speak properly to your employer. Only my aunt calls me dear Benjamin, and I don't expect to be lectured by a chit of a girl.' The tone was severe.

At least he was talking. 'So what shall I call you?' 'Misery' came to mind.

Yardley started walking up the track. 'You did well to get the sheep in so quickly. You can help me to mend the fence.'

Amy trotted beside her employer, trying not to laugh. 'It wouldn't do to get Banks Farm a bad name in the town, we had to keep them out of the gardens.' It was so good to be out on the land again, under the blue sky. Then too, she would put up with quite a lot if it meant getting away from Gran. It would be a pity to give up now, just because the farmer was a misery and called her a chit of a girl and 'you'. She could stand his rudeness for a week or two. She thought about his high and mighty ways and decided to call him Sir.

That night, Amy delivered an edited account of the day's doings to her mother and Gran. Molly cried a little when the animals were mentioned, but she said she was glad they all had a good home. 'But I can't be a dairymaid, there's no dairy. All the milk goes to the calves and pigs, but I suppose the pigs could have the skim milk if we did make butter.' Amy was still trying to work out the best way for dear Benjamin to make a profit. 'I wonder who bought our butter churn?'

Molly shook her head, but Gran knew

49

where it was. 'It didn't sell, so Bill put it in the shop with a few other bits and pieces.'

Amy was surprised. 'You mean – Uncle Bill put our churn in the blacksmith's shop out in the yard? And it's still there?'

Gran nodded. 'Waste not, want not. Your mother could sell it to the new tenant, if he'll take it. But some folks have to buy new, they're not satisfied with making do.'

She pursed her lips and took up her knitting again. 'Is the man still nasty?'

The house they lived in was the old blacksmith's, where Grandfather had once worked. The forge was still there in the yard, out of use for years and it was now a cobwebby relic of the past and a dump for unwanted pieces of furniture.

There was a choice. If Amy said nothing about the churn, she might be able to keep out of the dairy for longer, but it would be good to see the old churn back in its place. Dairy work was not too bad as a way of earning a living, as long as she could help with the cows and calves as well. Ma would be pleased to turn it into money.

Mrs Shaw was keen to start making butter and so Yardley came round with his horse and trap one evening to buy the butter making equipment and take it back to the farm. 'And a pleasant, well spoken young man he is, I'm sure,' Gran said to Amy severely. 'And you told us he's a misery. You should show more respect for your betters, my lass. Pride comes before a fall,' she finished darkly. Amy turned away before she made a face. Sir had evidently made a good impression; perhaps it took one misery to appreciate another.

He certainly was a misery, but you had to admire the way that Yardley got on with the job. In a few weeks, taking Amy's advice, tactfully given to his aunt, he had set up the dairy and Amy was making butter. The cheese would come later when they had more milk, but the big cheese kettle was ready and the store room shelves had been scrubbed. But all the time, Yardley seemed to be looking over his shoulder, apprehensive about what might happen next.

'The cattle plague's spread all through Yorkshire during winter like a roaring lion, they say. It's at Bedale now.' Yardley shook his head. They were milking in the cowshed, sitting on stools side by side. 'That's only – what, five miles away.' The milk squirting into the pail had a soothing sound.

'I heard about it,' said Amy thoughtfully. 'Folks are very worried, of course they are. Jim Salter's wife got holy water sprinkled on the cows by the parson– Whoa there, lass!' The cow moved restlessly, nearly upsetting the pail and Amy shifted her position. 'And at Bramley they've got a funny little wooden image in the cowshed window, heathen I suppose, and some folks have onions everywhere, to ward off the evil with strong smells. That's not likely, is it? But we could put onions all round the windows, if you want to try it.'

Yardley coughed and Amy wondered whether he was hiding a laugh. 'I'd like to see the pagan image, I wonder how many centuries that's survived. But you know, some of the folk tales are true and I think one day, science will prove the old wives were sometimes right. Onions, now, they are very healthy, but against rinderpest – I rather doubt it.' He sighed. 'Well, I'd hate to lose these old girls, and you know what the authorities do ... they kill all your cattle if you get just one with the rinderpest, to stop it spreading. They'd all be shot and burned, or buried in a pit with lime.' His face was grim once more. 'Sheep as well.'

Amy's cow relented and turning her head, gave the milker a lick with her rough tongue. 'It would be dreadful, but we can do something. Mr Fryer said so, the last time it came.' It was strange, but they seemed to be having a normal conversation.

'The vet in Bedale? Is he any good?' Yardley sounded sceptical in the extreme. 'I happen to know that with this type of disease, people can spread it as they go about. And what was the scientific method that Mr Fryer recommended?'

'A lot of cows were saved, folks were very grateful to him. We did what he said, my father didn't believe it at first but he did in the end. Mr Fryer said that little invisible things, living things called germs, spread the plague and that you can kill them with carbolic. You scrub the sheds and make the cows walk through it, in a footbath. Oh, and you keep folks away.' Amy grinned. 'He didn't say to do it with a shotgun, though.'

Yardley grunted and moved to empty his bucket of milk. 'I have some carbolic, as it happens. You can do the scrubbing, if you're so keen on it.' She was certain he was laughing at her, but perhaps it was better than his usual gloom.

'Thank you, Sir. There's nothing I'd like better.'

Amy scrubbed for three days and the smell of carbolic followed her home, got into her hair and even into her dreams. She tried to follow all her instructions. Yardley had told her quite forcibly that to protect the farm from the plague, she was to go straight home at night and not speak to anyone, least of all a farmer, and come back in the mornings the same way. Mornings were not a problem because she was out of town before most of the Masham folk had risen, but in the evenings she dodged round the back lanes to avoid trouble.

One evening as she passed the old bakery,

Patrick came out and he looked thinner than before, although he was still clean and neat. He grabbed her hand and pulled her into the kitchen. 'I thought you would have come to see me before now. Where've you been, little Amy?' The blue eyes looked intently into hers.

FOUR

Amy told him about the new job and the miserable employer and Patrick sighed. 'You deserve better than that. Well, I've had some luck at last. I'm hoeing turnips for Mr Brown on the other side of the town and I hope he pays me soon... I've still got some tea, would you like a cup? Not much food, though.'

Amy felt herself melting and moved away; this young man was too attractive. 'I didn't come to see you because I'm not supposed to talk to anyone. Sir made me promise to go straight home.'

'Goodness, Amy, I haven't got the cattle plague,' Patrick grinned. 'I'm off to the river to catch a trout. Living off the land is not as easy as it sounds ... but we'll have tea first.' Amy hesitated and then agreed; could tea with Patrick be so very sinful?

Only if Gran finds out, said her conscience.

That was one of many secret visits to the bakery. Every few days there was a good excuse to call in as she passed through the town. Amy saved newspapers for Patrick, so that he kept up with current affairs. She stole a jar of jam from Gran's pantry and then she found a book about cattle breeding, one of her father's, that might interest him. Patrick was so easy to be with, such good company and he seemed to be very knowledgeable. 'You've been to a better school than I did,' Amy confessed one day and Patrick grinned.

'All you have to do is to read more books, little Amy.' At his suggestion, she started to borrow books from Mr Yardley, much to the Misery's surprise. She read Mr Dickens in bed at night, amazed by his stories of people living in cities, a life so different to her own. There was now something to talk about at meal times. The Misery liked talking about books and he seemed to be happier when Amy was not giving him good advice, but listening to his ideas instead.

As she walked to and fro, Amy could see smoke rising from a farm up above them on the moor where the rinderpest was creeping across the land, the evil disease that could yet spoil their lives. Up there on that little farm, a family was in mourning for their slaughtered sheep. The smoke shadowing the hill was a grim reminder of the plague;

the shadow over the moor was coming nearer. What had any of them done to deserve such a thing? She decided not to mention the smoke to Sir; he was worried enough already.

At the Sunday morning service, the Vicar likened the rinderpest to a Biblical plague. It was a good chance to get his flock to repent, and he took it. Amy shuddered in her pew, Gran looked grim and the whole congregation was subdued; everybody depended on farming in some way and they were all touched by fear.

Masham sheep from that moor were famous; there was a cross bred animal called the Masham. Any animal with a cloven hoof would be killed if the plague visited your farm. Old Mrs Morrison's goats were in danger and even the deer in the Park. Farmers muttered about 'going arable' but Masham was a livestock area, with small fields and a fairly short growing season even on the river flats. And you could never grow crops on the moor. For thousands of years they had depended on stock and some of them might now have to give up farming and go into the town to earn a living.

The thought of Patrick's thin face haunted Amy and when one Saturday she was told by Gran to make a batch of scones, she managed to squeeze out a few extra for him. She cut a wedge of cheese and wrapped it

56

with the scones in a cloth, which she put in the bottom of a wicker basket. 'I'm going to pick some watercress,' she called to her mother and slipped out into the cool of the evening. There was cress in the little river Burn that ran into the Ure, and she could pass the old bakery on the way.

Patrick jumped up in delight when she walked into his kitchen. 'You're an angel!' he cried and kissed her cheek. 'Now, you must stay awhile.' He pushed her gently into a chair by the fire. 'I only wish we could go for a walk by the river, but I suppose not. I can't be seen and you ... it would do you no good, Amy, to be seen with a man.'

Amy shook her head. 'I shouldn't be here at all, Patrick.' She looked at a shelf of new books against the wall. 'Is this how you pass the time? These are school books, aren't they?'

'When I'm not hoeing,' the lad said ruefully and held up blistered hands. 'I'm trying to study scientific books, chemistry and biology, to learn about the theory of farming.'

Amy smothered a laugh. 'Chemistry and biology never enters the heads of Masham farmers–' she stopped in confusion when Patrick reached over and pulled her on to his knee.

'Now, Miss Amy, don't mock me. I'm just a poor lad, very lonely I am, and I need a cuddle. Has anybody told you how bonny you are? I love the freckles on your little nose.'

'I hate the freckles, it's with being out in the sun.' Amy tried to resist, but not very hard, and soon subsided into his arms. Patrick kissed her gently and she began to feel a rising tide of warmth as she returned his kiss. If only being with Percy felt like this!

'You do like it! I thought you would. You're a warm-hearted girl, Amy. Now kiss me again.' So Amy took the handsome face between her hands and kissed him on the lips, melting into him in a feeling she had never before experienced.

There was a sudden hammering on the front door of the shop and Amy jumped up guiltily. If she was caught visiting Patrick her reputation would be in ruins.

Amy left the bakery quickly and as she rounded the corner of the alley some children ran past her, shouting. They had knocked on all the doors in the street and were being chased by Mrs Betts the laundrywoman and two dogs. It was wise to walk demurely away from the scene and concentrate on picking watercress to take home. She was still breathless from emotion and blushing as she thought about what had just happened.

Patrick was hard to resist and although she had got used to visiting him and looked forward to it, she must not risk being with him again. If only Patrick was a normal young man with 'prospects' as her mother would say, and she could take him home to tea... 'I'm not going to fall in love with him,' Amy told herself sternly. 'He's not suitable.' But the warm glow persisted and she knew she was already half in love.

It seemed as though they had always known each other. She would need to calm down before she went back to Ma and Gran; better hurry down to the watercress bed.

Walking home by the river path, Amy saw the sleek head of an otter pushing upstream, followed by a faint V shaped ripple in the water. She had always loved the otters, although fishermen said they took the trout and people hunted them with dogs. Seeing the otter reminded her of living here in the old days. Before her father was ill, there were few clouds in Amy's sky. Nobody had minded if they took a trout from the river, and the otters were welcome to their share. Things had been easier then. It would have been wonderful to wander with Patrick by the river ... but it would only cause trouble and she wanted none of that. Imagine what Gran would say if she got to hear about Patrick; even Mother would disapprove.

It was hard to pass the baker's shop at first, but Amy tried not to think of Patrick. Of course he was lonely, he'd said so, that was why he was so pleased to see her. The trouble was, he had made Amy realize that

she too was lonely, in a way. To have someone hold you close, to have someone to
laugh with – is that what married life could
be? Not just obedience all the time, but a
loving partnership? Patrick had not been in
Masham for very long, but she couldn't
imagine life without him. He was so bright,
so happy. He made light of his problems
and took each day as it came.

Why did older folks keep young men and
women apart, so they couldn't really get to
know each other? If Patrick had been a local
lad and acceptable to Gran he might have
come to Sunday tea instead of Percy, but
they wouldn't have had much of a chance to
talk to each other. Several girls she'd known
at school had been courted in the proper
way by young men and they went into marriage not knowing how it would turn out.
Knowing how much money a lad had in the
bank told you nothing about what he would
be like to live with and some of the men
with money turned out to be very mean
with it.

Sometimes, doubt crept in. Amy and Patrick had got to know each other quite well
during their quiet talks, but did she really
know the lad? He was in a strange situation –
maybe he was hiding from something that he
hadn't told her about. One day he might get
a proper job and take her home to meet his
mother. It was something to dream about.

Amy kept away from Patrick after this, although she missed him and thought about him every day as she walked to and from the farm. Then came a wet day when a thunderstorm blew up as she was walking home from work. It had been raining and blowing a gale during the afternoon and Mrs Shaw suggested that she should stay at the farm until the rain stopped, but Amy knew that her mother would worry if she didn't get home in such wild weather. She splashed down the muddy lane to Masham and then through dripping streets, her curls in long strands, plastered to her head. By the time she reached the bakery she was wet through and had started to shiver. Just then, the forked lightning played round the church spire in a terrifying display of light and the thunder roared. Rain came down so heavily it was impossible to see.

Hardly able to breathe, Amy looked round for cover, but there was none; by the time her working day was over, most of the shops were closed. The only shelter was with Patrick until it was possible to go home. Dripping, Amy knocked at the back door.

Patrick looked horrified when he saw the bedraggled little figure on the doorstep.

'My poor darling! Come in and get warm.' Patrick led her to the fire, his face full of concern. 'You could catch pneumonia... I'm terrified of it, that's what kills so many people.' He took her cold hands in his warm ones. He was just the same, kind and affectionate and Amy realized how much she had missed him in the last few weeks. 'I think we'd better get those wet things off you and dry them by the fire.'

Amy was alarmed. 'Oh no Patrick, I can't possibly...' she was stopped by a fit of coughing. 'I'll just shelter for a few minutes and then go home,' she croaked. Patrick took charge and pushed her into a chair, then knelt and took off her wet shoes and stockings. He went out with a candle into another room and came back with a soft blanket, which he wrapped loosely around her.

'Now, take your things off under the blanket, Amy. Don't be embarrassed. It's serious ... you could get really ill.'

The rain was now a steady downpour, with thunder rumbling directly overhead.

Patrick's plates rattled on the table and livid forks of lightning lit up the room from time to time. It could be dangerous to be out in such a storm; Ma and Gran couldn't expect Amy to come home until it stopped.

In the firelight, Patrick's face was serious. 'Are you warmer now? I've missed you, girl ... but I suppose I know why I haven't seen you – a well brought up young woman like you shouldn't come here to a vagabond like me.' His grin was rueful. 'But I won't be a vagabond for much longer. I've got something to tell you, Amy. I'm leaving Masham soon.'

Struggling with her soaking wet dress under the blanket, Amy felt suddenly weak as though someone had hit her. Her body under the blanket was still cold as she shed the last of her clothes.

Patrick draped Amy's clothes round the fire. How shocking it was, to let a man handle her clothes – and to be alone with him, wearing only a blanket! Amy tried to feel guilty, but being with Patrick felt so natural that she failed.

What could she say? 'I'll ... miss you, Patrick. I'm sorry you're leaving.' Was this the end?

He looked across eagerly. 'Will you really? I wondered – but I was hoping to see you... It's bad news and also, good. I'm leaving – Mr Russell knows I'm here and he said I could stay for a week or two longer – but I've got a job on a farm near home and a place at a university for next year, so my mother has forgiven me. I'll be able to work on the farm for the summer and I'm going to study agricultural science!' His face was alight with excitement.

'I'm glad for, you, I really am,' Amy said between chattering teeth. Patrick noticed immediately.

'Now, how do you feel?' He stood over Amy and clasped her hands. 'Still feels cold to me. Let me warm you, my darling... I've wanted to do this for a long time.' Patrick picked her up easily, carried her through into the bedroom and laid her gently on the bed. A candle beside the bed threw strange shadows on the ceiling and at that moment, a terrifying clap of thunder shook the whole house. Amy hid under the blanket, she was not usually afraid of storms, but this was the worst she had ever seen.

'Don't be afraid, little lass,' Patrick said gently as he slid beside her and put strong arms around her. 'You're safe here, but I still feel you're cold. I need to warm you, Amy. Just relax, and I'll tell you how lovely you are.' Patrick bent over her, his handsome face full of concern. 'I love you, little Amy. One day I'm going to come back to claim you, when I've got established. And meanwhile, we'll write to each other, we'll be promised to each other. What do you say?'

'I – don't know what to say. I'm overwhelmed... I wish you were not leaving, I wish... I should not be here...' Amy felt his warmth beside her, gradually warming her through.

'Yes, you should. This is the best place in the world to be, here with me – would you wish to be anywhere else?' Smiling, Patrick took off his clothes and joined her under the blanket. Amy closed her eyes and breathed in the comforting scent of the man, the scent of soap and wood smoke. She relaxed against him and gradually, a rosy glow spread through her body. Nothing else seemed to matter. She and Patrick were one, the affection she had missed so much was hers. As the rain beat down and the thunder growled, Patrick and Amy gently made love. This was what married life would be like... Amy slept, while the thunder rolled about them.

Amy was left with mixed feelings in the days that followed. Her love for Patrick was a glow within her, and that fact that he loved her, they were promised to each other, had changed her life. But his absence was an ache that never went away. Would he write to her, as he'd promised? How long would it be before she saw him again? At last she had grown up, she understood what love could be, and it was nothing remotely like holding hands with Percy Coldbeck. But under the excitement of discovery, Amy had a vague feeling that there would be trouble – especially if she told Percy once and for all to go away.

There were only two more visits to the bakery after that. The last day before Patrick went away he held her tightly to him and again she felt herself melting until she had no resistance left. 'I'll write to you, my sweet,' Patrick murmured. She stroked his coppery hair, feeling happier than ever before, and also sadder. 'One day we'll be married and have a farm of our own. What should you like, Amy? A farm with a dairy?'

Amy could hardly imagine her future self as Patrick's wife, making butter in their own dairy. It was possible... 'Yes, I think we could rent a farm in a few years – Mr Russell might let us have one of the smaller estate farms. How lovely it would be!'

'I want to take you to bed again, to make love to you ... but we'll keep it until we're married, shall we?' Patrick's blue eyes were full of love. 'I don't want to get you into trouble... I never intended to take advantage of you that night in the storm – you understood that, didn't you?'

'I didn't plan it, either, but I don't regret it, Patrick.'

Patrick looked relieved. 'Oh Amy, I wonder how long it will be before we can get together ... maybe I should get a job on a farm with a house, and we could make it sooner. And then save up for our farm. Write and tell me what you think, Amy – I'll send an address as soon as I know where I'm staying.'

'Write to me care of the post office, Patrick. I don't want Gran reading your letters.'

Amy saw the carrier's cart making its slow way down to Ripon the next day and knew that Patrick was travelling away from her. When would she see him again? She had only known him for a few weeks, but it seemed as though they had been friends all her life. How soon would he write to her?

Granny Lowther, out in the sunshine one afternoon to see what went on in Masham, was shocked by the scanty dress worn by the girl on the vegetable stall. It was certainly a warm day, but there was no call for that expanse of bare arm and shoulder. 'If that Daisy was mine I'd spank her bottom,' she told herself fiercely. These young girls had no idea of decency. She headed towards the post office, which was always quite busy on market day. She would have to wait in the queue, but Molly needed stamps and there was usually somebody to talk to.

Gran leaned on her stick and looked round. She was surprised to see Amy ahead of her in the line, shamelessly standing there in her working clothes. There was mud, if not worse, on the hem of her skirt. How could a granddaughter of hers want to do dirty farm work? Gran looked down at her own neat, shiny little boots and patted her hat into place as Amy stepped up to the counter. 'Is there a letter for Amy Appleton, please?'

Gran's mouth fell open. Such deceit! Why would the girl ... what was she hiding? There must be a man in it somewhere ... maybe a married man. Gran had always had a lively imagination where other folks were concerned. She watched, concealed behind the large man in front of her, as the counter clerk shook her head and Amy walked sadly away. Gran knew it was her duty to get to the bottom of this.

After thinking it over, Gran decided to act. She went to the post office one morning when there were few people on the square. 'Letters for Miss Appleton, please,' she said firmly and held out her hand. Without looking at her, the clerk handed over an envelope. The mystery was in her hands and she could hardly wait to know more.

Sitting on a bench in the square, Gran looked at the envelope, addressed to Amy in square, confident handwriting. What should she do? She could give it to Amy and confront her with her underhand ways. She could throw it in the fire unopened ... or she could read it herself and then decide what to do. Her mouth set in a grim line, Gran slowly opened the letter and spread it out.

This was worse than she had imagined. The man had designs on Amy, it was clear. He wrote a lot of nonsense to turn her head and he implored her to write to him at an address in Boroughbridge. To protect the family reputation, Gran burned the letter as soon as she got home. She would say nothing just now and await events. Molly would need to know some time, but not yet.

Gran smiled her bitter smile as she realized she'd been right all along: Amy was up to no good.

Trouble came to Banks Farm three weeks later, on a pearly morning with dewdrops hanging from spiders' webs in the hawthorn hedges. It had been three weeks of anxious waiting for Amy, looking for the letter that never came. She kept thinking of reasons why his letter might be delayed ... or was it just that he'd been playing with her, enjoying her company but forgetting her as soon as he left? There was a feeling of lead in Amy chest, of impending doom. Patrick might even have been injured.

The Misery was full of doom too; he was bringing in the cows for milking with a face even more gloomy than usual. 'I'm afraid the plague's here,' he said briefly. 'Old roany, Marigold I think you call her, she's dribbling and she's down. Can't get up, she must have the cattle plague. It's all over with us.'

Amy felt herself go dizzy with shock. In spite of all the scrubbing, all the precautions, the disease had beaten them. Her first thought was of her father; thank goodness he had not lived to see his precious cattle slaughtered before his eyes.

Milking was a miserable affair that morning. The doomed cattle were just as usual, looking round for their oats, unperturbed by their dreadful fate. Amy wanted to run away and hide, not to face what was to come. It was too terrible. For the first time she felt sorry for Yardley, seeing the pain in his dark eyes.

After their breakfast of porridge, her heart sinking further, Amy tried to be practical as she carried the empty dishes to the sink. Sir didn't seem to have much experience of cattle; could he be wrong? 'What does Marigold look like, sir? Goodness, they're all so healthy! I never thought – has she got blisters on the mouth?'

'She's dribbling, that's a bad sign and she's down, of course, looking awkward with her belly pushed up... I should never have gone into cows, I knew nothing about all this until after I bought them.' The farmer was folding up his newspaper mechanically, but he was in a state of near panic. 'I'll have to go for the vet. You're not to go near her, you hear?' His face in the morning light was harsh.

Perhaps Yardley wanted to make it easier for his helper, to shield her from the horror of the disease. Folks said it was dreadful to see the animals in pain. But after breakfast he was slumped in his chair, a picture of despair and Amy asked his aunt to take care of the morning's milk. She sped down the lane to the cow pasture, with her heart beating in her throat. She must see Marigold for herself.

A cuckoo was calling across the hay meadow, a carefree sound at odds with the rest of the scene. There in the grass was a pathetic heap, lying in one corner by the hedge. When cows were lying down, their stomachs made a huge mound and they looked so helpless. Her eyes full of tears, Amy went quietly up to Marigold and as she did so, the cow sat up and looked round at her; she must have been asleep. The poor thing was conscious; bound to be suffering. The lesions on the mouth and feet would be painful. A little saliva drooled from her mouth.

FIVE

Wiping her tears away Amy stood looking down at Marigold, afraid to go nearer and confirm the dreadful truth. The worst had happened, in spite of all the scrubbing... Could it be her fault? Could Patrick have unknowingly carried the germs from the farm where he worked and passed them on to Amy? Could his caresses have been the means of spreading the deadly germs? It was a horrible thought. 'I hope it wasn't us,' she whispered to Marigold.

Gradually she was aware that something

was brushing against her skirt. Bess must have followed her, against all orders. Amy turned and found not the dog, but a small calf looking up at her, a newborn calf still damp, too young to know fear.

Marigold let out a soft maternal sound and struggled to her feet. The calf, a little red heifer, staggered over to the cow and was soon blindly nuzzling for the teat. Marigold stood absolutely still, so that the little animal could find the milk. Soon it was sucking noisily and she licked the calf tenderly as it drank. Once again, the miracle had worked.

Amy hardly dared to breathe as she watched the cow and calf. Did Marigold really have the plague and was the calf doomed as well as herself? Or ... was it possible that Sir had jumped to conclusions and she had just been lying down to give birth? The calf's coat was only now drying out and curling a little. It must have been born while they were milking. Yardley could have seen Marigold in labour before the calf was born and taken her distress for the cattle plague.

'Let's have a look at your mouth, girl.' She knelt in the damp grass and looked carefully at the cow's feet and her mouth, where the signs of rinderpest would be seen. As far as Amy could see, Marigold was normal; there were no sores, thank goodness. She was rather tired after giving birth, but that was all.

The sun was climbing higher and birds were singing in the hedges. Amy looked round at the pastures of green spring grass and felt a great weight lift from her. For now at least, the threat of plague had gone, and with it the nagging guilt that she might have been a carrier of the disease. If only it would go away altogether.

When Amy reached the yard again, Yardley was saddling up his riding horse to go for the vet. Amy danced up to him. 'She was calving, that was all! Marigold's got a calf!'

Yardley looked stunned. 'Are you sure? She's not sick? She looked pretty bad when I found her.' He seemed unable to believe that tragedy had not struck them.

'Cows do look very sick sometimes, when they're trying to calve,' Amy said soothingly. 'She may have had a touch of milk fever, old cows can get that when they calve. They lie out unconscious, with the head turned back to the shoulder.'

'She may have had that. I must try to get a book about animal health and disease,' Yardley muttered. 'Milk fever ... what's the treatment, then?'

'Well, we don't take too much milk out of her for a few days. Some folks feed the milk back to the cow. Mr Fryer said it was worse in bad weather, and that they need plenty of hay. He thought it was something wrong with the blood, when they suddenly start to make milk again. But there's not much you can do until they come round.' She looked at the shadow on the cowshed wall; time was going by. 'I've butter to make, I'd better get on with it.'

Yardley grunted that he would move the beef cattle on to fresh grass and fetch Marigold up from the pasture later and Amy promised to help him. 'We'll have to shut up a field or two for hay soon,' he said, almost to himself. Amy smiled; she had already decided which fields should be made into hay that year and was waiting for a chance to make him think that the plan was his. But she knew far better than the Misery which fields made the best hay and which ones needed a rest from cutting. It was better to cut hay from different fields every year, to take the scythe round the farm as her father had said. And this year's fields had a few thistles in them, which needed to be dug out before the grass was cut. There was a lot to think about, even when the weather was kind. They would need to keep the animals out of the hay meadows for at least two months, to get a good crop. If there were holes in the hedge, those sheep would find their way in and that would make Sir more miserable than ever.

She decided to concentrate on the job in

hand, instead of thinking like a farm manager. In the sunny dairy, Amy set to work with a light heart. She poured the thick cream into the churn, sniffing the pleasant ripeness. Cream had to smell right to make good butter, a sort of clean acid smell. Turning the handle deliberately, she allowed the cream to fall from one end of the churn to the other. 'It's the shock that makes the butter, not winding the handle fast,' her mother had always said. Then came the change, when quite suddenly the fat in the cream turned into little pieces like grains of wheat, floating in thin buttermilk and the sound in the churn became a liquid sloshing. She strained the buttermilk off and washed the butter grains with salt water, then scooped them out of the churn and heaped them on the worker, the old wooden butter worker that she and her mother had used in the old days. Time went by and she was making up the butter into neat bricks when a shadow fell across the doorway and Yardley came in.

For a few minutes the farmer stood watching her and then he sighed. 'When you're done, we'll fetch the cow and calf up.' He turned abruptly on his heel, but at the door he looked back. 'I suppose there's nothing we can teach you, Miss Know-all! But I wish you could tell me where my sheep are going. There's no gaps in hedges or open gates, but five more are missing today... I told the constable, but he wasn't much help. I get the feeling that sheep stealing's a way of life, up there on the moors.'

'Now that's not true, Mr Yardley,' Amy said quickly. 'The moorland farmers are mostly good folk who go to church or chapel. My father never lost sheep, except the odd one to liver fluke in a wet season, or a lamb taken by a fox.' Her father had been a pleasant and well-respected local man ... was that the difference? Did some local person have a grudge against Yardley, or had that grim personality of his made enemies already?

She would have to give some thought to the sheep problem. It was good to solve their problems and easy for her because she was a local lass. Last week, they'd asked about a girl to help in the house: Mrs Shaw couldn't manage all the housework by herself. Amy had suggested Rosie Slater and that had turned out well. But sheep stealing was a new problem in Masham and even Amy Appleton's experience didn't help.

Amy put the butter on the cool stone slabs in the dairy, washed her hands and prepared to follow Yardley, but he had not waited and she had to run down the track to catch up with him. How irritating he could be! He was probably annoyed that he'd been wrong, had panicked too soon. Only someone new to farming would have made a mistake like that ... but Amy remembered that it was the calf, butting against her leg that had given her the clue.

They went on without speaking and in silence they slowly walked Marigold up to the yard, followed by the calf. The cow kept stopping and waiting for the calf to catch up. Amy was watching the calf and gently persuading it to move along, but part of her mind was considering how to deal with her owner. It was hard for a man to admit that a woman knew better, she could see that. The clever thing would be to find something that he could teach her – but what? Amy had a lifetime of experience on that very farm.

When she was secured in the shed with the chain round her neck as they did for milking, the farmer touched the cow gently and then inspected her feet and mouth and like the old trouper she was, Marigold stood still. Still looking at the cow he said, 'It was a stupid mistake, but I'm so glad I was wrong. You have a very level head, young Amy.' Some of the strain had gone from his face.

'I hope we never have to face the plague on this farm,' the dairymaid said quietly.

She liked the way Sir handled animals; he was a born stockman, even if his experience was limited. It was a pity he had no sympathy with people.

As they reached the yard, Mrs Shaw was hanging out washing in the garden with the kitchen girl, Rosie. Suddenly the calf decided to try out its legs. It threw them in the air and went off at a run, blundering straight into the garden and coming to rest in a bed of rosemary. 'Don't worry, I'll get her out!' Amy called and was soon able to catch up with the calf. 'Come back to your mother, this way!' She grabbed the little animal round the neck and looked up at Mrs Shaw. 'Maybe we should call her Rosemary!' When her father ran the farm, Amy had always chosen names for the cattle.

'No, Rosie!' the maid called, and Mrs Shaw laughed.

Yardley took the cow and calf away and Amy explained to his aunt that the cow had been in labour and not in the throes of a dread disease, then changed the subject. 'You've improved the garden since our time, I can see that,' she said, feeling generous. 'There's more space for vegetables.' She walked down the path to the orchard at the end of the garden; there were three beehives under the trees and the bees were busy in the plum blossom. 'You've got honey! We never kept bees because my father swelled up whenever he got a bee sting.'

'Ben has always kept bees,' the older woman explained. 'He brought them up here to the moors for the heather every summer – that's how he found this farm.' She smiled. 'I hope that in time we'll be able to sell honey as well as butter and cheese in the market. But of course, it all depends on the season. Sometimes there is no honey to spare – the bees need it all.'

Bees were a mystery to her. 'I would love to learn about them,' Amy said truthfully. The next time Sir worked with the bees, she would ask if she might watch.

It might be tactful to show her ignorance of some part of their work. This would be something that he could teach her, if he had the patience.

After their lunch of bread and cheese, Yardley sat back in his chair and looked at his dairymaid. 'I think our farm adviser should be more involved with the sheep,' he said, smiling, but in a rather sarcastic way. So far Amy had worked very little with the sheep, having plenty to do in the dairy. 'I've kept sheep for years but I must admit to failure this time ... are there any savage dogs round here, do you know? Something or someone is taking the sheep. But if they were dying we'd find the bodies, wouldn't we? And then I'd be worried about the rinderpest.'

And dogs would leave part of the carcase, blood, some clue. It couldn't be dogs, she knew. 'I'll check the sheep now, if you haven't seen them today,' Amy said quietly.

'Yes, take a walk down there, Amy, and see if you can spot anything unusual. I did wonder whether thieves could come down the river, but I think the Ure's too shallow for boats. It's a mystery.'

The sun had disappeared behind dark clouds and a light rain was falling as Amy wrapped a shawl round her shoulders and set off down the well remembered path to the river. The sheep were kept on the river flats and in the remotest fields; it would take too long to walk the milking cows up from the river at their slow pace. Lambing was over and shearing had taken place before Amy had come back to Banks Farm.

All the sheep were happily grazing and not one was lame; Yardley was certainly a good shepherd. Lameness was the result of neglect; Amy always hated to see limping sheep and ewes grazing on their knees because their feet were sore. She counted them, but she had to be quick. Their heads came up in alarm when they saw her, ears swivelled in her direction and then the flock took off, scampering away to the far corner of the field. What had made them so nervous? The last time she'd walked by the river they had been calm and quiet.

Amy walked quietly through the field, but the sheep didn't come back to inspect her, which their own flock would certainly have done. These sheep formed a tight bunch with the lambs behind them, watchful and defiant. But there was nothing else out of the ordinary. She searched the mud of the gateways for footprints and cartwheel tracks, but there was nothing.

The shower passed over and the sun came out again, gilding the wet leaves of the trees by the river. Amy saw a flash of blue as a kingfisher dived and thought how lucky she was to be back at the place she loved. She went down to the water's edge and saw footprints, presumably those of fishermen who patrolled the banks, mainly in the evenings after work was done.

In one spot there was an old willow hanging out over the water; Amy's father had kept a little rowing boat moored to the tree. Although much of the river was shallow as Yardley had said, there was a deep stretch downstream from Banks Farm for a mile or two and Amy and her father had sometimes rowed quietly along, enjoying the peace of the river. The old boat had been forgotten, but when Amy parted the willow curtain it was still there. No doubt it would have been offered at the farm sale if anyone had remembered... Hitching up her skirt, Amy hopped into the boat and untied it. Just for a few minutes she would revisit the past.

Moving down the river with the current, Amy thought dreamily how Patrick would have enjoyed the afternoon. Perhaps one day when his troubles were over, he would be there with her and they could be happy.

Where the Banks Farm land ended there was a bend in the river. Amy had always enjoyed seeing the fields from the water, getting a different perspective on the farm...

'Oi! What you doing here? This is private!' A raucous shout made her start as she rounded the bend. The peace was shattered and only a few yards from Yardley's land, someone was objecting to her presence.

A rough, red faced man stood on the bank opposite, waving a stick. 'My, it's a lass ... well, didn't want to fright you, Miss, but don't come no further.'

'And who are you, to order me about?' Amy demanded. They had never been stopped for rowing on the river. Once after heavy rains they'd gone all the way down to the village of Thorpe.

'Don't you know a water bailiff when you see one?' the man blustered. 'Get off the river, go back to where you came from and keep away, or it'll be the worse for you.'

Carefully Amy turned the little boat and rowed back upstream until the bend hid the man from sight. Then she leaned on her oars and wondered what her father would have made of him. Water bailiffs were there to prevent salmon poaching and they used to treat her father as an ally. She had never seen this one before, or any as rough as he was. They were usually polite; bailiffs had the power to stop and search a boat if they thought something illegal was going on, but Amy hardly looked like a poacher. Thoughtfully she made her way back to the willow and tied up the boat again. Things had changed on the river since last year. Even the sheep were uneasy. It had always been a peaceful stream, reflections shimmering in the deep pools, dragonflies hovering in the dappled light and often, the hum of bees. It was troubling to think that the river's peace had been shattered.

Amy meant to tell Sir what had happened on the river, but he had gone out shopping with his aunt when she got back to the farm, leaving a note on the door. She scrubbed out the dairy and then it was time to bring the cows in for milking. She was nearly finished when Yardley returned with a box of tools and some rolls of netting; Mrs Shaw had bought a set of china cups and saucers. They both seemed pleased with their afternoon and went off to unload the goods, leaving Amy to finish off the dairy work. By the time that was done it was quite late, so she waved to Yardley and went home.

The next day, Yardley shrugged off the story of a watcher on the river. 'I suppose it's none of our business what people do downstream. But you wouldn't get far on the Ure in a boat, would you? I've never had the time to play about on the river.' Maybe he thought that Amy had been wasting time during working hours, rowing her boat when she should have been working. 'I wondered whether it had anything to do with the disappearing sheep,' she offered.

'I've thought they might get across the river when it's low, but the farms on the other side would let us know quite soon if our sheep were eating their grass,' Ben said.

'I can just imagine the ewes picking their way across the stones and the lambs going across on their backs,' Amy said, and raised a smile. It was going to be hard work to lighten the mood at Banks Farm.

SIX

Some of Amy's efforts at lightness worked. Mr Yardley was a fraction less grim in the days that followed, especially since there were no more local outbreaks of cattle plague. Cloud shadows came and went across the moorland, but there was no more smoke, no more burning pyres of animal remains. The people of Masham held their breath and hoped that repentance had saved them from the worst, although some believed that the hot weather might have killed whatever mysterious forces were at work to spread the disease. June came in with a warmth that they had forgotten since last summer.

Amy took on the job of going to the Wednesday market with the butter and as they had all hoped, it sold well. 'Well, lass, is it as good as your mother used to make?' the housewives asked her as she stood in the cobbled market square, just like old times.

'Of course it is, mother taught me,' Amy smiled, enjoying the role of saleswoman. Mrs Shaw had made her new, blue print dresses to wear to market, and given her a little cap to keep the fair hair out of her eyes. Perhaps the past reputation of Banks Farm would help Mr Yardley to establish himself, together with a smart presentation on the stall. Butter was sold in tall one pound bricks, with the grooves of the scotch hands on the sides and a distinctive pattern on the top, made with a carved butter stamp. Her new employer had no stamp as yet, so Amy carved a Y for Yardley on the top of each brick. She kept them cool in brine as long as she could and her butter looked fresh and bright, with a wholesome smell and no white specks in it. When you broke a brick clear moisture oozed out, which meant it would keep well. Milky butter did not keep. To show off these points, Amy gave a taste from a small pat of butter to anyone who questioned the quality.

Gran came round the square on her usual tour of the market stalls and was amazed when she saw the transformation in Amy, but she could not bring herself to be gracious. 'Never seen you look so tidy,' she said sourly. 'Better late than never, I suppose.' She sniffed and tapped off with her walking stick, going uneasily on the stone cobbles.

Amy couldn't resist a reply this time. 'Cleanliness is next to godliness, Gran,' she called after the bent back, and earned a laugh from Daisy at the next stall.

The baskets were empty when Ben Yardley came back to collect Amy at the end of the market. He hitched the horse to a rail in front of the King's Head, exchanged greetings with a couple of farmers and bought a few plants for the garden before approaching the butter stalls. Amy thought he looked almost human, but she knew he could turn into a misery again in two minutes. Life was a serious business for Mr Yardley.

'It's a good job we brought a pail of brine, it was so hot the butter could've melted,' Amy told him cheerfully, handing over the money she had taken. It was hot and seemed to be getting hotter; perhaps there would be another thunderstorm.

Amy jumped up into the trap and they clattered out of Masham square and took the road home. She was thinking about the next job, milking, when Yardley said suddenly, 'I have to make a call on the moor road, so we'll be a little late for milking. Do you mind? It's just a little way over the moor.'

'N-no,' Amy stammered, surprised. It was true, she didn't mind anything that kept her out on the farm for a little longer. Since the fear of cattle plague had subsided most people were going about their ordinary business again. She looked around at the unfamiliar view; from high in the vehicle she could see over hedges and walls. The late afternoon sun shimmered on the fields and woods of the valley. Sheep lay panting in the shade of the trees and the wilting roadside flowers, the frothy Queen Anne's lace, were covered in the fine peppery road dust that stung eyes and got into throats, and made a long journey into an ordeal.

As they went, Yardley explained that he had arranged to buy some poultry. 'It's time we had our own eggs, and it's a good time of year to start.' He shot a sideways look at his passenger, who was sitting up straight with her hands in her lap. 'I suppose you know all about hens and rearing chicks, Miss Knowall?'

'Well,' Amy began cautiously, 'it was my job at home. I used to put eleven or thirteen eggs under a broody hen – always an odd number, was the old rule – and let her hatch and rear them. But if you want eggs right away you'd best buy some young pullets, just ready to lay.'

Yardley shook his head. 'I must admit I've never kept poultry. How do you make a hen go "broody" as you call it? I suppose she has to decide to incubate the eggs.'

Amy sighed warily; she mustn't lecture him too much, he didn't like it. 'Folks sort of share them round, in summer. It's nature's way, I suppose, of breeding up more poultry.' She looked at him out of the corner of her eye, but the dark face was neutral. 'F'r instance, if I have a hen that goes broody, she won't lay any more eggs, she just sits tight and clucks. She's no use, unless I want to hatch some chicks. So I'll lend her to someone over the moor who does want chicks but has no broody hens. I used to like watching the hen teaching the chicks to scratch for food.' Amy grinned at the Misery, willing him to smile. 'I could ask round for a clucker if you like.' Market day on Wednesday was the best place for this sort of information.

'Well, we might do it if there's time, but we'll need a male bird for fertile eggs, I suppose. How long is the incubation period?' Yardley was showing some sort of interest and he sounded very scientific sometimes. Had he been a scientist in York?

'Three weeks, it takes.' Flies buzzed round the horse's head and Amy brushed them from her own face. 'They don't all do it, but some hens just naturally start to cluck and sit tight in spring and summer ... there'll be plenty round Masham just now.' In her mind's eye she could see little fluffy yellow chicks, clustered round a mother hen. 'We could rear some this summer – there's a little hen coop we could use.' She stopped suddenly; she must remember not to tell him what to do. 'But this heat's not good...'

Yardley was hardly listening; he was looking at something on the road ahead. They were leaving the green river valley behind, they had passed the high walls of the Park and the road wound up a hill. Hedges were giving way to stone walls and the sloping fields had a look of the moorland. 'What's that? It looks like a body!'

Amy peered over the side of the trap and saw a black bundle on the ground, covered in flies. It was probably just a pile of old rags, but... Yardley jumped down and Amy did the same. He threw the reins to his assistant. 'Hold the horse.'

Gently Yardley touched the bundle and moved the black material back to reveal a face. Amy edged nearer and saw that it was a bruised face. The eyes were closed and the long dark hair was matted with blood. 'Is she ... dead?'

An hour before Yardley drove up towards the moor, Sara West had stumbled down the dusty road with one idea hammering in her brain. Saul might find she was gone and come after her, and if he did, he would kill her this time for sure. Weighed down by a heavy winter coat, she tried not to breathe in the hot dust. It had been stupid to bring the coat on such a day, but the pockets carried a few possessions.

A buzzard circled above her in the brassy sky. How many more miles to Masham? She should get off the moor road, Out of sight; she desperately needed water ... it was almost a relief when she tripped over a stone and fell heavily. Just a little rest and she would get moving again.

Eyes closed, Sara could still see her husband towering over her, feel his hands on her neck. This last time he had very nearly killed her in his rage. He had seen her talking to a pedlar who sold lengths of cloth and unfortunately, the man had said something to make her laugh. Saul, half drunk, accused her of being unfaithful. Once again, he had forced himself on her brutally; she never wanted to go near a man again. Why had she married him? Because her parents approved; young, handsome and rich, Saul was impressive. He knew how to be pleasant when it suited him and he'd seduced her. She had thought he loved her then, but he wanted a slave, he wanted to beat, to humiliate his woman and she had not realized the truth until it was too late. And now that her spirit was broken, he despised her.

Then the thought faded, the heat receded and everything went dark for a while.

Coming to herself, above the heavy buzz of flies Sara was dimly aware of a woman's voice... 'Is she dead?'

Yardley shook his head and as he did so, the woman opened her eyes and flinched, bringing her hands up to shield herself. 'Don't hit me!' Her hands were badly bruised.

The farmer got up and looked briefly at Amy, his face grim. 'She's afraid of me, poor soul. You speak to her.'

Amy handed the reins to Yardley and knelt in the road. 'Sara Lawson! Whatever has happened to you, Sara?' But the woman had drifted into unconsciousness again. It was important to speak gently, to keep the horror out of her voice. To Yardley she said quietly, 'Sara and I were at school together. She married a man who owns a lot of the moor.' The girl's eyes were closed and she seemed not to hear what they said. 'We've got to get her to a doctor, but can we carry her into the trap? Maybe if we tie up the horse and both lift her...' The flies buzzed as they moved the inert body; she was heavy to lift. 'Why would she wear so many clothes on a hot day?'

Yardley shook the reins and they set off back down the hill to Masham, all thoughts of poultry forgotten. 'We'll take her home with us,' Yardley said firmly. 'To Banks Farm.

91

The heat has affected her of course, and she's badly bruised, but we can treat her ourselves.'

Amy supported the girl as they clopped slowly through the dust and heat, wondering how Sara had come to this. Who had inflicted such injuries and why?

She'd married only last year ... surely it couldn't be her husband? All she knew of him was the name, Saul West, and that he had a big moorland estate with a lot of sheep and a whole army of workers.

Sara was only dimly aware of being lifted gently into a vehicle, of moving slowly through the hot day. Afterwards, she remembered the scent of hawthorn blossom as the stone walls gave way to hedges on the lower land. That told her, confused as she was, that she was off the high moor and back among farms and people again. It was a comfort; there were too many shadows on the moor.

Some time later Sara found herself in a cool room, with a strange woman bathing her face and wrists with cold water. The heavy coat was gone. Gratefully she drank when the woman offered her a glass of water. Then a tall man came in and with a rush of terror, Sara's arm came up to shield her face.

'Don't worry, I won't hurt you,' the man said gently. 'I'm Ben Yardley and this is my aunt, Mrs Shaw. What's your name?'

Silence was best, Sara thought. Was she

safe here? Would they take her back to the moor?

'There might be concussion,' the man said quietly.

'Sara,' the girl whispered at length, to prove she hadn't lost her memory.

A smile lit the man's dark face. 'That's what Amy said. Do you remember why you were on the road, Sara?' She was aware then of another face watching her, a young woman with untidy fair hair, whose features seemed to rearrange themselves into a familiar face. Amy ... Appleton. How much did Amy know?

Amy said fiercely, 'Who did it to you, lass? The police should know about this. You never did anybody any harm!' She looked across at Yardley. 'Sara's a landowner's wife, he has a big place up at Carlsmoor and he owns a lot of farms. But there's marks on her neck! Someone tried to strangle her!' She paused, still staring at the farmer. 'Should we get her to the doctor?'

'No!' Sara's hoarse voice was as forceful as she could make it. 'I mustn't be found...'

'We can treat her, Katherine and I know what to do.' Yardley's deep voice was very reassuring and Sara felt herself relax a little.

Amy seemed very confident with these people. 'So now I call you Doctor Yardley, do I?' There was a hint of mischief in her smile.

93

The man shrugged. 'Don't be daft, Amy. I'm a tenant farmer, as you know.' He moved away impatiently. 'Rest, that's what you need, Sara. But we'll see to the damage first.'

Sara drank milk that the other woman brought, but said nothing. She was gently washed by Amy and her cuts and bruises treated with salve. Amy said she worked for Yardley. 'I was looking for a job after – after Father died, and they wanted a dairymaid, so here I am.' She patted Sara dry very gently with a towel. 'So – what happened to you, lass?'

Sara shook her head and winced with pain. She was not going to tell anyone about the humiliation, the sheer horror of being married to Saul. His threats were real and they haunted her; they would always haunt her. He knew how to silence her. He had a reputation as an upright man and no one would believe her if she told them what he had done. Saul West, the prosperous, well educated landowner who went to church on Sundays and gave money to charity; that was the other side of the man. The violence was hidden and in their isolated home, where servants were housed separately, there was no one to hear her screams. Sara had found that rich men can make their own rules.

Amy went out with the bowl of water and sun moved through the sky towards evening.

None of Sara's bones seemed to be broken, but her wrist had been cruelly twisted and Yardley bandaged it; the cuts and bruises were soothed by the salve. Yardley gave her a small dose of something to deaden the pain and after taking a little soup, she was put to bed between cool sheets. Sara slept.

Waking to moonlight, she was confused before she remembered where she was. These people had saved her life; she would have died on the road very soon if they hadn't found her. If ever she could help them in return, she would do it. Thank goodness they had come along. Her life was ruined, degraded, but somewhere deep inside Sara there remained the will to live.

Back in Masham Amy lay awake, looking at the moonlight. She tried to remember all she knew about Sara West, formerly Sara Lawson. They had been friends at school, but Sara's parents were teachers and had sent her to a private school for the last year. After school, Amy had worked at home on the farm and only occasionally had she and Sara met at the market, or a concert in the town. Sara had been training as a teacher herself at the new college in Ripon until she gave it up when she married, last year.

Amy had not been invited to Sara's wedding ... what was the man's name? Saul West, that was it. He'd come from north of

Darlington to buy an entire moorland estate, complete with rented farms and shooting rights. The grouse shooting was important and attracted rich people from all over the world and the sheep runs extended to thousands of acres. So in Masham it was known that Sara had done very well for herself and Saul was said to be handsome, which was a bonus. Something, though, had gone badly wrong, that was clear. The pitiful creature they had picked up out of the dust was hardly the same bright girl that Sara used to be.

The other surprise was Ben Yardley. He'd handled Sara confidently and very kindly. Why couldn't he always be pleasant?

Sara looked worse than ever that morning when Amy visited her after milking, but she said she was improving. The bruising was lurid purple, yellow and orange all over her face and arms and there were still livid welts on her neck, which she tried to cover up. 'So – where were you going, Sara? What's up?' Hands on hips, Amy looked down at her friend. 'You can tell me, you know.' Sara said nothing and after a minute, Amy tried again. 'Are you running away from your husband?'

Sara nodded and looked away.

'He can force you to go back, of course. He has the right.' What a terrible situation for the poor lass. He must have belted her ... whatever she'd done wrong, she hadn't de-

96

served this. And what a terrible law, that would force a woman to live with a man who treated her like this.

'I've got to get away, Amy. My parents can't see me like this, I'll go home later. My mother has a weak heart, it would be too much of a shock for her ... I must look like a monster.' The swollen lips smiled a little. 'And also, he'll look for me there. I have to get away from him ... but I can't travel in this state.' Sara was fighting back tears. 'Amy, I was wondering ... do you think I could stay with you, just for a day or two? I can pay my way, I've got some money.' The dark eyes were frightened, pathetic.

Amy sat down on the side of the bed, a thing she'd been told by Gran never to do. 'If only I had a little house of my own, yes, of course, lass. But Ma and me, we live with my Gran.' Amy sighed and shut her mouth tight in case any criticism of Gran escaped her. Gran would have a fit if she took anyone home, but of all things a woman running away from her rightful husband would bring out the worst in Gran. She could already hear the hard voice, telling Sara her duty.

'Oh, dear, I didn't know you lived with her. Yes, I remember your Gran. She was always – strict.' Sara understood; there was a pause, while Amy tried to think of something useful to say. Where could the poor girl go?

'There's one place I can think of, but you mightn't like it...' She stopped as Mrs Shaw came in with the patient's breakfast, a lightly poached egg.

The older woman put the tray in front of Sara and stood looking down at her. Sara said she was much better, thank you and then Mrs Shaw said gently, 'Would you like to tell us what happened? Sometimes it helps – to talk about your troubles.' The silence lengthened. 'But perhaps a warm bath would be what you need.'

Sara put down her cup and pushed back her thick brown hair. 'I – I can't say anything.' She kept her eyes down. 'But thank you, thank you so much for saving my life. All of you.'

'We are pleased that you were found in time! You could easily have died, out there in the sun. But those bruises need more salve and you should stay here and rest for a few days. Have you anywhere to go after that?' She must realize that Sara was not going to go home.

'I'm going to organize that,' Amy said. 'If Mr Yardley will leave us on the square in Masham, I can take Sara to – a safe place.' The old bakery was now empty and Patrick had left what furniture he had. Sara could stay there for a while, but she would need permission first. She must feel safe.

That evening Amy went through milking

as fast as she could and then walked swiftly back into the town. Instead of going home she turned down the road off the square that led to Mr Russell's house. Bob and Maisie Russell would be just sitting down to their evening meal and Mrs Russell would not be pleased to hear the doorbell ring.

'I'll tell them you're busy,' Amy heard her say as the door opened. She looked down at Amy on the step, who tried to smooth down her hair. 'It's Molly Appleton's lass, isn't it? Will your business wait until tomorrow? Mr Russell has had a hard day.' She prepared to close the door.

Amy stood up a little straighter. 'It's very important, Mrs Russell, but it won't take very long.'

SEVEN

Three days later, Ben Yardley dropped off both girls in Masham square. Sara looked round nervously. 'I don't like being here ... someone might see me.' She was swathed from head to foot in several shawls that made her look like a much older woman.

'This way,' Amy said cheerfully. She led the way round a corner to the old bakery, Sara lagging uncertainly behind. 'Mr

Russell said I could rent it for a while ... it's got some furniture, too. I said we might start up the bakery business again. Of course I didn't mention you, Sara.' Mr Russell had smiled indulgently at Amy and she had promised to spring clean the entire building, in return for a few months' rent free use of the premises.

Sara stood in the middle of the neat little kitchen. 'It's lovely, Amy ... just so long as nobody knows where I am.' The late afternoon light streamed in through the window; all Patrick's things were still in their familiar places. Amy felt a pang of sadness as she looked round.

'Well, a friend of mine lived here for months and nobody knew he was here except me and Mr Russell, and I actually walked in one day. It's tucked away, somehow behind the yard walls and the lights don't show out at night. The front of the shop is different, of course, but these rooms at the back are very safe. I'll come to see you as often as I can.' Amy lit the fire and filled the kettle at the sink 'We'll need to get you some food, of course.'

Sara subsided into a chair wearily. 'The only thing I've got is some money. I knew where he kept the money and I – stole some...' she shuddered.

'That's not stealing, Sara,' Amy said firmly. 'Your husband's money is yours.'

Sara shook her head, but then went on, 'I need some clothes, maybe you could get some stuff and I can make a dress or two and some underwear. Yes, and some food – bread and cheese would be good, and maybe a few eggs. Mrs Shaw gave me some honey. They're so kind, Amy, and so are you... I hope to repay you one day.'

'Nay, I don't need help, lass. It's good that we were there when you needed us. Now, would you like to look round? This here's the bedroom, it's nice and clean, but the working part of the bakery is all cobwebs and rust. You won't need to go there.' Amy explained that she had thought briefly of reviving the bakery business, before she got the dairy job. She wanted to talk about Patrick, but not yet.

Yardley had said that she could forget about the evening milking just for once, so Amy went off to buy some food. But horrors, there right in front of her was Gran at the grocer's. 'What are you doing here at this time of day?' the old lady rasped. 'You should be working. "For Satan finds some mischief still for idle hands to do".'

'Doing errands for Mrs Shaw. "How doth the little busy bee improve each shining hour", that's me.' Amy quoted gleefully from the same poem, one of the pieces she had learned by heart at school and once performed at a concert. Amy loved poetry but it

101

was lost on Gran. She only liked the dark bits, the doom and gloom and hell fire. The grocer winked at Amy as though he sympathized and Amy thought once again that Mr Coldbeck was far more human than his son Percy.

Taking the food back to Sara, Amy thought of something else. 'If I get a few books, that will help you to pass the time, and you'll need patterns for the dresses.'

She almost ran across the town to Mr Jackson's little shop, that sold tobacco and newspapers, sheep dip and candles, and many other essentials of life. In the back of the shop was a small, well-thumbed lending library. Amy paid a penny and came away with several books and two dress patterns.

'Mr Dickens is popular just now, he's been in Leeds doing readings,' the old man told her. Mention of Charles Dickens reminded Amy of Patrick and their talks about books. Patrick, where are you?

Amy ran back to the bakery and then thought of candles, so she went back to the shop again. By this time milking would be over and she would be expected home for the evening meal. She looked at Sara and smiled. 'The bruises are fading! I'll call in the morning on my way to work.' She was out of breath and felt rather giddy, which was strange.

The next day Amy went to check up on the patient and was pleased with what she saw. 'Who's Patrick? I found a book with his name in it today.' Sara was livening up a little, taking an interest in her surroundings. She smiled. 'I suppose he's the lad who lived here before me – is he a friends of yours?' Amy blushed and Sara added, 'I can see he is. Have you heard from him?'

'No ... he said he'd write, but I've heard nothing. Sara, I'm worried...' and sad and heartbroken too. 'I asked him to write to me via the post office, but nothing has come through.'

Sara nodded in sympathy. 'I wish I could help. It's been a few weeks, but that's nothing to worry about.'

'I'm selling butter today, it's market day, so I'll be in town before the post office closes.' Amy could feel her fragile happiness slipping away; Patrick might not come back, after all. He might have forgotten all about her.

When all the butter was sold, Amy slipped over to the post office but once more, there was no letter waiting for her. If only Patrick had left his address! He'd said he didn't know where he would be living.

It was July, time to cut the hay at Banks Farm. Amy was scrubbing out the cowshed with her usual vigour one morning when a

103

shadow fell across the doorway. Yardley was in the hayfield, supervising the long awaited mowers and presumably praying for good weather, but Amy wasn't sure about that. Ben Yardley never seemed to go to church. Mrs Shaw had gone to Ripon in the carrier's cart and now, Amy was alone and there was a visitor. She laid down the broom, smoothed her hair and looked up at him.

The visitor smiled pleasantly and Amy found herself smiling back. He was rather below average height, but so slim and well proportioned that it was hardly noticeable.

'Are you the lady of the house?' he enquired, raising his hat. Behind him she could see a tall thoroughbred horse tied to a rail; strange that she hadn't heard him approach.

'No, I'm the farm adviser,' Amy said brightly, and then regretted it. 'But I'm the only one here at the moment. Can I help you, sir?' She was used to dealing with salesmen, but this man was well dressed, almost elegant and his shiny leather boots must have been polished by a servant. Business, it must be, and only Yardley could deal with him.

'I hope you can advise me then, Miss,' the man said with a slight smile. The handsome, tanned face turned to look round the yard and Amy admired the pure profile. 'I'm looking for news of my wife, who has had an accident.' He turned to Amy with a serious look. 'My shepherd was on the moor just above the town three weeks ago and he tells me he saw the Banks Farm trap on the road. I think you may have been a passenger. Now, did you meet anyone walking on the road that day? I have been making enquiries far and wide, distracted with worry, as you may imagine.' The man paused and then went on, 'It was a faint hope that you might have seen something, some clue as to where she might have gone.'

Amy gazed at him with interest. How smooth he was; no wonder Sara had been deluded into thinking he was a normal, gentle man, kind to children and animals. First impressions were not always true ones; Yardley appeared to be sour and mean, but he was quite kind underneath.

Amy gathered her wits for the answer, she must be careful what she said to this intelligent man. 'I'm sorry to hear about your wife, sir. No, we met no one walking that day.' It was strictly true. They had found a pathetic bundle on the road. 'But I will enquire in the town for you, if you like.'

'My name is West. My poor wife was originally from Masham, you may have known her ... Sara Lawson, she was.' He paused and Amy nodded. 'She has, I'm afraid, become deranged. There was always a slight mental weakness, I understood that all along, but the mind has slipped in the past year.'

'That must be dreadful for her, and for you,' Amy said politely. Could he be speaking the truth? She searched her memory for evidence of Sara's weakness. It wasn't likely; Sara was training to be a teacher, before she met Saul West.

'It is, and this is why she must be found. Three weeks ago she fell and hurt herself during one of her ... fits, you see. I had arranged for her to see a nerve specialist and she was violently opposed to it, but ... it's the only thing to do. Poor Sara is no longer able to decide for herself, and its my duty to look after her. But she actually ran away from home when I talked of the specialist, and now she seems to have vanished. Her parents, her friends – nobody has seen her.' West shook his head sadly. 'I'm so afraid she has come to harm. I've done my best, she has a beautiful home, the best of everything. But for the illness, she would be very happy.' There was a break in his voice; it was beautifully done and Amy almost found herself feeling sorry for him.

'Yes, I remember Sara from school. I'll certainly try to help, Mr West. Some of the other girls in the town might know something.' What if this were true and Sara was deluded? It was a dreadful possibility and in one way it was more likely than Sara's story. Her husband seemed genuinely upset.

106

'Of course, my men have been scouring the district ever since she disappeared...' Amy maintained her polite expression, but she was quaking. What if West's men stumbled on the bakery?

Ben Yardley swung into the yard with the dog at his heels and came up to the visitor. Amy tried to give him a warning look, but he ignored her. Mopping his brow he said, 'We hope the rain holds off for a week, now the grass is being cut for hay. Good day to you, that's a fine mare you have there. I'm Yardley,' he added.

West looked at his horse complacently. 'Yes, I paid a fortune for her at Newmarket, I'm going to breed from her. Mr Yardley, how do you do, I am Saul West. I have just explained to your ... helper here, that I am searching for my wife. The young woman tells me that you saw no one walking on the moor road three weeks ago, on the day we lost Sara.'

Yardley shot Amy one swift look and agreed. 'No, we saw no one walking on the road that day.' He looked the man in the eye. 'Was she unhappy? It was unusual, was it not, for such a lady to be walking alone so far from home?' The tone was neutral, but it was not quite that of a tenant farmer. Amy wondered once again how Yardley came to be so confident.

'She was not well, I'm afraid. She had fallen

107

and hurt herself and the underlying cause is – I hate the word – insanity.' The eyes that looked back at Yardley were troubled. 'To be truthful, I am distraught.'

Yardley's eyebrows rose, but he said only, 'I sympathize, you're in a difficult situation.' There was a pause and he changed the subject. 'Have you lost any ewes lately? But I suppose your shepherds will keep a sharp eye out for trouble. We've thought that the odd ewe might fall into the river and so on, but too many have gone – I'm twenty down this week and something must be done. Trouble is, I'm new here and I don't know many other farmers. Have you any idea what can be done?'

West moved towards his horse. 'I must keep going. Well, I haven't noticed any problem with the sheep, but on the moor we only gather a few times a year, so we don't count them often. That's bad luck for you when you're just starting up... I will tell my men to report any thing unusual.' He unhitched the reins and swung easily into the saddle. 'And of course you will let me know if you hear anything of Sara.' It was not so much a request as a command.

'You knew Sara when she was younger. Did you know about any mental problem?' Yardley demanded as soon as West had trotted out of the yard. 'Her school mates would have spotted anything unusual, surely?'

108

Amy looked at him. 'I was going to ask you about it. Sara was a clever girl, but sometimes she would just stop whatever she was doing – speaking, or walking, anything. She didn't hear us speak to her, sometimes she staggered a little. In a few seconds she was normal again and didn't seem to know that anything had happened. Have you heard of anything like that?'

Yardley looked grim. 'Falling sickness, by the sound of it. Sometimes the victims have a full blown fit and injure themselves, but those with the mild form don't always. I wish I knew the truth!' He hammered his fists together. 'It's a logical explanation, but it doesn't quite explain the sheer terror on that poor girl's face.'

'Either poor Sara is really ill, and blaming her husband, or...' Amy stopped.

'Or West is a good actor and a lying villain who abuses his wife,' Yardley finished for her, his tone hostile. 'Her falling sickness would be a perfect excuse for him.'

'Didn't you like him, Mr Yardley?' Amy picked up the broom to finish her work.

'No, I didn't. But then I don't take to people easily.' Yardley strode into the barn and started to take down hay forks from their rack.

'So I've noticed,' Amy muttered, but not so that he could hear. Sir didn't seem to take to people at all and maybe that was why he had no wife.

Yardley came back to Amy in a few minutes. 'You'd better be here early tomorrow morning. We'll need to turn the hay, I expect you've done it before. And then I'll have to sort out the bees. The clover honey is ripe and we need to clear out the hives before they go up to the heather.' He sighed as though the thought of making hay made him feel tired.

'Can I help you with the bees? I would like to learn about them,' she said demurely. This was her chance to learn a new skill, and to let Sir do the instructing. It might cheer him up, Amy thought.

Yardley looked at her closely. 'You won't panic or anything, will you? There's a chance you'll get a sting or two. But if you really want to learn, bring a hat with a brim tomorrow and a dress with long sleeves. Then we'll see.'

Amy called in as usual the next morning at the old bakery to see Sara on her way through the town, even though she was earlier than usual. 'You're looking much better ... we'll have to go for a walk one evening, Sara, you need some fresh air. You can wear the shawls and a bonnet and nobody will know you, even if we see someone by the river.' She felt suddenly giddy; the room was turning round her and she sat down at the table.

110

Sara moved the boiling kettle from the fire.' I'd like to go out – but do you think it's safe?' She poured boiling water into the teapot with a hand that was quite steady.

Sara was neat in a print dress, her thick brown hair was smooth and there were few traces left of the bruises. 'You're right, I am improving. Have a cup of tea, Amy, if you've time. You're looking pale this morning.'

'No time today lass, we're haymaking. I'll try to spend a bit more time with you when I can, it must be lonely here on your own.' Amy stood up with an effort.

'Don't worry about me, look after yourself. I think you're doing too much. Now, just have a look in here.' Sara led the way into the big bakery kitchen and Amy gasped. All the cobwebs were gone, the floor had been scrubbed and the walls whitewashed. 'I found some whitewash in a cupboard. So when you want to start your bakery, it's almost ready. I just have to get the rust off the ovens. Can you buy me some vinegar?'

Sara was evidently trying her best to do something to help and so far, there had been no signs of insanity. But Yardley, who thought he knew everything apparently, had told Amy that some patients were very clever at hiding their delusions and that even falling sickness would be hard to spot unless it happened right in front of you.

111

Amy sighed as she turned in at the track to Banks Farm. All they could do was wait and see... At that moment she felt her stomach rising and turned aside into the hedge to be sick.

Now what had she eaten to cause this? Feeling rather shaky, she drank some clear water from the little beck that flowed into the river. By the time she reached the farm, things seemed to have returned to normal and she sat down with the milking stool and bucket quite happily. Yardley spoke very little in the mornings and Amy was left to her own thoughts, but by the second cow the thoughts had become uncomfortable. She had been so busy with other things that she'd neglected to notice what was happening to her own body. What if ... what if she was going to have a baby?

Amy went cold. But surely not ... she and Patrick had only made love that one time, and she knew that her parents had been married for years before she was born. But – it was possible. Oh Patrick, why haven't you written?

Haymaking went on as usual, but Amy was not able to enjoy it. She was strong and healthy, but the threat of pregnancy weighed her down. With no hope of contacting Patrick, she was on her own. Amy's thoughts went round in circles but she had no idea what to do, except to wait and hope that next

112

month the flow would start again and she would be free.

The nausea came over her frequently, but at different times of the day. One morning soon after she got dressed to go to work, she had to run to the outside privy and when she came back in, there was Gran waiting for her with a face like thunder. Gran always got up earlier than anyone else and was proud of it. 'What's the matter with you, then?' she demanded, her eyes raking over Amy from head to foot. 'Not in trouble, are you?'

Amy felt faint. The blood drained from her face and she turned away. 'I've got to go to work, I'm late.'

'If you've gone and got yourself into trouble, if you're in the family way, I'm not having you in this house. We've no place for a fallen woman here. Just think on, then.' Gran shut her mouth like a steel trap and started to walk up the stairs. She looked down at Amy from the stairs and added, 'I reckon you've got a fancy man somewhere, so let him take you in. I've done with you. And your mother will be the same. We will never be able to hold up our heads in this town again. I know what you've been up to, you hussy.'

Amy looked up at the old woman but could find no words.

'And I shall have to tell your poor mother.

Now, if you're expecting I give you a week to get out of my house. And after that I'll never speak to you again.'

EIGHT

'I can't help worrying about Amy.' Katherine Shaw looked up from her sewing one evening, after a day in which Amy had suffered bouts of retching and was looking as pale as a ghost. 'Ben, she's a pleasant girl and I don't think she's immoral, but ... she must be pregnant. She's ill and she's so quiet, too.'

Ben Yardley looked up from the newspaper he was reading and sighed. 'I was hoping it was only a digestive problem and she would recover ... but you're probably right. Time will tell, and we may lose our dairymaid if she gets married – which I suppose I hope she does.' A smile flitted across the dark face. 'Young Amy will make some man a good wife, you know. You chose well, Kate – she's a grand lass, as they say in Masham. We got the hay in good time, just before the rain. Amy wasn't well, but she worked hard.'

Mrs Shaw laughed. 'Amy would be shocked to hear you say that! You're very grim sometimes, you know, I think she tries

114

to cheer you up. But when I chose her for the job, one reason was that she had no follower and no plans to marry. And do you know, I believed her.'

'I think she's truthful, Kate. She must have met somebody since she came to work here – I wonder who it could be? It's none of our business, I suppose, but she may need help.' After a while Yardley passed the newspaper to his aunt. 'Now, I want you to look at this. There's a farm for sale, quite near here and I'd rather like to buy it.'

They both looked at the sale notice, which told them that a hundred acres on the edge of the moorland was to be sold because the farmer had decided to retire. 'What would you do with it?' Mrs Shaw frowned a little. 'It would be a lot more work for you, Ben, and I can't help you on the farm. In fact, I need young Rosie in the house for another few hours a week. I'm glad you found her, she's a treasure...'

Ben looked over the paper at his aunt. 'Well, ask Rosie for more hours if you like, Kate. I can afford it. It was Amy who recommended her, of course.' He looked at the paper again and sighed. 'I could hire a labourer or two if we get more land... It's always a good investment. We could turn some of the river flats here into arable and grow oats and turnips, keep more cattle and sheep. Sheepcote is only a couple of miles from here, we could move stock up there from here.' He paused and then added, 'We've done quite well here at Banks Farm so far, thanks to you and Amy. I was very new to it all when we started, but now – well, I'd like to expand, and have some land of my own. Haytime's over and we have very little corn, so...'

After a silence Mrs Shaw looked up again. 'There's a house with that farm, you could hire a man and wife, if we lose Amy. The wife could perhaps make butter and cheese.' She wanted to see Ben organized before she went back to York

'It's a good day to harvest the honey, you can help me if you like.' Yardley handed Amy a piece of black net and showed her how to drape it over her straw hat to protect her face from stings. They walked down to the hives together and Amy could hear the soft buzzing of many bees in the flower garden. 'The best time to open the hives is on a warm day, with most of the bees out foraging. They don't like us to take their honey, and you can't blame them.'

'Why are they not all out in the sunshine?' Amy wanted to know. She would concentrate on the bees as a way of forgetting her problems for a while.

Yardley was busy lighting a fire in a tin with a tiny bellows on the bottom. 'Because the

116

queen bee never leaves the hive, she lays eggs to hatch out into more bees. And then the younger ones, they feed the queen, and feed the larvae – the grubs – when they hatch, and some of them make the wax to build combs for storing the honey. It's highly organized, life in a beehive.' He looked up through a haze of smoke. 'The smoke calms them. I'll lend you a book about bees, if you like.'

'Yes, please.' Amy peered over his shoulder as Yardley prised open the lid of the hive with a metal tool and sent a puff of smoke over the frames. 'Beeswax makes polish ... we use it for the furniture. I suppose you can take the wax as well as honey?'

Yardley grunted and lifted out a wooden frame filled with wax cells. 'Often we put the old combs back so they can use them again. This is how they store the honey, see?' Several bees buzzed angrily and Amy stepped back, but Yardley carried on, just brushing them away gently. 'Always move quietly, and don't harm a bee if you can help it. It makes the others more aggressive.'

Several frames of honey were loaded on to a wheelbarrow, leaving some behind for the bees. Then they moved on to the next hive. When they got to the third, Yardley tucked in his collar and cuffs and put on gloves. 'This hive is harder to handle, they're a swarm I took last year, not so quiet as mine. Stand back, Amy, they're coming out.'

It was too late; bees surged from the entrance in an angry cloud. Amy was stung several times on the arm and the pain was intense. Tears came to her eyes, but she made no sound. 'Don't touch the stings!' Yardley warned her. He stopped what he was doing and, holding her arm, scraped away the stings with a fingernail. 'It's worse if you rub them, the sting stays in the skin and keeps pumping in poison,' he explained. 'We'll put a drop or two of lavender oil on them when we get back to the house. Pull your sleeves down, you forgot what I told you.'

So it was her own fault she was stung; trust Sir to see it like that. Amy tried to smile. 'Thanks. I'll remember to stay well away from hive number three.'

They took the frames of honey back to the dairy, followed by a few bees, and closed the doors and windows. Amy was afraid that this part of the process would make her feel ill again, but the honey was fragrant, smelling like clover, the essence of summer. It was a miracle that the tiny insects could preserve the sweetness of clover as food for the winter.

Yardley cut the caps off the wax cells by slicing through them with a big knife and the honey oozed out. A square of muslin was fixed over a large bowl and the wax was scraped with a spoon; the honey started to filter through the material and into the bowl. As she stood watching, Yardley said quietly, 'Amy, forgive me if I'm wrong, but perhaps we should have a talk. Have you a problem that we can help you with?'

His eyes were on the work, but Amy felt herself blushing. She watched the golden honey trickling into the bowl and wondered what to say. Had he guessed her guilty secret? Should she lie, or pretend she didn't know? She took a deep breath and decided to be honest. In any case, he and Mrs Shaw should be told, it would affect them too eventually when their dairymaid couldn't work. What a pickle she had got into, through being weak and giving in to a handsome lad who now appeared to have forgotten about her! 'Well sir, I'm afraid – I might be expecting a baby.'

Yardley looked up and she saw not irritation but concern on his face, although most employers would have been annoyed. 'Oh, dear. We need to know – it will affect your work.' He paused and then said gently, 'I'm not judging you, not at all, but perhaps you need some help. I know a bit about it, you see, can recognize the signs. You will need to see Dr Andrews, of course.'

The kind, quiet tone was too much for her and Amy broke down in tears. Yardley quietly took a clean spoon and held out a spoonful of the golden liquid for her to eat. 'This will calm you,' he suggested and the fragrant sweetness was comforting; she did feel better after it.

After a while, as the honey slowly dripped through into the bowl, Amy told him what had happened; Patrick had gone away, he'd said he would write to her, but there had been no letters and she couldn't contact him. 'And in any case,' she had to face facts, 'he probably wouldn't be able to afford to get married ... not for ages. But we are promised to each other.' Or we were, she thought bitterly. 'I never expected this to happen, it was an accident, really, that we–' She stopped. All the silly lasses who fell would probably say the same thing.

Yardley was quiet for a while, scraping the wax cells and periodically tipping the sticky wax into a bucket. 'Let's look on the bright side,' he suggested with one of his rare smiles.

This from the man she called the Misery! 'Is there a bright side?'

'A new baby should always be good news. You're a healthy young lass, you shouldn't have too much trouble and I'm sure you'll be good at looking after a baby. It's just the other people and what they say, isn't it? Especially in a small town. It's always the other people – and of course, the father, if he's not keeping in touch. But there may be a reason for that. It could all end happily, Amy.'

This was so unlike the grim farmer Yardley; it was more like the side of him she admired, his gentle touch with animals. Amy sat on a stool, her head resting on her fists as she watched. 'Gran's sending me away, of course. She found me out and she doesn't want the scandal in her house. Maybe I could stay in the bakery with Sara for a while.'

Yardley sighed and picked up another frame of honey. 'I ... had a bad experience, once, and other people condemned me. Judged me without knowing the true story and it completely spoiled my life for a while. I might as well tell you that the woman I was to marry had no faith in me, she preferred to believe the critics. And then, when I decided to come here she didn't want to be married to a mere tenant farmer. So it all ended happily.' He cut through the caps neatly with the big knife and Amy thought how expertly he worked. 'Morals are all very well, but judging other people is wrong and it leads to so much unhappiness. I've never understood why unmarried mothers should be ruined for life, just for the lack of a ceremony, but I'm not very conventional, I'm afraid.'

So that was his story; what Sir had just said might explain the gloom that seemed to descend on him very often. Mrs Shaw had hinted at trouble; she was here because of

121

Sir's low spirits. And now Amy, who had been trying to cheer him, was in low spirits herself. 'I suppose most people have troubles in their lives,' she said. 'I shouldn't have ... done it, but then we are – were – promised to each other. But I don't know what to do.' She could appeal to her mother, but Molly would never stand up to Gran, who had bossed her all her life.

Yardley straightened up and looked down at Amy. 'On the practical side, I know what you should do, Amy. I suggest that you come to live here at the farm with us, for now. It will save you a lot of energy, walking through Masham every day, and it will keep you away from prying eyes.' He grinned like a lad. 'And when a cow's due to calve, you can take a turn at getting up in the middle of the night.'

'Are you sure, Sir? It would be easier.' Amy hadn't wanted a 'live-in' job, but now it seemed like a wonderful idea. It would be much easier if she didn't have to walk the four miles to work and back. But would Mrs Shaw agree? And what would she think of Amy's trouble? She was a regular church-goer and might object to Amy living in the house on moral grounds, like Gran.

'It's common sense. When winter comes we'll have snow, and that will make travel more difficult. And now, will you line up the glass jars? Fetch me some hot water and a cloth, and we can pour the honey.' Yardley was smiling at his solution to the problem.

Amy went into the kitchen for a kettle of hot water, where Mrs Shaw was shelling young peas from the garden. Perhaps she should face the question straight away. 'Mr Yardley said that perhaps I could live here, for a while, instead of going back to Masham at night. Would you be you happy about that, Mrs Shaw? I-I'm expecting a baby, you see, and ... the man I'm going to marry has gone away and I can't contact him. You might not want me here, when ... when it happens.'

There was silence for a minute and Amy thought she might get a moral lecture, or the sort of revulsion she'd had from Gran. Then the older woman smiled. 'We, Ben and I, would like to have you here. You'll be welcome, Amy, and when your time comes we'll be able to help you. I have two children, both grown up now of course, so I do know what to expect.' She looked at Amy and added, 'It's unfortunate, of course, especially if your man isn't here – he must bear at least half of the blame! But it's not the first time it's happened, you know. Try to keep cheerful, won't you? For Ben's sake as well as your own.'

The room started to swing round alarmingly and Amy sat down suddenly at the table. 'Thank you, thank you,' she said faintly. 'I didn't know where to turn ... and I don't know what Mother will say. I haven't

123

talked to her yet.'

That night Amy managed to get her mother alone in the scullery after supper and told her that she was going to move to the farm. 'And I suppose Gran's told you the bad news.'

Molly sighed. 'Aye love, I was right sorry to hear you're in the family way ... but it's not the end of the world, in spite of what Gran says. You can tell me all about it when you're ready. I've been wondering for a while whether we should find a place of our own, away from Gran, so you can have a bit of peace. It's not easy for you here.'

Relief flooded through Amy like a warm tide. 'Oh Ma...' She should have told her mother about Patrick at the start. 'I'll go to the farm for now, keep earning my wages while I–'

'What are you two doing in there? Come out and stop wasting candles.' Gran wrenched open the scullery door, blew out their candle and glared at the two guilty faces. 'Oh what a tangled web we weave, when first we practise to deceive,' she grated. 'What about my hot bricks?'

Without a word, Amy took two hot bricks from the oven at the side of the fire, wrapped them in a cloth and carried them upstairs to warm Gran's bed. She felt lighter than for weeks; her mother was on her side and Gran didn't matter.

At the beginning of August the whole

124

country was declared free of the cattle plague and the Masham folk heaved a sigh of relief. Ben Yardley decided to sell some sheep once the markets were open again. 'A few lambs left over from last year,' he explained to Amy. He seemed to be energized by the good news. On the day he went over to look at the farm that was to be sold, he called at Gran's and picked up Amy's trunk of clothes and possessions. She had been given her old bedroom in the farmhouse and it was wonderful not to go back to Gran's house after the day's work was done.

Mr Yardley's good mood did not last very long. He returned from the livestock market at Ripon, swearing and muttering that something must be done about the sheep. 'There was a pen of ewes in the market and I reckon half of them were mine, but I can't prove it,' he growled. 'Their ear notches had been changed, but I knew them all right. I'm going to try to trace them back, I've asked the auctioneer to help me. He's going to look into where they came from.'

'Nothing wrong with those sheep, Mr Yardley,' the auctioneer told him the next week. 'There was a lot of stock in, folks have been waiting for the marts to open again. That pen you mentioned was part of a big consignment that came down from the High Side, from Mr West, Carlsmoor. He's a big man in these parts and he wouldn't handle anything that was come by dishonestly. I'd stake my life on his reputation. You must ha' been mistaken, sir. But of course, he might have bought them in to sell on, that's probably what happened.'

'I wonder about West,' Yardley said as he drank a cup of tea before milking. 'He's well thought of and very charming, but then who mistreated his wife?' Amy had been thinking the same thing; Sara was often on her mind. 'Those bruises and wounds couldn't have all been self inflicted.'

Sara was improving, but her nerves were still bad. Molly had agreed to call in on her often, after Amy had taken her there one Sunday afternoon and explained the situation. Sara's parents had been there once or twice, but that was all. The fewer visitors she had, the less likely it was that West would find her.

'I won't be in Masham so often when I live at the farm,' Amy had explained to Sara. 'But you need supplies and a bit of company. It'll be a nice change of company for Mother too ... but Gran mustn't find out.' She shuddered at the thought.

'I was lonely all right, on the moor,' Sara said. 'But I don't feel lonely here at all.'

Amy soon got used to living at Banks Farm again. She was invited to sit with Yardley and his aunt in the parlour after supper, but she felt it invaded their privacy and there was plenty of room in the kitchen. When he mentioned the sheep one evening she offered to walk down to the river, to check them before dark.

'It beats me how they get spirited away,' Yardley said for the twentieth time. 'Yes, you go, the walk will do you good.' He and Mrs Shaw were often thinking of things that would do Amy and the baby good, such as extra helpings of Yorkshire pudding, and it was becoming a joke between them. 'Most females don't walk enough.'

Amy jumped to the defence of the lazy females who rode everywhere. 'But it's not ladylike to take walks on your own,' she said lightly. 'My Gran was always telling me how shocking it was.' She blushed when she remembered that Gran had suspected her of meeting a lad ... and had been proved right. Females who walked about on their own were likely to get into trouble.

As she walked down the farm track Amy was thinking about Patrick. She would be selling butter again on Wednesday, a chance to call at the post office and perhaps – just perhaps find a letter waiting for her. How she longed to see him again. Would he be pleased to hear about their baby? Amy herself was more reconciled to the idea by now, but she still found it difficult to imagine it as a person, a new human being.

The sheep were all bunched up in the far corner of the paddock, even before they saw Amy. Quickly she switched her mind to the task in hand. Something had disturbed these animals recently, but the sun had dropped behind the moor and it was not easy to see far in the soft afterglow of the sunset. A last gleam touched the river and Amy's eye was attracted to ripples on the water. A boat was pulling quietly away from the bank, a big shallow boat with two men in it. Two men, and she could also see several little heads ... sheep's heads, going downstream. So this was how they got the sheep away.

NINE

Of course she should have rushed back to the house and told Yardley, but by the time they got back to the river it would all be over. Quietly Amy went down to the old willow and stepped into the little rowing boat. She would give the men a few minutes to get round the river bend and then she would follow, to see where they went.

Amy wondered where the sheep would be landed; they couldn't go far. The river swung out in a long curve at the village of Thorpe, where it became wide and shallow again, no use to a boat. The twilight deepened and an owl hooted in the wood on the opposite bank. She fitted the oars and slid the boat out into the middle of the river.

About a mile downstream, they came to level fields on the river bank, dotted by clumps of willow. At one of these Amy hid her boat and scrambled onto the bank, hampered by her long skirt. She crept along silently. Ahead she could now see the bigger boat it was making for a stone barn in a field on her side of the river. She watched as the men tied up the boat and lifted out the sheep between them. The animals were tied up with ropes round their legs and necks and were helpless, although they were trying to kick. Six or seven of Yardley's sheep, pedigree breeding ewes and their little lambs, were being thrown about roughly. Rage swept over her at the way the animals were being treated and at the loss to a hard-working farmer. These men should be tied up themselves and thrown into jail.

Suddenly Amy was grabbed from behind in a strong grip. There was a smell of beer and onions and a rough voice growled, 'What you doing here, you bitch?'

She froze with horror and then tried to collect her wits; who was he? Amy managed to wriggle round enough to look up at the man. It was the 'water bailiff' who had accosted her before, a huge coarse man with ginger hair and a red face. 'If you're really a water bailiff, arrest those men! They're stealing sheep! Don't worry about me, go and do it! Those sheep belong to Mr Yardley, they've been stolen!' But her heart sank as she said it; this was no law officer. He was one of the thieves.

The man laughed in her face. 'You seem to know a lot about it. Too much, maybe. Pity you had to come along just now, but–' He stopped and turned as the other men shouted something to him. The last of the daylight was lingering near the river, but the bank where they stood was in shadow.

'Come on, Bert, we need you now!'

The man called Bert gave a sudden heave and Amy overbalanced into a deep pool at her feet. She heard him give a hoarse laugh and then she felt herself going down, down into the dark, icy cold water. The river was swollen with recent rain and the current had swirled into the pool, carrying leaves and twigs with it. Grimly she struggled, determined to get out, but her heavy skirt held her down. She couldn't hold her breath any longer; frantically she tugged at the skirt, but it was clinging to her. She was going to drown. So this was how it would all end … before the baby had even started to live. She had let him down.

Yardley was in the stable that evening, cleaning harnesses and wondering how much the new farm was worth and whether he should buy it. He was lucky, he had money to invest but it must be spent wisely. If he had more land it would justify more labour and then he wouldn't have to clean his own tack... He didn't need a full time groom, but a man who worked with horses would be useful, they would need to plough in the autumn.

From time to time he looked out to the river track expecting to see Amy coming back from her walk, but there was no little figure in sight. What had kept her? A cold feeling crept over Yardley as he realized that far from taking a quiet walk by the river, Amy had gone to make sure that sheep were not being stolen. But perhaps they were, and perhaps she was in trouble. The thieves could be dangerous if disturbed – what would they do to a young woman who caught them in the act? He should not have let her go, it was thoughtless, dangerous – and she was pregnant, she should be taking care.

Yardley put the newly cleaned bridle over Mary's ears, the bit into her soft mouth and without waiting to saddle up, jumped on her back. Mary was a steady eight-year-old mare and she had not been worked too hard lately. A little gallop would do her good.

As she flew down the river track the mare's hooves thudded on the soft ground. There were no gates to open, the field gates were to the left and right of the track, which led by a winding route to the river. Amy should be safe, she must be safe. Yardley was surprised how agitated he felt. 'Must be getting old,' he told himself.

Bending down from the horse's back to open the gate of the sheep paddock, Yardley could see nothing amiss; the sheep were grazing quietly at the far side. He cantered across the short grass to the river bank and took the walking track that led downstream. If Amy was not here, she must have gone down the track, although there were no little footprints in the earth. Then he remembered the boat; she had told him about it...

A mile downstream, Ben Yardley was ready to give up. He must have missed Amy, she'd be back at the farm by now. Looking down the river, he saw a pinpoint of light in the distance, like a bobbing lantern. He strained to listen; on the breeze came the high wail of a lamb. It could be from a farm across the river, but there was something going on ... a hoarse shout, then a little scream and a splash. He dug his heels in and the mare surged forward.

In the fading light he could just see that a big man was running away towards a stone barn, but there was nothing else, except ripples on the river. Throwing his bridle over the horse's neck, he ran forward and, looking

132

down into the water, he thought there was something white ... a little hand. Amy was down there.

Lying on the river bank, Yardley felt under the water until he grasped an arm, but he had to jump into the river before he could make any progress and the pool was deep. Amy was lifeless, a dead weight hampered by her clothes. The main thing was to take off her heavy skirt and it took all his strength to hold her and free her legs from the heavy, wet material. Treading water, he did so and was relieved when her weight eased a little. Holding onto a tree root with one hand, he eased her to the bank and managed to drag her clear of the water. Turning her to lie face down, he grimly started to pump the water out of her lungs.

By now the daylight had gone; the moon was rising, touching the river with silver.

Yardley worked frantically. 'Amy, can you hear me? Please Amy, start breathing!' he muttered, but she was white and still.

If only he hadn't let her go off to the river on her own! He should have known it was dangerous. If Amy was lost, nothing would be worthwhile. Water dribbled out of her mouth as Yardley worked, firmly pressing and releasing her rib cage to get the lungs working again. He knew it was touch and go; had she been in the water too long? Surely not, he'd heard her fall in, but still... But she didn't fall;

she'd been pushed, because she'd seen his sheep being stolen. He would never forgive himself, never.

After what seemed an eternity to Yardley, Amy coughed, spluttered and her breathing came in ragged gasps. After a while she tried to sit up and she grabbed at his hand, thanking him with her eyes. As soon as she could speak she gasped, 'Thank goodness you came. Oh sir, they're stealing your sheep!'

'So I gather,' he said grimly. 'And it seems you were taking risks. You ought not to have done it, you know.' Amy was not drowned, he had pulled her out in time.

'Will the baby be hurt?' Her eyes were huge in a pale face framed by her wet, plastered hair. She held both hands to her stomach, cradling it.

'The baby will be fine, they can put up with quite a lot.' She should never be allowed to take risks again. The breeze blew through his wet clothes, but Yardley felt happier than he had for years. He'd sounded severe again. 'But I do appreciate that you were trying to help.'

Amy felt her cold legs. 'Goodness, I'm in my petticoat!' She looked like a little waif in the moonlight. 'A big man threw me in the river... I don't think he wanted me to get out again, it was very deep just there.' She looked up and tried to smile. 'Thank goodness you came when you did. If you hadn't been there,

I should have drowned, I couldn't get up again.' She tried to look round. 'I suppose we've lost the sheep, poor things.'

Yardley felt weak with relief. 'Don't worry about the sheep, Amy. We'll follow them up another day – now we know they go out down the river, I can tell the police to look out for them. Now, let's get you out of here. Can you stand up? That's good. Now, the horse is here, you can ride home. Mary will warm you up.' Yardley decided not to sound too sympathetic; she might cry. 'Tell me about it when you're warm and dry.' And if she had drowned, nobody would have known what happened – except the thieves. When she was found eventually, the coroner would have called it suicide. Sometimes a lass threw herself into the river, rather than face life as a fallen woman. It was a chilling thought.

Amy was very quiet and Yardley walked beside the horse with his long stride, going as fast as he could. 'Soon have you home now,' he said cheerfully. 'You didn't know that lout who pushed you in?'

'No... I've seen him once before though, remember I told you? That man who told me to get off the river. He said he was a water bailiff.' Amy shivered in a sudden breeze. 'But at last now we know how they're leaving. Oh sir, the boat is down here, I came down in it tonight and I nearly forgot it.

Shall we–?'

'Tomorrow,' Yardley promised. 'It should be safe until tomorrow. Now, did you see anybody who looked like Saul West? I keep coming back to it, those sheep of mine were sold by him at the market.' They had come to the boundary gate and the horse stopped. 'But I suppose he'd be too important to be running about after a few sheep in the dark. I wonder what really goes on.' He opened the gate and led the mare through, back into the safety of Banks Farm.

The next day Amy insisted on working as usual. Being pushed into the river had been terrifying, but she hadn't been in the water very long, thank goodness. She tried to forget the sensation of being dragged down in the water by her heavy skirt. If Sir hadn't come along when he did, she would surely have drowned. She was beginning to feel that she owed dear Benjamin a great deal.

Butter making seemed to take longer than usual that day. Amy felt tired and rather weak, but work was better than sitting in the shade thinking about dying, either in the past or the future. On her mind was a nagging worry: had the baby been affected by her time in the river? 'Unborn babies are well cushioned,' Mrs Shaw assured her.

Mrs Shaw reminded her nephew at lunch

that the promised poultry hadn't yet arrived. 'When will you be able to collect them, Benjamin?'

'Well, I can go there today, if you like. I assume they're still waiting for us. Then I could take a look at the hive site on the moor. I always visit to check it before I move the bees, in case anything has changed since last summer.' Yardley himself looked tired, Amy thought, but he wasn't grumpy at all, just rather thoughtful.

'Do you go to the same place every year?' Amy asked. She had seen hives on the moor when the heather was in bloom, but never given them much thought.

'I've been taking the bees to the Harlands's farm for some years now, for the heather harvest. For the rest of the year they were on a farm at Tanfield, over the river from where we are now.' Amy nodded; she had been wondering how he could bring bees up here all the way from York. Yardley looked almost pleased at the thought of a trip to the moor. 'I came over from York when I could, and got to like Masham. So when this farm was vacant I asked Russell to let it to me.' Yardley helped himself to another plate of soup. 'Have some more soup, Amy, it'll do you good.' But Amy shook her head.

'Take Amy with you, she can choose the hens,' his aunt suggested. Amy was happy to go, and rather pleased that they should value

137

her opinion. Together they had cleaned out her father's old poultry shed and mended the wire on its run, which was green with weeds. Yardley had bought a bag of wheat and Amy had suggested a small tray of grit, which she knew was something to do with the birds' digestion.

'Our biggest problem was to keep the hens out of the garden,' Amy had explained. 'But they need to scratch about in the yard, to get insects and things.' The farmyard didn't look quite right without a few hens.

As soon as the meal was over, Yardley went out and Amy followed him after she had helped Rosie to clear the table. It was a bright afternoon with a few high clouds and a soft breeze. 'Have you a crate or a box to put the hens in? I can hardly hold them on my knee all the way home.' Amy looked into the empty trap, thereby earning a black look from her employer, who was yoking up Mary to the vehicle.

'Do you think I'm completely stupid, woman?' Sir was back to his normal grumpy self. It was odd, but Amy realized she was getting used to it.

Another vehicle came into the yard. It was a smart pony and the trap was piled high with sacks and parcels. Percy Coldbeck jumped down heavily and lumbered over to them. 'Flour and sundry items, delivery for Mrs Shaw,' he announced importantly. 'And how

138

are you, Amy? I haven't seen you for weeks. Your mother told me you are now living at the farm, of course. I would have thought that you would inform me yourself.' In the flat Yorkshire accent his formal words sounded odd, but that was how Percy always spoke.

Amy blushed and glanced at Yardley, who was trying not to laugh. 'You may have met Percy, Mr Yardley.' To the lump himself she said quickly, 'I'm sorry we can't stay to talk, we're going out.' Percy looked disappointed.

Yardley let her down at this point and Amy was dismayed to hear him say, 'Take a few minutes to talk to your friend, Amy, while I find a crate.'

It was time to get it over with; she now had the perfect excuse for getting rid of her suitor, painful though it was. Amy walked across the yard with Percy to his pony and patted its smooth nose. 'I'm sorry Percy, but you won't want to see me again. Not after what I must tell you. I'm – I'm expecting a baby.'

The lad's mouth dropped open and he stepped backwards. 'I don't believe it. How could you ... this is not like you at all!' He paused as the full horror sank in. 'I knew your grandmother was upset about something you'd done, but now I can see why! How very dreadful! Well, Amy, I wish you well, but I must distance myself from you, naturally.' He backed away again, as though she had a disease. 'I would hate anyone to think that I was involved with you in any way. It would not do, you know, I have the good name of the business to think of.' He looked round the yard. 'Mr Yardley doesn't think it's my fault, does he?'

'Mr Yardley doesn't think about people very much, only animals.' That wasn't quite fair, but it let Percy know how little interest Yardley was likely to take in him. The farmer reappeared with a wooden crate, which he stowed in the trap. 'Mrs Shaw is in the kitchen, you can knock on the door over there,' he said to Percy.

As they swung out onto the road Yardley shook the reins and Mary broke into a trot. 'The pompous grocer had designs on you, did he? Thought you'd be a handy lass on the cheese counter, I suppose.'

Amy managed a laugh. 'The good thing about all this is that Percy has just dropped me like a hot cinder. I've been trying to get rid of him for years.'

In fact, Percy's shocked reaction was hard to bear, but she would have to face the disgust of the whole town in the end. A fallen woman could expect no sympathy; she suddenly realized how unusual her employers were, how understanding. Many farmers would have turned off a dairymaid who was pregnant, in case the scandal reflected on their good name. As it was, gossips might suspect Yardley of being the father... What a terrible thought.

Mary plodded steadily through the town. The site for heather honey production was the first objective and to get there, they had to follow the moor road, the horse pulling steadily uphill past little grey stone farms sheltered by trees; past the place were they'd found Sara that hot day. Honeysuckle wafted from the hedges at first, but then there were only stone walls and soon they could see the vast sweep of the moorland, the first tinge of purple like a haze over the heather. They went through a gate and so came to the open moor. Amy breathed in the clean, cold air and looked across the top of Nidderdale. After the green Ure valley with its tall trees, the moorland had a bleak, bare look, in spite of the purple heather billowing in endless waves to the horizon. There were few farmhouses and the low stone buildings huddled in little valleys they called gills, trying to keep out of the wind; cloud shadows chased each other over the slopes in patterns of light and shade.

Amy tried to imagine life on the moor for someone like Sara, who was used to the bustle of a little market town. With a good husband it would be quiet enough, but with a brute it would have been so much worse, unimaginable. Why did West insist on living in the wilderness, if he was rich? They could have lived in comfort on the lower land and Sara could have kept in touch with her family.

The folks who were born up here were used to isolation, Amy knew. For weeks on end in winter, you would be cut off by snow from the rest of the world, entirely dependent on your own resources. If you were expecting a baby, you would go to stay with a relative, somewhere in civilization. Then there was the summer heat, and sometimes fires in the peat that burned for weeks, covering the moorland with smoke. 'We're only a few miles from Masham, but this is a different world,' she said, and Yardley nodded.

'A more primitive world, I think. People would have lived in the same way here for hundreds of years.' Yardley reined in the mare and took a deep breath. 'Can you smell the heather?' They sat for a moment and Mary looked round too, as though admiring the view. Then as Amy watched, the mare's ears went back and she snorted in alarm.

A horseman appeared over the nearest ridge and when he spotted them, altered course. He pulled up beside the trap, a man in rough tweeds and riding a big, raw boned grey. He looked flushed and it was a few minutes before Amy recognized Saul West,

Sara's elegant husband, looking less than elegant in his working clothes.

He sat his horse and scowled at them. What had they done?

Amy wondered whether they had strayed on to West's land and were trespassing, but the moorland was unfenced and the moor roads ran through the various properties.

Perhaps he was worried about his game birds; it was the grouse season and shooting parties would be out. Yardley had warned her to keep a look out for them, although the butts were a long way from any of the roads.

'Yardley, it's you. What are you doing up here?' The tone was not very friendly.

West's horse moved nearer and tried to bite Mary, but she threw up her head and avoided him. Yardley bit his lip and backed her off a little. 'I'm about my business, the same as you are, I suppose.'

'You have no business here,' the landowner sneered. 'Get back to your rented farm.'

TEN

Amy sat very quietly, watching West. The change in the man was amazing. Gone was the charm and the handsome face was twisted in an ugly expression. This must be Saul West as his wife knew Kim, whereas before, they had seen the face he presented to the world. Why was he showing his other side today?

Yardley moved irritably on the seat beside Amy. 'We bring the bee hives up to the heather every year, you'll know about that. I'm just going to check the site before we move them.' Ben sounded cool and he had his usual grim expression, but Amy knew he was angry.

West frowned and jerked at his bridle. 'It will have to stop. My tenants do as they've always done, but they'll have to learn that they've got a new landlord now and things are changing. In future the tenants will be told not to take bee hives. I hate the damn things.' He wheeled the horse sharply but Ben held up a hand and he paused.

'What have you got against bees? They're a very old tradition on the heather. They do no harm up here.' Amy wished that Ben would move on, but he seemed interested in West.

'Had a bee sting once, nearly killed me. I swelled up and couldn't swallow. Doctor said to keep away from bees and that's why they're not wanted here.' He glared at Ben. 'Leave them at home, Yardley.' It sounded like a threat.

A young, half grown sheepdog came trotting up to West and his attention was diverted. 'Come here, you mongrel!' he growled and the dog flinched. He put a chain through the animal's collar and savagely wrenched it until the dog was choking. Amy felt sick.

Ben shook the reins and Mary moved on; Amy looked back, longing to help the dog. West left abruptly, dragging the dog along behind the horse and the encounter was over. Amy felt better when he had gone. 'Will you still bring the hives up here after that?' she asked. 'One of his men might tip them over, or smash them. I wouldn't trust that man with anything. You won't be able to protect them, or visit them often.'

Ben laughed. 'Yes, of course I'll bring them. Most folks will leave bees alone, for fear they get stung. West doesn't frighten me, although he would like to, he thinks he can bully a tenant farmer like he bullies his dog. It's interesting to have moved down the social scale and observe the different reactions... I wasn't a tenant at York, you see.'

145

'Well, my dad was the tenant before you, but nobody treated him like that,' Amy said fiercely. 'He was well respected and I always thought that folks judge you on what sort of a person you are – and maybe how well you farm – rather than how much land you own.' But then there were people like Gran, who judged you on their view of morals.

'There are a few like West who patronize the lower orders, although things might change now that most men are able to vote.' Yardley looked at Amy. 'Did you think the man had been drinking? I thought so, too. It doesn't matter – he and his men won't go near the bees. As a matter of fact, they won't be on West's land, so he can't do a thing about it. His Lordship, my landlord of course, owns this stretch of moor over here and that's where we're going. Mr Russell the agent knows all about it.' He waved an arm over the sea of heather, but Amy could see no boundary. For a mile or two they went on in silence, broken by the call of a curlew and the occasional whirr of a grouse from under the horse's feet.

Eventually Yardley pulled off the road and took a track beside an old building. 'We don't put the hives too close to the road,' he explained. They went on for a few minutes and then he stopped at a ruin. 'There was a farmhouse here once, a long time ago.'

The little stone house was roofless, the

windows blank like sightless eyes. Bushes sprouted from the stones and in the front was a ruined garden, with a straggly rosemary bush that had survived the years. 'I wonder who lived here?' Amy whispered. Could a woman have been happy, shut away in this lonely fold of the moor, gathering rosemary to cook with the mutton that would be their main diet? The herb suggested that a woman had lived there once, perhaps a woman who spun and wove the wool of the little upland sheep. Of course, if Amy lived there with Patrick, it would be different. But even then, it would be a cold and lonely place. No wonder it was empty of all but its ghosts.

'They're a special type, those that farm up here. They have to be bred to it, I suppose. I wouldn't like it.' Yardley got down and peered into the ruined house.

Amy thought about poor Sara, brought up here by her husband to somewhere not far from this isolated place. 'Will the hives be safe here?'

Yardley laughed. 'Safe as anywhere. It's a tradition, taking bees up to the heather and we, beekeepers that is, have an understanding with the farmers – we give them a few jars of honey.'

'Yes, and some of them use it to make bochet.' Amy's father had told her all about it. Yardley looked puzzled and she added, 'They ferment it and make a sort of mead.

It's very strong, bochet. But it's maybe better for them than gin – that's what they drink all winter.'

Yardley nodded, swinging up into the driving seat. 'If I lived here I'd be tempted to do the same! Now, Miss Amy, why do you think this is a good place for the hives?'

Realizing this was a lesson, Amy considered. 'Right among the heather, for a start, they won't need to travel far, and there's a little beck over there, so they'll have water, I suppose even bees need water. Those stone walls will stop the westerly winds and – they'll get plenty of sunshine. But it's a bit cold, I think your little bees will be glad to get back to Masham when it's over.'

'Sadly enough, some of them won't come back. Bees only live for a few weeks in summer, Amy. Then they're replaced by younger ones from the nursery.'

Yardley turned the trap carefully for the return journey. He was a good driver, Amy thought, considerate with horses – and he was even sympathetic to bees.

They called in at the farm on the way back and saw the shy farmer's wife, telling her that the hives would be in place in a day or two. Her face lit with pleasure when Yardley produced a jar of clover honey from the batch that Amy had poured. 'That's grand, Mr Yardley, thanks.'

As they regained the main road, Amy watched figures on the skyline, coming closer. Shepherds were on the move, a fairly large flock of sheep pouring over the slopes, bleating as they came down like a woolly tide, washing up at the sheep pens near the road. Somewhere they heard a dog barking, a sound that changed to a howl and then a scream of terror. A man could be heard cursing.

Yardley increased their pace. 'That poor dog's catching it... Most of these moorland folk think the world of their dogs. I wonder if it's that man again?'

Soon, it was all too clear. West had dismounted and still had his dog on the chain. He had one foot on the chain and was whipping the poor beast with a riding crop, shouting and even redder in the face than before. The dog cowered, but could not escape. It was hardly more than a puppy and Amy was afraid it would be killed. In the background the grey horse waited, flinching.

'Don't kill the poor dog!' Amy shouted. The man looked up and then hit the dog even more viciously. Yardley jumped down and, avoiding the whip that was raised against him, managed to overbalance the man so that he stepped off the chain and the dog was freed, but it lay still. Amy got down from the trap; the poor animal seemed to be lifeless, but when she laid a hand on its

149

head, it opened one eye and looked at her. Amy never forgot that look.

Yardley stood directly in front of the man, who was shaking with rage, and said quietly, 'You'll die of apoplexy if you don't watch out.'

West half raised his whip against Yardley. 'You've no right to tell me what I can do with my dog,' he shouted. 'I'm going to kill the swine. He was hunting grouse when he should have been working.' He raised the whip again and then staggered.

'We are taking the dog away, you're not fit to own him,' Yardley said through set teeth, as furious as West but with an icy calmness. West was a short man and Yardley towered over him. He gently picked up the dog and put him in the bottom of the trap with the whip curling round his shoulders, but West came no nearer. They left as quickly as they could, Amy holding her breath, or so it seemed until the moor gate was closed behind them. Yardley looked at Amy with a grin. 'Good job he was drunk, if he'd been able to stand up properly I'd have got a whipping.'

'If he'd touched you, I was going to get your whip and hit him from behind. I would have enjoyed it.' The big whip sat upright in a holder at the side of the trap, but it was never used. Amy looked at the dog. He was a black and white collie, rather too thin and he had big bleeding welts all over his body. One ear was half torn off and he lay quite still, hardly breathing. 'But now we're criminals. We stole a dog.'

'I will offer to pay for the dog,' Yardley promised. 'Poor Sara! This is the man she was living with.' He shuddered. 'And now, we'd better get home as fast as we can, the weather's changing.' He looked up at the sky, where black clouds were gathering. The moorland was bleak and sombre now, a hostile place. 'The RSPCA should pay a visit to Mr West.'

They called very briefly to collect Mrs Shaw's pullets; Amy was afraid that the dog would die if they delayed too long. She quickly tried to pick out the hens that looked the healthiest, but they all looked equally healthy and they were all the same age. Amy counted ten of them carefully into the crate, squawking in protest as they went. She picked them up gently with a hand at each side of the little bodies, holding the wings down and the pecking beaks away from her. 'So that's how you do it,' Yardley said. 'I thought you picked them up by the legs and held them upside down.' He brought out his wallet and paid for the hens.

'Only when they're dead,' the farmer's wife said firmly. 'Treat them gently if you want them to lay.' Amy wondered how he would have got the hens into the crate with wings flapping, if she had not been there. There would have been more panic and a lot more pecks... Sir still needed her assistance.

When they got back to Banks Farm, Amy led the horse away and unyoked it while Yardley carried the dog into an empty stable. Gently he bathed the terrible gashes and the animal feebly licked his hand. After some time, Amy encouraged the dog to drink water. She gathered chickweed leaves and mashed them with a little lard to make a green ointment for his wounds and Yardley nodded his approval. 'An old Yorkshire remedy, eh?'

The hens were tipped gently into their new home, cackling in alarm, but they soon settled down to scratching for grains of wheat. They were a mixture of colours from white to deep brown – plump birds with very red combs. 'They're Leghorns,' Amy explained. 'We'll have eggs in a few weeks.'

The dog was left to rest, but by morning it was more active and they gave it some beef broth. 'The poor thing might survive,' Mrs Shaw said cautiously, as worried as Ben was about the creature. Her young hens were established in their new home and she seemed to be pleased with them.

'You really need a rooster,' Amy told her. 'For the proper farmyard sounds, I mean.'

The next day was market day and when

Amy had sold her butter with time to spare, she crept quietly round to the back of the bakery to see Sara and tell her that they had met Saul West. 'Anyone who'd seen him beating the dog would be horrified!' Amy told her. And they would believe Sara's story, not Saul's.

'That was my puppy! Saul took him from me to be a sheepdog. I called him Jake, he was company for me. I was lonely up there on the moor.' Sara looked at Amy through tears. 'Now you've seen for yourself what Saul can be like when he's drinking. He has bouts, he's unpredictable...'

'The little dog should get over it in time and one day you can have him back, Sara.' Amy felt tears coming to her own eyes. This story had set back Sara's recovery, reminding her forcibly of the terrors of the moor.

'And now, Amy,' Sara was looking at her closely, 'You'd better tell me about your troubles.'

Amy sat down and covered her face with her hands. 'I've been meaning to tell you about Patrick ... but you've had enough grief of your own to bear.' Sara sat quietly beside her and said nothing and after a minute or two Amy continued, 'Patrick and I are promised to each other. He went away and said he would write to me, but I've ... heard nothing. I keep going to the post office, but nothing. I don't know where he is, and now

I'm expecting his baby... Oh Sara, what a mess!'

Her friend took a deep breath. 'I guessed about the baby. What does Mr Yardley say? And Mrs Shaw?'

Amy relaxed a little. 'He told me to look on the bright side. They're very good people, they treat me better than I deserve. But I don't want to be a burden to them.'

She sighed. 'It's not right to bring a baby into the world without a father.'

Sara's face was soft as she said, 'The baby will come when he's ready... I lost mine, you know, when Saul hit me – before I ran away. But about Patrick, there must be a reason. If he was a decent lad, and I'm sure your judgement of men would be better than mine, his letters must have gone astray. Now...' She paused. 'I think somebody else could have picked up your letters, Amy.'

They looked at each other and said together, 'Gran!'

'She might have worked it out somehow...' Amy said slowly.

'I remember your Gran was always keen to know folks' business, and she actually – would you believe it – asked me if I was in the family way, the week before I got married. She wondered why Mr West would marry me, else. I was annoyed, but I didn't say anything.' Sara looked out of the window at the garden. 'My problem was, I didn't know Saul at all well at that time. It would have been better if I had.'

'I know Patrick as a person, we spent some happy times talking, but I don't know his family and really, he was only here for a few weeks. I made a big mistake, that night of the storm, and I'm going to pay for it.' Amy stood up. 'But I will face up to Gran, I'll go there now and make her tell me.' Amy's fists were clenched, but then she thought of her mother. 'I should see Ma this week. She comes to see you sometimes?'

Sara smiled and nodded. 'I call her Molly, now.'

Molly was not at home when Amy walked firmly up the path and Gran was knitting furiously. 'I'm not talking to you no more,' she said and turned her back on Amy. 'I've finished with you – you're as daft as a brush.' The needles clicked reproachfully, reminding Amy that now she was not at home, Gran had to knit socks to make a living.

'Well, I am speaking to you, Gran.' Out of respect, Amy spoke quietly. 'I would like to know whether you took my letters from the post office, and what you did with them.'

The old woman looked round sharply 'What letters? I'll tell you what, my lass, if I did find any letters of yours I'd throw them on the fire! It's devil's work, that's what it is! You've no right to be getting letters from men. But I know what I'm going to do. I

155

shall go to see Mr Benson and cut you out of my will. You'll get not a penny from me, not if you're in the gutter you won't.' She came to the end of a line and moved the knitting over impatiently.

'So you did pick up letters ... from the post office ... and you threw them on the fire.' Amy gave her grandmother a murderous look

'If I did, it's nowt but what you deserve. "Hinder the Devil when you can", that's what I say.' Gran's thin lips shut tightly and she counted stitches.

Amy stood over the old woman. 'If you kept them, give them to me now!'

'I've nowt of yours, they're all burnt up. And when that gaffer of yours at the farm finds out what you've been up to, you'll be turned off without a character. Best you go away and leave us in peace. I'm off to change my will tomorrow.'

At that moment Molly opened the door and Amy saw her stricken look. 'I've been to the churchyard, put flowers on his grave. I wonder what your Dad would have thought of the trouble we're in.'

Poor Ma... Amy felt guilty once more. Ma must be finding it hard to put up with Gran these days; telling her what had just happened would only make her feel worse. 'Come out with me for a walk, Mother,' she said and for once, Molly agreed.

Amy headed across the market place, talking as they went. 'Let's go and see Sara, it'll get you away from Gran for a while. I'm right sorry, Ma about the pickle I'm in. But I think Patrick has written to me, only Gran burnt the letters.'

'I just hope the lad turns up, for your own sake,' Molly said sadly. Then they reached the bakery and the talk turned to making dresses for Sara.

'Mr Yardley will be coming into the square for the butter baskets, I have to go now,' Amy said quickly, and as the church clock struck four, there he was.

Amy said nothing on the ride back to the farm, but there was a thread of happiness underneath her anger with Gran. Patrick had been faithful, he must have written to her and Gran had burned his letters; she was sure of it now. There had been guilt on the old woman's face as well as the usual dislike. Why couldn't she have had a loving, comfortable Gran? Her other grandmother was just a distant memory, but Amy dimly remembered a kindly soul who gave her biscuits when she was a small child. The question remained; how could she contact Patrick? He would be having doubts himself by now, wondering why Amy didn't write to him.

A few days later, Sara decided to make a dress for Amy. She would cut it generously

157

to leave room for the baby, and it could be altered afterwards. She made a pattern, cutting it out of an old newspaper, and pinned it to a length of dark green material, one of the lengths that Amy had bought for her. Working like this made the days go quickly, but when would she ever be able to go out again? The bruises had faded, but she knew that Saul would not have forgotten about her and what had happened to the poor dog Jake was typical. Saul was dangerous, more so when he was drunk, and if she went home to her parents, he would surely find her.

Sara took up the scissors to cut out the dress and as she did so, she heard a sound in the yard. It was only the black cat, shooting out from under the lilac bush, but what had startled it? Then the kitchen door opened and a man slipped into the room.

Standing by the table with scissors in her hand, Sara summoned her courage. She felt like screaming, but that wouldn't help. 'Go away!' She waved the scissors fiercely.

ELEVEN

The young man put down a pack he was carrying and laughed. 'Good day, Miss,' he said cheerfully. 'Those scissors look dangerous. How about a cup of tea?' He looked at the kettle boiling on the fire. He was a well made youth with hair of a dark copper colour and blue eyes; his clothes were clean and neat.

Gradually, Sara relaxed. She was not being invaded. 'You must be Patrick,' she said.

'I am, and I didn't expect to find anyone here... I was going to stay for a few nights, you see. Sorry to intrude, Miss. Do you ... do you know Amy Appleton?' His voice was anxious. 'I must get in touch with her.'

Methodically, Sara made a pot of tea. She nodded. 'I'm Sara, keeping quiet here for a while. As you did at one time – Amy told me about you. Amy has been waiting for weeks to hear from you ... and nothing came. Did you write, Patrick?'

A shadow passed over the young man's face. 'I did, every week, but there was no answering letter. So I've come to see– Is she well, do you know? I so want to see her!'

Sara poured the tea and sat down, smooth-

159

ing her apron, surprised at how calm she felt. She was facing a stranger, which was unthinkable only a week ago. At least the bruises were nearly gone – she was not quite such a horrifying sight as before. Should she tell him about Amy? To gain time, she asked Patrick about his work and smiled at his enthusiasm for farming; it was so like Amy's interest in crops and stock, but more romantic. 'I love the haymaking season, the scent of the hay and the feeling that people have been harvesting like this for centuries – working with horses in the sunshine.' Had he ever tried farming in the winter, Sara wondered.

Soon, Patrick went back to the subject of Amy. 'I'm very glad to hear the real reason why she didn't write to me, although I can't imagine what happened to my letters. She didn't get a single one? I've been so worried ... she's a lovely girl, isn't she? I felt so helpless, hiding away here and not being able to go out to look for her. I didn't even meet her mother. But you see I had to find work on a farm and plan a future before my family caught up with me. My mother would have come here and made a scene if she'd known where to find me. This was a perfect place to hide, as you must have found, Sara. So now, what has Amy been up to?'

After a while Sara said, 'I should let Amy speak for herself ... but I'll tell you what I know. She's living at Banks Farm where she works, the folks are good to her. Amy's very worried about you and very sad that she hasn't heard from you. She went to the post office every week, hoping for a letter. I think someone else collected them and didn't hand them on – it was cruel. I'm so glad you've come to see her.' She paused; should she tell him? And then plunged on. 'And ... there's something else. A surprise for you, Patrick. She has found out that she's expecting a baby.'

Patrick froze with the cup half way to his lips. 'A baby! Oh lord!'

After a minute or two of silence Sara thought he was going to back out, to deny his part in making a baby. It was bound to upset the lad, if he had plans for university as Amy had told her. But Amy was rather shy, she was not at all forward or bold. She would have been seduced by this handsome, confident young man. In fact, he would have been hard for a lonely girl to resist. Was he another charming man with a hidden side, like her own husband?

Sara hesitated. Should she say anything more? It was up to Patrick to stand by Amy now. As Amy's friend, one who owed her a great deal, perhaps she could influence his thinking. 'Your baby too, Patrick,' she said gently. 'You're in it together.'

Patrick put his head in his hands, but his next words surprised Sara. He was thinking of Amy, not of himself and his own predicament as the breadwinner of a family. 'The poor girl, with no husband and no support! Losing her reputation, and then she might lose her job... All by herself!' He drained the tea and stared into space. 'People judge unmarried mothers very harshly, I know my own family does.'

'That's true, but if you love each other, you'll be able to work through the problems.' Before her marriage, Sara wouldn't have been able to talk to a young man so freely. Her recent experience had made her appreciate the good in people, and made her look past etiquette and convention.

Patrick was pale. 'I had no idea, of course... Amy must have suffered. Especially when she didn't hear from me, she must have thought I'd run away to sea.'

'That made it much worse – but it wasn't your fault.'

'Well, it is a shock, I don't know what to think. I desperately want to marry Amy, but I'd planned to save some money first. I must go to see her right away. It's my responsibility too, as you said.' He squared his shoulders. After a few minutes' silence he stood up as though he had made up his mind. 'You know what? It's a blessing! That's the right way to think.' He looked down at Sara and smiled, a real smile that reached his eyes. 'A new baby, of our own! We'll be a family! It's wonderful news, Sara. Everything will work out well, I'll get a job with a house. You look worried, but don't worry about us. We'll be so happy!'

Patrick left his pack at the bakery and strode off to see Amy at the farm. Sara was left feeling breathless; this young man seemed to live at a fast pace. She took up the scissors again with a smile. If all the lads who fathered a baby were as pleased as Patrick had decided to be, lasses would have a much easier time.

The next few weeks passed in a flurry of activity at Banks Farm and for Amy, in a blur of happiness. Once Patrick walked into the cowshed where she and Yardley were milking, everything changed. She jumped up and spilled the milk from her bucket. Yardley tactfully turned his back and they clung to each other. Amy could hardly believe that he was really here.

Patrick was just the same as she remembered him, but bigger and handsomer and he was delighted to see her well. She felt shy with him at first, but not for long. 'I – didn't know how you would feel about the baby,' she confessed.

'I will take great care of you both, from now on,' he promised. Patrick said he was working on a large farm at Boroughbridge and once they were married, he would find a house there for them. He now planned to

163

study agriculture in his spare time and try to achieve status as a farm manager eventually. He had to go back to his work in a few days, but there was the question of the wedding.

Somehow the milking was finished and they all went into the house for supper. Mr Yardley was rather glum. He said he was pleased to see that Patrick was taking his responsibilities seriously, but could he not find a job in Masham? 'I don't want to lose my worker,' he said as if he meant it. 'There's a farm I'm looking at – if I buy it, I'll be able to offer you a job and a house.' He looked as severe as ever, and Amy was surprised that he wanted her to stay.

'What was it you said about me on my first day here? "She'll be no use at all."' Amy kept her face straight as she looked at her grumpy boss.

'"Better the devil you know than the devil you don't". Didn't your granny teach you that one? I don't want to have to train another girl...' Ben Yardley tailed off as Amy glared at him. 'Maybe I should say that I don't want another girl to train me.' He looked at Patrick, sitting close to Amy on the sofa. 'I think you should have a look at the other place with me tomorrow, my boy.'

Patrick said quietly, 'I do feel obliged to my employer in Boroughbridge, I promised to stay...'

'That's loyal of you, Patrick, I appreciate

it. But the baby changes everything, you know. Now, we'd better plan the wedding and Katherine will help us. I know nothing about that sort of event.' Yardley looked across at his aunt, who nodded happily.

'I know just what to do. Now Patrick, we can offer you a room here if you would like to stay.'

The wedding was a quiet one and Yardley was thankful for it. Amy's dragon grandmother did not attend, but Molly and Patrick's mother were there. Molly wore a smile and a flowery hat, she seemed to be charmed by her son-in-law, although she shed a few tears to think that Amy's father would never meet him. She had put her own grief aside to share in Amy's happiness and Yardley admired her for it.

Patrick's mother, Mrs Seaton, wore unrelieved black and a sombre expression, but Patrick whispered that she had been in strict mourning ever since his father died. She was distant with Amy, but no doubt her son's sudden marriage had been a shock to her respectable soul. Sara came out of hiding, disguised in a big cloak and a hat with a veil. The vicar, who had christened Amy, might have guessed why the wedding was so quiet, but he kept it to himself.

Ben Yardley had offered to take the bride down the aisle, since Amy had no father and he took care to dress for the occasion in a well cut suit, which seemed to impress the bride. Of course, she'd never seen him off the farm, she didn't know his other self.

The farm chores were over very early and they all drove to church together. Amy, Ben thought, was looking much better since Patrick had turned up at last. The bouts of sickness were rare now and the healthy bloom was back in her cheeks. Sara had made her a pretty pink dress for the wedding, and she whispered to Yardley that she was praying for a happy marriage for her friend.

'So am I,' Yardley said with feeling, and looked across at his dairymaid. It was time to go into the church with her. Amy placed her little hand on his arm and he realized that he was dreading the moment, the business of giving Amy into Patrick's keeping. Patrick would be in her company for the rest of their lives; he would enjoy her mischievous smile, her lively sense of humour and the cheerful willingness that Amy brought to everything she did. Yardley's face was grimmer than ever as he looked down at the girl on his arm. He wanted her to stay with him, keep smiling at him and never go away... But she was marrying Patrick.

They moved slowly together towards the altar, where the vicar was waiting.

'Cheer up, Sir,' the bride whispered, and squeezed his arm gently. 'Soon be over.'

How like Amy to be concerned about how he was feeling, at this moment when all attention should be on her, as the bride. She must think that he dreaded the ceremony and so he did, but not in the way she thought.

Lovely little Amy ... and now he must give her up, he might not even be able to keep her as a worker. 'Amy...' he whispered back. The organ was thundering and no one could hear them. 'If things go wrong for you, I'll always be here.' He got the sweetest smile in reply, and then the marriage service began.

After the wedding Patrick went back to Boroughbridge. He explained that he had to earn a living, so he would need to stay in his job until he found another, either with Yardley or someone else. 'I'll look for a nice house to rent for my little wife,' he promised. He would come back in a few weeks and they could discuss the future then. Amy was pleased that the baby's future and name was safe, it would be born legitimate and have two loving parents. Patrick was sure it would be a boy. They all went back to Banks Farm for a meal before the groom went off.

Amy insisted on walking to the square to see Patrick off on the Ripon carrier. When they had gone, Katherine Shaw looked at her nephew and sighed. 'They're so young! But I like Patrick, don't you? I think they'll be happy.'

Ben Yardley sighed. 'I fear he's not realistic. He's obviously from a middle class background, family in the Church... He doesn't know what he's in for. Supporting a wife and child on a labourer's wage won't be easy. Amy's a sensible lass, but she's been brought up here, she was an only child and they were comfortable. You know, Kate, I think they'll struggle. Patrick was irresponsible, seducing her and then going off like that.' He frowned.

His aunt laughed. 'Maybe it will be rather like your experience, Benjamin? You came from a profession to be a tenant farmer. Down in the world socially, you might say.'

'Not like me at all,' Ben snapped. 'I knew what I was doing, I have capital and I have no dependants.' He paused. 'Sorry Kate, but I'm worried for Amy. Patrick's pleasant enough, but does he appreciate her?'

'Well, we'd better make sure that they do come to live at Masham.' Mrs Shaw started to clear the table of dishes. 'I'm sure Amy would far rather live here, near her mother and her friends. A girl with a new baby needs her mother, and she's attached to the farm, you know.'

'Yes, she's attached to the cows and the dogs,' Ben said bitterly, but then he smiled. 'Especially little Jake. She's nursed the pup back to health and now he follows her around like a shadow. I only hope West thinks that the dog died. If he asks for it back, he's in the right I suppose, but we're not going to hand it over.'

The heather was fully in bloom and the hives had gone up to the moor, but Amy was not there to see it because Yardley drove them there one morning before dawn. It was better to travel with bees at night, he said, because most of them would be in the hive. 'I hope you don't meet Mr West up there,' Amy said with a shiver. She reminded herself that Yardley had got the better of him. It showed there was an advantage in looking naturally grim.

'The hives are not on his land, remember... I think we came across him because all the shepherds were gathering their sheep at the same time,' Ben said soothingly. As usual, they were talking as they milked, the sunlight of a hot August afternoon filtering into the shed through the aggressively clean windows. The Boss had been quiet lately and Amy was trying to get him to talk, to lift the look of gloom from his face. Maybe he was worrying about the fact that the police had made no progress in finding the stolen sheep. When Mr West's name was mentioned, they were sure he must be mistaken. Mr West was a gentleman, not a thief and he was probably losing sheep to the villains himself, the sergeant had said. Yardley had come home fuming about class distinction.

Yardley tipped his bucket of milk and went to the next cow. 'After milking, Katherine and I are going to have a look at the place that's for sale – Sheepcote farm, they call it. I suppose you know it?'

'My dad was quite friendly with Josh Brown, they helped each other at times. Yes, I know the farm, he's a good farmer. Hedges and walls are tidy and he's always put plenty of manure on the land.' Amy thought a moment. 'But of course it's on higher land, almost on the edge of the moor. That means–' she didn't have to tell him, she knew by his expression.

'Poorer land and a shorter growing season. Well then, in your capacity of farm know-all, you're invited to go with us to see the farm.' Yardley sounded sarcastic, but Amy took no notice of his tone. She was hoping fervently that he would buy the farm and then offer a job to Patrick and they could live there, in that snug little stone house.

They drove there in the trap, in the cool of the evening. Yardley said little as they looked round, but he made a few notes. It was all neat, as Amy had said.

'Do you mind telling us why you're leaving, Mr Brown?' Mrs Shaw turned her eagle eye on the farmer.

'Well, it's not that I've failed, or ought of that,' the man told her. He was a rugged little

170

man of about sixty. 'I could go on for a few years yet. But my nerves are bad, what with cattle plague coming and going, and then I've lost quite a few sheep – stolen, mind you. Not strayed. We can't afford to lose any more, can we, lass?' He looked at his wife. 'I've had enough, to be truthful. But a younger man like Mr Yardley here, he'll do well.'

Mrs Brown nodded and then looked round the farmyard as if afraid that some-one might be listening. 'Nay, although we've a fair idea of where the sheep go, there's nowt we can do about it.' Her voice dropped to a whisper. 'West and his men, they're in charge of this moor now, but the police won't believe anything wrong of their boss – you know all that, I'm sure.' She looked earnestly up at Ben Yardley. 'It's a grand farm, but we've had enough. If you do take it, think twice about keeping sheep here, that's my advice.'

Yardley shook his head. 'I really must get to the bottom of this sheep stealing, it can't be allowed to go on. They take them down the river from my place – I've told the police but no arrests have been made. We haven't lost any lately, but I think it's only a matter of time before it starts again. And I too have a fair idea – I saw some of mine in the market, with changed ear notches. But I couldn't prove it, so I kept quiet.' The Browns nodded, but said no more.

They looked round the farm house, which was just as Amy remembered it. The rooms were clean and neat, she and Patrick would be very comfortable. She loved the big kitchen and the cooking stove, heated by either wood or coal. It was exciting to think of being the mistress of her own kitchen. Amy had been taught to cook by her mother, but she had worked on the farm more than in the kitchen.

As they were leaving, Josh Brown detained Yardley with a hand on his arm. 'We've bought ourselves a little place at Tanfield with a few acres, but we need to pay for it right away. I'd drop the price, Mr Yardley, if you was to take farm from Michaelmas.'

Yardley nodded. Michaelmas was a quarter day, the twenty-ninth of September, a significant day in the rural calendar, sometimes with a Michaelmas goose, fattened on the stubble in the cornfields. 'That's only a month away ... I'll think about it,' was all he said. But a few days later, he visited the Browns again and the deal was done. When Patrick came to see his new wife the next Sunday, he was offered a job and a house – and the new wife was looking at him in a way that made it hard to refuse.

Amy was finding work rather more difficult as her pregnancy advanced and it would be so much easier for her if Patrick came to work with them. Sheepcote had come along just at the right time, she told Patrick

They were walking by the river in the precious time they had before Patrick had to leave and when they came to the place where Amy had been thrown into the water, she laughed and told him the story. 'But we still can't prove anything...'

Patrick was horrified. 'When I come to work for Mr Yardley, I'll make it my business to find these ruffians,' he promised. 'In my spare time, if need be.' He looked down at Amy. 'But please keep well out of it, my girl. We can't have you and the infant coming to harm. The sooner I move over here, the better, I think.' His young face was stern.

TWELVE

Patrick was so worried about Amy that he left his job earlier than they had expected and was given a spare room to share at Banks Farm, until the married couple could move into their new home at the end of September. 'I left on good terms with the boss,' he said. 'We could buy oats or barley there for a good price, if needed.'

'I will file that away for future reference,' Yardley said and Amy thought he meant it.

173

'We're grateful to him for releasing you from your agreement.'

Patrick said to Amy, when they went to bed that night, 'Mr Yardley doesn't speak like a tenant farmer, does he?'

Did he think tenants were peasants? 'When we farmed this place, Father wasn't ignorant, you know. He read books and he kept up with the new ideas on good farming.' How could she explain her father, a kindly, cheerful man who would she was sure, have heartily approved of Patrick? Father would have taught him all about farming.

'I didn't mean to say that tenant farmers are peasants, but you know, Mr Yardley, Ben he said I should call him, he's better educated than any of us. What did he do before he came here?' Patrick jumped into bed beside her.

Amy said sleepily, 'Dear Benjamin is a misery most of the time, he's a worrier, he reads a lot but – I quite like him, he's a very kind man. Now let's go to sleep.' Curling up with Patrick, with his arm round her, Amy felt happy and secure. It was strange how she'd got used to dear Benjamin's ways, but she was glad he liked Patrick.

A few days later the Browns held their dispersal sale, which had in fact been arranged for some time. Josh Brown told Ben to put some stock on his land immediately and not wait until he was the legal owner. They had

174

been scaling down their business for the last year and there was grass to spare. 'Might as well graze it before the frosts kill the grass,' he said and so Ben and Patrick moved dairy heifers up to the new farm in the big farm cart. They debated for a while before moving sheep, after Mr Brown had warned them that he'd lost sheep to the poachers. In the end Ben bought a batch of young ewes and decided to send them straight to Sheepcote Farm.

Amy and Patrick delivered the sheep to their new home, Patrick driving the farm cart. He was a confident driver, even though he was new to the work. Looking at him sitting beside her with the reins in his hands, Amy could hardly believe how lucky she was. Only a few months ago she had been cramped and stifled in Gran's little house, and now she was back on a farm, with a handsome husband. Patrick was tanned by the summer sun and his hair shone with coppery glints. Would her baby have that glorious hair colour? Amy hoped he would.

'You're taking a risk, lad, with them sheep. Tell that to Mr Yardley,' Josh Brown greeted them as they rolled into the yard.

Patrick jumped down from the cart and laughed. 'Don't worry, Josh, I'll keep an eye on them.' He had made friends easily with the Browns in his light-hearted way. 'Mr Yardley's bought a new horse that I can

175

ride, so I'll come over here very often.'

The older man sighed. 'Aye, well – it'll maybe take a young man like you to get the better of them.' He dropped his voice. 'But you do know what you're up against? Yon villain is a rich man – it's dangerous to cross him.'

Having met Sara and heard her story from Amy, Patrick knew that West was violent. He laughed and promised to be careful. On the ride home he said to Amy, 'Whatever we say, the police can't do anything without evidence. So if the villains come for our sheep, if, mind, and I can follow them, I'll be able to tell the police where to look. No,' seeing her anxious look, 'I won't tackle them myself, lass.' He reached over and covered her cold little hand with his big one. 'We'll beat them, you'll see.'

Amy enjoyed the cooler weather and the tang of autumn in the air. As the days got shorter, Mrs Shaw was busy in the garden and orchard, harvesting fruit to preserve for the winter. Yardley gave Patrick a few lessons in horsemanship, warning him that Dan, the horse he was to ride, was young and un-schooled. But Patrick said lightly, 'Don't worry, Ben, I've got good balance and I've ridden before, a little. If I fall off I'll just get back on again.' He patted Dan's rough neck. The gelding was a dark bay, young and energetic like Patrick himself.

Patrick was just as cheerful about learning to milk cows. There had been no dairy on the farm at Boroughbridge and so he had no experience, but he was sure it would be easy. Amy laughed when he crouched on a milking stool with a bucket between his knees and attempted to extract milk from Marigold, who looked round at him with a puzzled expression. Patrick squeezed and squeezed, but no milk came. 'This is harder than I thought,' he admitted.

Amy showed Patrick how to hold the teat at the top and move the milk down with his fingers. 'Pull down, but gently, you don't want to hurt her,' she said. Marigold shifted her weight from one hind foot to the other and sighed noisily. 'Stand still, Marigold, everybody has to learn some time. Now you try, Patrick, but keep an eye on her tail, we don't want it in the milk bucket.'

Patrick persevered over the next few days and his wrists were swollen and red by the end of the week, but he was getting into the milking rhythm. Yardley seemed more cheerful when Patrick was about and Amy thought he was good for the boss.

Slowly the heather flowers began to die back and the purple of the moor faded to lavender. Shooting parties were out after grouse; there were gamekeepers and beaters everywhere. Ben talked about moving the bees back to the farm, but they were busy

177

with other work. 'It won't hurt to leave them for a little while longer,' he said to Amy.

'As long as Mr West doesn't see them!' Amy had an uneasy feeling about Saul West.

Patrick went up to Sheepcote farm on the new horse to check the sheep most evenings and he also kept an eye on the Banks Farm sheep, but Ben had moved them away from the river. Amy worried at first about Patrick, but he was so confident that she concentrated instead on knitting little coats and mittens for the baby. It was not due until March, but you couldn't start early enough, her mother told her. Now that Amy was safely married, Molly allowed herself to look forward to the coming grandchild.

Sara at the bakery was sewing for the baby now, helped by Molly, who visited her once or twice a week. Amy had worried about not being able to see Sara and was glad that her mother had taken her place. Poor Sara still wondered when she would be free, but at least she was safe.

Michaelmas was approaching and the next concern was furnishing the Sheepcote farm house. Mrs Brown asked to see Amy and as they sipped tea in the kitchen, she explained that their new house was smaller than this one. 'So we're leaving some stuff for you, dear, I'm sure it's the best thing to do. Your Patrick can talk to Josh about how much you owe him, but it won't be much.'

There was a huge old four poster bed in the main bedroom, together with a big oak wardrobe, a linen press at the top of the stairs and some smaller pieces. Their home would look heavy and old fashioned, but that would not worry them. Amy loved the old bed with its feeling of history. As a gift, Mrs Brown handed her some creamy coloured, rather rough sheets, smelling faintly of lavender. 'These go with the bed, to my mind. They're nettle cloth, love, made by my granny long ago. Nobody makes nettle cloth these days, it's too much work to spin and weave.'

When she told her mother about the furniture, Molly sat up straight. 'I'd nearly forgotten, but there's some stuff of ours in the old blacksmith's shop at Gran's. You'd better come and have a look, love.'

It was the first time Amy had been back to Gran's house since she had been told to leave, but she gritted her teeth and went over the square after the butter was all sold on the following Wednesday. Gran had no say over Molly's furniture, Amy told herself. She was hoping not to see her grandmother, but inevitably, Gran came out of her house to see what they were doing and to give advice.

'Don't be giving yourself airs and graces, just because you've got a tied house,' Gran sneered from the depths of a big shawl. 'It

179

goes with job, you'll be turned out if lad gets the sack. Look at you, married to a farm labourer who's no better than he ought to be... Appletons have gone down in the world, that's for certain. Well, you haven't got all your bread baked yet, lass,' she finished darkly. 'Things will likely get worse and it's only what you deserve.' It was hissed like a curse and Amy's mother looked close to tears.

Amy turned her back on Gran, willing her to go away. She looked at the dusty furniture and it brought back her childhood. There were remembered tables and chairs that would be useful, but Gran had spoiled the moment for her. 'I'll come back with Patrick, we'll borrow the trap,' she said to her mother, and left as quickly as she could. She couldn't blame Molly for not standing up to Gran, but it would have been better to support her daughter.

Back at the farm, Amy tried to shake off the feeling of gloom, but Gran's spiteful face kept floating back into her memory. The cows were milked quickly with three of them on the job and at supper, Amy mentioned her mother's furniture. 'If we can borrow the trap, Ben, we could collect it one night before dark,' Patrick suggested. 'But not tonight, I've planned to check Sheepcote farm again.' Straight after supper, he saddled up and clattered out of the yard.

180

Amy washed up the supper dishes and put them away, then sat down by the kitchen fire with her knitting. What would they call the baby? It was hard to imagine him as another person, an independent soul. Patrick's middle name was James and that was a good, manly name, but what if the baby turned out to be a girl? A flower name like Rose or Violet would be pretty. Certainly not Gertrude, that was Gran's name and Amy had never liked it.

Some time later Amy fell into a doze and was wakened by Ben coming into the kitchen. 'I'm off to bed. Ask Patrick to lock the door when he comes in, will you? Good-night, Amy.' He looked down at her for a moment with a faint rueful smile, then turned away.

'Patrick should be home soon, I'll wait up for him. He's probably talking to Josh Brown,' Amy told him. It was after nine and Patrick should have been home before this. She dozed again and when she woke, the kitchen fire had gone out. Uncomfortable with sitting so long, she walked round the kitchen. There were a few months of discomfort ahead, as the baby grew. She should go to bed ... but where was Patrick?

By midnight, Amy was seriously worried, but what could she do? She was relieved when Ben came downstairs, fully dressed. He had been waiting, listening as she was

181

for Patrick's return. 'I'm going to look for him, I'll saddle up Mary. No. Amy, you stay here. Light the fire, will you and make a cup of tea.'

Amy stood at the door and watched him go, his stern face pale in the moonlight. Perhaps Patrick had been caught by the sheep stealers... She shuddered as she thought of the man who'd pushed her into the river; he would not have cared if she'd drowned. If only Patrick could come home safely, she'd never let him go after them again.

Back in the kitchen, Amy walked up and down, with a sick feeling of apprehension as the time went by. There were so many dangers out there for a young man who took danger lightly. There always would be, for Patrick; Amy felt that she could never rest easy again. She hadn't realized that this was what love did to you, this agony of worry and care. Her love for Patrick was hurting her now.

Ben Yardley urged his horse along as fast as he dared to Sheepcote and the mare responded willingly. Amy's little face, pinched with worry, stayed in his mind. 'When I catch up with Patrick, I'll tell him to take more care,' he told himself fiercely. It was all very well to be carefree and cheerful, but Amy's young husband would have to take life more seriously. It was thoughtless of him

182

to leave Amy alone, worrying, so late at night, and when she was expecting a baby, too. She needed rest and peace, not anxiety like this.

The road shone pale in the moonlight and soon Ben came to the farm. After hesitating a moment, he took to an old drover's road that led off in the direction of the moor. Josh Brown was sure that the sheep had gone out that way... He looked for tracks of horse or cart, but the surface was stony and there was nothing to see. It was not wise to ride an unfamiliar road in the dark, but this must be where Patrick had gone – typical of the young fool to chase after criminals. If he'd seen sheep on the move, he should have come home and reported it. The whole idea was to have something to tell Sergeant Taylor at the police station, not to rescue the sheep himself. Ben felt himself growing warm with annoyance.

The lane wound steeply uphill and surprisingly soon, he came out on the open moor. Sheepcote farm had grazing rights on the moor, but Ben had not realized how close it was – perfect for sheep stealing, come to think of it. What now? He looked around, but there were no tracks.

The moorland was bare under the moon, the heather dark, hiding treacherous bogs.

It was dangerous to go haring off across country, but it looked as though that was what Patrick had done. His horse suddenly tensed and pricked her ears enquiringly. Ben slackened his grasp on the reins and Mary pulled to the right and whinnied softly. From the dark came an answering neigh. 'Well done, lass!' he said softly and patted her neck.

Ben rode over towards the sound for a few hundred yards and came to an open rickety gate in a stone wall. Through the gate a track dipped sharply down into a hollow, but there was still nothing to be seen. He slid from the saddle and tied the mare to the gate. He kept to the side of the track, walking downhill noiselessly on the rough moor grass.

Mary whinnied quietly again from above and Ben saw a dark shape moving towards him. It was the young horse Dan, but without his rider, his bridle hanging down. Ben caught him quickly, led him to the gate and tied him up beside Mary where the two horses had a reunion, nuzzling each other; Mary had taken to Dan and the two had adjacent stables at Banks Farm. 'Keep quiet, will you,' Ben whispered irritably and set off down the track once more. Patrick must have left the horse roaming free while he investigated; a stupid thing to do.

The land sloped down on all sides and at the bottom Ben could hear a small beck trickling over stones. He could dimly make out stone walls, almost hidden by bushes. The acrid smell of fresh sheep dung hung about the place, but it was silent. Sheep had been here recently, but they were gone. Patrick had been here, which must mean that they were stolen sheep. On the softer ground at the bottom of the slope were faint traces of cartwheel tracks.

Something brushed his face and Ben whirled round, straining his eyes into the darkness. It was only a bat; several bats were flitting round him, but there was no other sign of life. Patrick, then, must have followed the sheep ... but why on foot?

Ben rode wearily home on Dan, leading Mary who was quieter than the young horse. He had failed to find Patrick and now he had to face Amy and tell her so; he felt sick at heart. All the possibilities crowded into his mind, but he had failed. They now knew where the sheep had been taken initially, but that was all and they had no proof.

'You'd better get some sleep, Ben,' Amy said heavily when he told her what he had found. Oh Patrick, what have they done to you? Fears for his safety kept giving way to anger; best keep to the anger, it would give her energy.

'I'll go up there first thing in the morning, take the trap...' Ben was taking off his boots.

'I'm coming with you, I can't stand waiting at home.' Amy was so determined that

Ben nodded. 'Rosie's coming today – she can milk the cows if we get them in for her. She used to be a dairymaid.'

For a few hours the house slept uneasily, but at first light Amy dressed and went out to round up the cows for milking. Then she backed Mary into the trap and was waiting when Ben came out to the yard. Silently he passed Amy a glass of milk and she drank obediently. They climbed into the vehicle and took the road to Sheepcote farm. Neither spoke until they reached the farm, where Mr Brown was standing in the yard. Ben told him what had happened and he shook his head.

'You didn't hear or see anything last night?' Ben asked him.

'Nay, we're both hard of hearing these days, I'm sorry to say. Didn't hear the young lad go through, or owt else.' He looked at Amy. 'It's a bad job, lass. I hope you find him.'

They passed up the drover's road and came out on the moor. Ben looked round and then spotted where he'd turned off the night before; it all looked different this morning, less sinister. A pale sun was struggling through the clouds and a brisk wind was pushing them along, creating the familiar pattern of sun and shadow on the moorland. Tension mounted as slowly Ben took the horse and trap through the gateway.

186

'Patrick must have come down here, it's where I found the horse,' Ben said quietly.

They were halfway down the slope when Amy cried out. 'What's that?'

Between the gate and the sheep pen there was something on the ground. Her heart started to thump. Ben jumped down and threw the reins to Amy, but she scrambled awkwardly down and went to where Ben was kneeling. They had found him.

THIRTEEN

Patrick lay partly under a bush, one arm flung out – it was his light jacket that Amy had spotted. His neck was at an unnatural angle. He was cold, lifeless. They were too late; the bright potential of Patrick's life was gone.

A curlew's haunting cry echoed over the little valley like a lament. A shadow passed over the sun and Amy felt that all the light in her life was gone with it, in an instant of time. With a wild sob she took the body in her arms, trying to warm life into the cold limbs, but Ben gently put her aside. 'It's no use, lass. He hit his head on this stone... He's gone, poor lad ... must have died instantly. I suppose he came off the horse.' He

187

paused and then said slowly, 'The other possibility, I suppose ... is that they wanted him out of the way.'

'How do you know? He might be still breathing, you can't tell–'

'I do know, Amy.'

Amy was dizzy and faint; she felt numb. It was all over, their marriage was over almost before it began. With a strange calmness, she whispered, 'He'll never see the baby.' Ben covered her hands with his own, but said nothing.

Ben struggled to his feet and Amy found she had to comfort him. She held his hand as they both looked down at Patrick's body. The big man was choking back tears. 'I should never have let him go out on that horse, or chase those sheep... I blame myself, Amy.' He turned to her then. 'It's the worst thing for you just now but you must protect the baby, try to stay calm. Think of the baby, love.'

'You're not to blame, Ben... Patrick never thought about danger, he's not – he wasn't careful enough.' No, he was not and his happy personality had cost him his life; it had ruined Amy's, and made his baby fatherless. Under her grief a sad anger persisted. If only Patrick had been more responsible ... but she had loved him for his sheer enjoyment of life.

They went back to Sheepcote and a shocked Mr Brown helped Ben to move

Patrick's body onto a shutter and into the trap. Amy was near to collapse, but she insisted on going with them to bring him home. They travelled in silence for a while. The older man struggled with emotion as he said, 'Well, the horse was a youngster and lad was only just learning to ride.'

'Yes,' Ben said stonily. 'I should never have let him do it.'

'But – I can't help wondering who else was down there last night in that damp little gill. Summat to frighten the horse, like, or make Patrick fall. You can see there's been sheep there...' He wiped his eyes. 'This must be where they took my sheep, not far away, but I never found them. I blame myself as well, Mr Yardley. If I'd found out what was going on...'

'Nobody's to blame.' Amy looked at them both through her tears. 'It was an accident.' But she kept thinking of the big man who'd pushed her into a deep pool. If he had met Patrick last night, he might have helped to arrange an accident.

The death was reported and the doctor came. 'There's not much point in telling him that Patrick was looking for stolen sheep,' Ben said as the doctor rolled into the yard. Amy agreed. The less said, the better.

Dr Andrews looked sorrowfully down at the still body and listened to the story. 'There was nothing you could do,' he told

189

Ben. 'The horse must have thrown him. A young horse, you say? Up at Sheepcote? The cause of death was obviously an accident.'

Then there was the undertaker, all the trappings of death. Amy's numbness persisted for days; she was exhausted, but needed to work and so she went into the dairy and made butter. She could not erase from her memory the sight of Patrick's still body where they had found him. She went through her work mechanically. If only she had begged him to stay at home! Dizziness came over her at intervals and she sat down for a moment or two before going on with the work.

There was a terrible feeling of having lived through this before. Just two years ago, her father had died and Amy had kept on with the work, because it was there. But, much as she had loved her father, this was different. Patrick had been the centre of her life; they had so much to share, they were going to bring up a child. Even in her grief Amy smiled at the thought of Patrick as a father. Would he have settled down, taken more responsibility? She would never know. He had been so joyful, so eager to plan their future, but he'd never worried about practical details.

The baby was now Amy's reason for living; for him she ate and drank and slept, went through every day. But she could not imagine the days ahead. Where could she go now, what could she do?

Ben Yardley looked across at Amy in her plain black dress, sitting at breakfast three weeks after they buried Patrick at Ripon. 'Katherine and I have discussed the future, which will be hard for you to think of at the moment, Amy. But we want you to know that we plan to make no changes at present.' His face was closed, with no emotion showing.

Amy tried to smile, but her face was stiff. 'But you'll need to replace me. I'm getting slower and when the baby comes I'll be hampered. I can't expect you to look after me, either of you. How many weeks after the baby comes will it be before I'm able to milk the cows again and then, how could I leave him for hours at a time?' It was kind of them, but not practical.

Mrs Shaw looked up from her plate. 'But Amy, if you leave, where will you live? I gather your grandmother doesn't approve of you and I – well, I don't want to intrude on your private affairs, but I don't suppose Patrick left very much money to support you.'

Amy blushed. She had been told straight after the funeral by Patrick's uncle, the clergyman who conducted the service, that her husband had left no assets at all, and his family was not able to help to support the

191

baby. They were polite and distantly sympathetic, but wrapped up in their own grief; Patrick had been much loved. Amy even had the feeling that they thought she might be to blame. They probably thought he had been seduced by a dairymaid and led to his death. 'Everyone knows farming is a dangerous occupation,' the clergyman said. 'That was one reason for his mother's objection to it as a career for Patrick.' He sighed. 'No doubt your own family will look after you, my dear. I understand you have relatives in Masham.'

Mrs Shaw was right. 'N-no, Mrs Shaw, I don't expect anything. I'll have to earn my own living and the baby's, too. I'm hoping that Mother might join me, we could find a cottage somewhere.' That was, if Ma could be persuaded to leave Gran. The old tyrant was getting more dependent on her daughter as time went by, so it would need to be very near Gran. But Amy's grief and anger for Patrick was much bigger than any fears she had for herself. What did it matter what happened to her? Amy was tired of thoughts that went round and round, getting nowhere. Ben had done his best to find out what had really happened, but with no result.

Ben poured himself another cup of tea. 'You're needed here, as it happens,' he said brusquely. 'We'll employ a man or a married couple in due course, for Sheepcote. Your place is here with us and I'm going to ask Mr Russell if the estate will allow some alterations to be made to the house, for your accommodation.'

'But you can't do that! Tenants never alter buildings, the estate won't allow it.' Perhaps he didn't realize how much he was at the mercy of the landlord. The Park estate, like most others, had strict rules. Amy sighed; there was still a lot that Ben didn't know. 'What did you think of changing?'

Buttering his toast the rebel tenant murmured, 'We'll see. Mr Russell is very good to deal with, as I'm sure you know. We thought of making a separate part for you and the baby, with a small kitchen of your own – the apple loft and the old store room under it would give us plenty of space within these stone walls.' Looking up, he glared at Amy's shocked expression. 'It would be for everybody's convenience, of course. You can help in the house if the outdoor work is too heavy at first. But I want you back in the dairy, my girl, for next summer. Our butter has a good reputation.' The firm mouth closed as though that was the end of the argument.

His aunt nodded her agreement. 'My plan for a dairy is working out well, Amy, with your help. Ben can keep more cows next year and we'd like to expand it, make cheese as well as butter.' Mrs Shaw looked at Yardley and added, 'Of course I must go home to York eventually, but I would like to keep an interest in the farm and visit when I can.'

They were waiting for Amy to speak. How could she churn butter with a bairn on her hip? It didn't seem possible. 'I'd like to stay here, thank you for taking thought for me.' She looked at Yardley; he was glum as usual. It was flattering that they valued her work; Amy realized she had turned out to be good at something, in spite of Gran's predictions. 'But what about the baby?' That would change everything.

Mrs Shaw was not a very warm person, but Amy felt that she was an ally, almost a friend. 'I'm sure you'll manage the baby very well. Once they settle down, babies sleep a lot. They don't need constant attention. And then, your mother might be very pleased to look after him at times – grandmothers are like that, you know.'

Mrs Shaw didn't know Amy's Gran, obviously. How could she ever repay them, except by working hard and helping them with the farm business? She wanted to thank them, but could find no words. 'I'm speechless,' Amy stammered and Ben said that that was a change, she usually had an opinion on everything. They all smiled. The terrible hush of the last few weeks was beginning to break up a little. Things would

194

never be the same again, but life would go on.

It was amazing, but Ben got his own way. He explained to the agent how much the farm would benefit from having servants' quarters attached, since it was so far from the town. He threw himself into the project with energy, making sketches and talking to builders as soon as Mr Russell had told him that His Lordship had no objection to the alterations, providing Ben paid for the work himself and it was done by a builder the estate could approve.

The winds were blowing colder and folks at the market brought out the old joke: somebody's left moor gate open again. Ben said uneasily that it was high time the hives were brought home from the heather, but Amy could not bear the idea of Yardley going up there on his own. The thought of going back herself to that bleak and desolate place where Patrick died was horrible, but to stay behind and wait would be worse. There were too many shadows on the moor. 'I'm sure no harm will come to Benjamin, but I understand how you feel. I will come too,' Mrs Shaw said unexpectedly. 'I've never been up to the moor.' Nobody mentioned Saul West, but he was one of Amy's worst fears.

In the end Ben agreed that they would all three go there in the trap one evening and move the bees as soon as darkness fell. He chose a warm, still evening and later, there would be a full moon. 'The hives will be heavy, but I'll get young Tom Harland to help me to lift them. He's the farmer's son,' he explained to his aunt, who looked relieved.

The moorland was tranquil in the evening light, softer than in the harsh light of afternoon. It was a slow journey in the farm cart, with the heavy horse Prince, an old plodder with huge, feathery hooves. As they passed the little farms on the moorland road, the scent of late flowers wafted over them from the gardens that were so lovingly tended and protected from the cold winds. Ben talked quietly, pointing out various landmarks to his aunt. Looking back, they could see the lovely Ure valley with its chequered gold and green fields and in the centre, the spire of Masham church.

Amy sat rigid, her hands clenched with all the tension of the last few weeks. Oh Patrick, if only you were with us! Sometimes she found it hard to remember the outlines of his dear face. Since he died she had tried to recall everything about him, the way he laughed easily and the enthusiasm that carried him through every day.

Ben glanced over his shoulder at his helper as they passed the place where West had beaten the dog. 'Don't think we'll see the ruffian tonight,' he said comfortingly. 'This is where we took responsibility for young Jake,' he explained to his aunt. But Amy felt that something was going to happen; she had been uneasy all day, dreading the trip to the moor.

'What a lovely sunset! I had no idea this place was so beautiful.' Mrs Shaw looked round her at the scene. From the high ridge of moor between the two valleys, they looked to the west where the sun was going down over the Nidd, leaving a reddish glow that tinged the dying heather and softened the harsh stones. In the distance the far hills were faintly blue, but to Amy, the sun was the colour of blood. The moor was a violent place. Good people like the Harlands were powerless to stop the bad elements doing what they pleased – men like the huge Bert and madmen like Saul West. She never wanted to come here again.

The farmer's son was waiting for them as they clopped up the track, having seen them winding up the hill. Amy remembered Tom Harland from their schooldays, but the lad had changed. There was a worried look on his thin face and his big cap was pulled low over his eyes. Tom had always been a happy lad, known for the tricks he played.

'Aye, I'll give you a hand, gladly,' he said, but without the grin that Amy remembered. He now worked for his father on the farm; perhaps the loneliness was affecting him.

Poor Tom, ageing before his time.

The women got out of the cart and Ben backed it as near to the hives as he could. The last bees were coming in as dusk fell. Mrs Shaw walked away from the hives to where she had a better view of the sun as it disappeared and Tom sidled up to Amy, who was standing on her own. 'Sorry to hear about your husband, lass,' he said awkwardly. 'A real shame, it was.'

Fighting tears, Amy watched Ben moving the cart carefully, the horse taking small steps backwards in spite of its great size. 'Thank you Tom, it's hard to bear,' she said quietly.

Tom seemed to want to say something more, but he hesitated and Ben came to join them. Prince stood patiently without being tied up, waiting for the next move.

After about ten minutes, Ben decided that they could close the hive entrances and the men lifted the boxes carefully on to the cart. 'A good yield of honey this year,' Ben grunted. 'I can tell by the weight.'

'Aye well, we've had fine weather,' Tom said. 'Some years, the bees can't fly for the rain.' He settled the cap straight on his head. 'Ma says to come your ways in for a drink of tea, Mr Yardley.'

Ben looked at his aunt and Amy. 'Would you mind getting home a little later?'

Mrs Shaw had no objection; Amy was

tired, but because it would be a grave breach of moorland manners to refuse, she smiled at Tom.

'No, Mr Yardley, we'll go in.' They got into the cart and Ben stopped by the farmhouse door. Tom's mother, his father and the dog all came out to greet the visitors and Amy had to go through more anguish as they offered sympathy. She had often wondered what to say to others in this situation; how can you offer any comfort when a loved one has died? But now she realized that although it was hard to talk about Patrick, it would be worse if he had not been mentioned. In a strange way, it was a comfort to know that these kind people felt her suffering. They were with her in spirit and it was a kind of support, a lessening of loneliness.

Amy was the last of the guests through the door, with Tom coming in behind her.

She sat wearily at the back of the room. Mrs Harland offered chairs to the others and Mrs Shaw sat by the peat fire. 'I love the scent of peat,' she said. 'It reminds me of Scotland.'

Jim Harland was talking to Yardley as his wife made the tea, his mind still on the recent tragedy. 'Yes, it's a bad job about that young worker of yours,' he said sadly. 'Just married, an all.'

'I want a word with you about that,' Tom

199

said quietly in her ear. 'I know summat that – that you should know, Amy. About what happened.'

FOURTEEN

The tea was drunk and everybody went out to the big stone barn to look at Mr Harland's new Swaledale ram, his pride and joy. They stood in a pool of lamplight, surrounded by dark shadows. The ram held his black face and handsome horns up for them to admire while Ben asked many questions about the Harlands's plans for flock improvement. 'I'm trying to do the same thing myself,' he said.

Tom pulled Amy aside, but then it seemed as if he didn't know how to begin. He still looked serious, so to cheer him, Amy said, 'How's your Sally, then? You'll be getting wed before so long.' She wanted to hear what he knew about Patrick, but she was afraid of it – afraid of knowing worse things still. He could have little comfort for her.

Tom's face cleared a little. 'She's a grand lass, I'm lucky. We've asked Mr Russell if he can find us a little farm. But...' he frowned, 'I've got to tell you summat, Amy. I'd been to see Sally the other night and I was coming

200

home from Masham, late it was, with moon lighting the road. I was hurrying along on our pony when I ... saw what I saw.' He swallowed and looked round, but the others were still immersed in sheep. 'Lights over the moor, folks droving sheep in the dark. Why would honest men do that? What with talk of stock going missing and that, though we've lost none, I thought to find out what was going on.'

'So did Patrick,' Amy whispered. 'It cost him his life.'

'And I know how, lass. It were no accident, that. I went for the lights, quite a way off over towards Carlsmoor. But I were too late, lights disappeared and I didn't know which track they'd taken. You hear about fairies and witches over yon side, but that's bairns' talk. They might be doing it to keep folks away!' Tom was pleased with this thought. 'Aye, that might be it.'

Amy was waiting. 'So what did you do?'

'You mind on top of the ridge there, there's three ways join? I saw a lad on a horse going down one of the tracks, as if he was following the lights.' He paused and looked round, but the others were still talking sheep. 'So I went on behind him, he didn't look round and see me. We went down into a gill and I remember wondering if there was a way out. I didn't want to be trapped and I didn't know who was down there.' He paused. 'It was dark, there were trees over the track... All of a sudden there was a commotion, a clatter of stone and a shout. A horse neighed and then it came galloping past me, the horse the lad had been on, with stirrups swinging. He must have come off, somewhere down there. So I went down there on foot, it was quite steep and I saw, I swear it, a rope across that track. Just at the height to catch you in the neck if you was on a horse. Somebody meant mischief. There's a ruin down there Amy, used to be a little farm. They must have put sheep in there for collection.'

'And then?' Amy could scarcely keep still.

'Well, I could see nowt but I thought lad might need help, he might have broken bones. But I was turned away by a big fellow who came out of the dark at me, shone a lantern in my face so I couldn't see him. He said there'd been an accident, but lad would be all right. By the way he growled at me it seemed better not to ask questions. Of course, I never knew who the poor lad was. From what the big bloke said he might have been one of them. So I went home, but I was worried about whole thing. I was right sorry when I heard he died, I guessed it would be your lad ... of course I never knew him, but Josh Brown told me he was working for Mr Yardley and he'd just got married to you.' He looked haunted. 'Yes lass, I'm right sorry,' he repeated. 'I should ha tried

202

to help him. And to think they left him there for his boss to find, and went away. They're right villains, whoever they are.'

There were no words to describe such men. She stood in silence for a while and then looked at Tom. 'It could have been you they caught, Tom,' Amy said gently. 'And maybe you couldn't have helped him ... Mr Yardley thought he'd died straight away. We found him the next day.'

Tom shuddered. 'You found him? You poor lass! Did you see rope then?'

'No. There was no rope when we got there.' Amy looked at Tom; he was honest, she believed him. What next? 'Have you told anyone else?'

Tom turned away. 'You'll think I'm a coward, Amy, but – that big prize fighter, he has a broken nose, he works for Saul West. Likely you'll have heard of him, though he hasn't been round here for long. West's a man with money and land and it's not wise to cross him. I-I was warned off when he first come here. Just picking bilberries for Ma, that's all, but I was over the boundary and that was enough to get me horsewhipped before I could get away – West was in a bad mood that day. I won't say no more, and I hope you won't neither. There's absolutely nowt we can do about it. Only it's right that you should know.'

'Time to go,' Ben called and the visitors

went back to the cart, where Prince was waiting patiently, shifting his weight from one huge foot to another. Ben lit two lanterns for carriage lights and they trundled slowly off down to the valley with their load of bees.

Watching the twinkling lights of the town far below, Amy's thoughts were racing. Tom obviously wanted her to say nothing, but she owed it to Patrick to tell somebody what he had seen. What would Patrick have said? Patrick would say they shouldn't get away with it, or they'd do it again and somebody else might get hurt. Ben and Mrs Shaw talked quietly together, but Amy was too busy with her thoughts to hear what they said until she was spoken to directly.

'Tom seemed to have a lot to say to you.' Ben kept his eyes on the road. Should she tell him? Ben had a right to know. He whistled when Amy told him what the lad had said. 'As a matter of fact, I did notice a rope, coiled up on the top of the stone wall. I didn't think any more about it. Poor Patrick may have been thrown from the horse by that, rather than because Dan's a young one.'

Or because he wasn't a good rider, Amy thought. She knew that Ben had reservations about Patrick's horsemanship.

'How I wish I'd never let him go off like that, trying to find my sheep, because he knew I was worried about losing them. I think it's time to go to the police again.'

'Don't blame yourself, Ben. Patrick liked the adventure, he probably liked the danger.' Amy wondered whether Patrick had ever known fear.

The next morning at milking, Amy was still thinking about what Tom had told her when Ben suggested that she might like to help him with the honey extraction.

'Heather honey's different, it's very thick and hard to extract. We need a very warm room to thin it a little, and we might have to squeeze it through the sieve.' So after lunch Amy was to build up the fire in the kitchen and clear away chairs and rugs.

Amy was making butter in the dairy when Ben opened the hives and she didn't see him until lunch time, when he appeared looking battered, with swellings on his face. 'Hive number three's in a bad mood,' he muttered. 'Should have left them a day or two to settle down. I've never had to deal with such aggressive bees.'

Mrs Shaw put lavender oil on the stings and gave him a plate of hot soup. 'This should make you feel better. It's a good job Amy wasn't with you. You're not going to put up with that hive much longer, I hope. Get rid of them, Benjamin.'

The beekeeper shook his head. 'A hive's too valuable to destroy. They say that if you change the queen, it can make a lot of differ-

205

ence. All the workers are related to her, so if she's quiet, the next generation might be better. I'll see if I can find a new queen.'

Mrs Shaw went into the sitting room with her sewing, saying the kitchen was far too hot, Ben was in his shirtsleeves as he carried in the frames. Amy spread sheets of newspaper over the floor and they put a large tub in front of the fire, with muslin over it. As Amy settled down to scrape a frame of honeycomb carefully into the sheet of muslin, she heard a loud buzzing sound. The kitchen window was dark with bees.

Ben checked that the windows were all closed and there were no gaps through which bees could get into the house. 'It's frightening,' Amy shuddered. 'Are they swarming? They don't usually come into the yard.' What if they upset the cows when they came in for milking? The heat was making her feel faint.

'They're after the honey,' said Ben briefly. 'I think the best plan is to take some out there for them, distract them. It's the number three hive again, I expect. Not a swarm. When bees swarm they are usually docile, busy looking for a new home.' He took a section of comb outside and left it some distance from the house. Most of the bees followed him and took to the honey.

The heat from the fire made the honey easier to extract, but the work proceeded slowly. It was milking time before they were finished and Ben could take the frames back to the hives, where he said the bees would clean them up. Amy went out and prepared the milking pails, Ben hosed down the cowshed floor and they both looked up as a trap bowled into the yard and pulled up sharply by the cowshed. A well-dressed man jumped down from the driving seat. 'Yardley, may I have a word with you?' A patronizing smile flitted over his face, but he looked determined to have his own way.

Amy's heart sank. Saul West was the driver and beside him sat the big, red-faced man who had thrown her into the river, possibly too the man who had told Tom Harland not to worry about Patrick

'Good day, West.' Ben was a tenant farmer, but he was not going to call the man mister or sir. 'There are several things we might have a word about. Such as the death of my worker, on your property.'

West seemed surprised and he stepped back a pace. He looked up at the trap. 'Come here, Dickens,' he snapped. 'Tell the man what you told me.'

Dickens lumbered heavily over to Ben and towered over him, while Amy held her breath. Ben still had the cowshed hose in his hand and looked as though he might turn it on the man. 'I know nowt,' the man said. 'Never saw the lad at all. He must ha gone down there in the dark and horse threw him. What would we be doing there on the moor at that time of night?' He sniffed.

'What, indeed.' Ben was evidently controlling himself with an effort. 'You know, of course, that Patrick was looking for the thieves who stole sheep. My sheep. I have told the police the whole story. But what I cannot understand is why none of you tried to help the lad, or came to tell me if he was beyond help...' His voice broke. He went on, 'He was found where he fell, under a bush. But you knew he was there! And you stretched a rope across the track. Thieves and murderers.' He shook his head, not able to go on.

Amy was weeping. Poor Patrick, to fall in with hardened men like these! But nothing could be proved and the police were too much in awe of West to push the matter very hard.

Both men advanced on Ben. 'It's you are the thief, Yardley,' Saul West shouted, all pretence of politeness gone. 'You took my dog. I want my bloody dog back and I want it now!'

Amy quickly looked round at the dogs. Bess was sitting by the gate, waiting to go for the cows with Amy, as she always did at this time of day. Jake, West's young dog had retreated to the kennel and was cowering and shaking with fear. Jake knew who had come into the yard and he remembered,

208

evidently, what that man represented.

'How much do you want for him? I'll buy him,' offered Ben, not looking towards the kennel.

'That dog is not for sale.' West had not even noticed the dog, who was now out of sight. In one way he had right on his side; they had taken his dog, stolen it, you might say. How terrible if he had to go back! Amy had to restrain herself from rushing over to protect him.

Dickens took the whip from its rest on the trap. 'Mr West wants the dog, alive or dead. Give it over.' He strode forward, his little eyes alight with malice.

West called him back and arranged his own features in a more pleasant expression. 'Not so fast, Dickens, wait a minute. Now let me explain, Yardley, I will make it plain to your limited understanding. That dog's pedigree is exceptional and now that I have the right bitch, I want to breed from him.' West seemed to be sober, but he spoke slowly, exaggerating his words as though talking to a young child.

'You should have thought of his value when you were beating him. It's obvious that you have no feeling for animals.' Ben seemed to be holding back his anger with an effort. 'If you breed dogs, there will be more for you to ill-treat. You are not having this one.'

209

West went on as though Ben had not spoken. It seemed that what other people thought or said was not important perhaps he didn't even hear them. Amy thought it was a mental problem and she was now sure that Saul West was mad. 'I expect you fancy him too, but he's mine and he's too good for a tenant farmer. You wouldn't be able to afford to buy him. Now hand him over, I can't hold Dickens back for ever.' He smiled thinly. 'Bert enjoys exercise, he doesn't need much excuse to teach you a lesson. You've had one coming for a while. I would have been here before now, but I've been in the north.' He paused. 'For your own good, do as I say, Yardley. I am not accustomed to failing. I have come to collect the dog and I give you five minutes to produce it.'

Bert looked disappointed and retreated a little.

'You are not having Jake,' Ben said quietly. By his expression Amy saw that he immediately realized what he had done.

Amy flinched as West swung round immediately. 'How do you know the dog's name?' So he did listen to what was said, after all. Shaking with fear, Amy quietly filled the milking pails with water. It was the only thing she could think of to stop the bully, if he did attack Ben. Then she saw that West was also threatening him, holding a short riding whip in his hand. Ben had nothing to defend himself with, having put down the hose. Should she hand over the dog, to save Ben? But that would be putting the poor animal in danger again.

'You have been talking to my wife. Where is she, Yardley? Is she here? I shall beat the truth out of you.' Now the man was working himself up into the mad rage they had seen on the moor. 'You've got my wife! You're probably living with her. She'll be your slave, I know your type!'

West motioned Dickens forward and the big whip slashed across Ben's back, just as the marauding bees from hive number three came back into the yard in an angry cloud. They must have finished the honey Ben had given them and come back for more. Amy was afraid they would still be able to smell honey on her, but West's horse was sweating and they went straight over the yard, to buzz angrily round it. The horse danced and half reared and the trap rattled.

West started to flail his arms and hive number three turned some of its attention to him, while Ben and Amy watched in horror. The man had said he hated bees; he was panicking. The change in the landowner was amazing. He scrambled back into the vehicle and screamed at his assistant. 'Get up, quick! We're leaving!' Dickens went over and was heaving himself into the trap when the horse reared, having been stung several times. West

211

hung on, but Dickens fell down.

There was a scream as some of the bees around West found their mark. Amy was stung on the arm and scraped the sting out immediately. West was yelling, thrashing about wildly. 'Get me out, you idiot! Drive away!' The horse settled down a little, Dickens rubbed his head and pulled himself up into the driving seat. West's face was red and beginning to swell; most of it was covered in bees.

Ben ripped off his own shirt and jumped up into the trap. He tried to wrap West with it, to protect him from the bees, but the man fought him as well as the insects.

He seemed to think that Ben was trying to suffocate him. His breathing was laboured and his eyes were disappearing in the swollen face. 'I'm trying to help!' Ben yelled. 'Amy ... honey! Quick!'

Honey was the only way to control them. Amy ran to the house and came out with more honeycomb, which took the main body of bees away as they followed her into the garden. With the help of Dickens, who seemed impervious to stings, Ben brushed most of the remaining bees away from West. When she came back, she noticed at once that West's breathing was extremely laboured and he hardly seemed conscious. Ben methodically began removing stings from the man's face and hands. 'He needs a doctor,' he said to Dickens. 'Get him there as soon as you can.'

The man shook the reins and wheeled out of the yard with his employer slumped in the back of the vehicle. The threat was over – but for how long? Sara was in danger now, as well as Jake.

'How bad is he, do you think?' Amy wondered.

Ben shrugged. 'He was hysterical, it's hard to say, but he was certainly in a bad way. The difficulty in breathing may have been sheer panic, or it could have been a reaction to the stings. If so, there's not much the doctor can do, except cool him down.'

Ben put on a clean shirt and they all had a cup of tea; Amy's hands were shaking and they both had several stings. It couldn't be good for the baby to have happenings like that, Amy thought. She had heard a lot of older women talk about such matters when she worked on the butter stall; the market place was the chief centre of gossip. And there was a school of thought in Masham that suggested you should look at beautiful things and think good thoughts, if you wanted a beautiful baby. To Yardley she said, 'Will my bee stings affect the baby? I hope not.'

Yardley looked concerned. 'You scraped them out straight away, as I showed you? Good. You'd better keep away from the bees

213

from now on. I've read something about it...
I must say, I didn't think you would be anywhere near stinging bees when I got you to
help me with the honey. Let me know
straight away if you feel ill, Amy.'

Mrs Shaw said, 'You are a healthy young
woman, Amy. Your baby will be healthy too.'
That was more reassuring, but did she really
know? 'Now, about the poor dog. What will
you do?'

Ben admitted that he was not sure what to
do about the dog. 'It's his property, but I hate
the way he treated it and we've no reason to
think he'll be better in the future. I should
report him to the RSPCA. Cruelty to animals is illegal, thank goodness.'

'He might report us for causing his stings,'
Mrs Shaw said quietly. She was rather afraid
of the bees and had kept well clear of the
yard for the whole afternoon.

After milking that evening, Amy asked the
beekeeper what he planned to do with hive
number three. 'I've decided to get rid of
them,' he said reluctantly. 'Tomorrow, I'll
put poison into the hive.'

Strangely enough, the bees took matters
into their own hands and by the next afternoon, hive number three was nearly empty.
Most of the bees had swarmed, gathering in
a compact black cloud and then taking off in
the direction of the river. Amy hoped that she
would never see them again.

Soon after the bees had gone, the local doctor came to Banks Farm. Dr Andrews had been sympathetic when Patrick died and Amy had visited him for checks on the baby. 'Looking after yourself, lass?' he asked in a kindly way. 'Just thought I would call in, as I'm passing.' He looked at her and Ben and then said, 'I thought you should know that Mr West died yesterday. There was nothing I could do to save him.'

FIFTEEN

Amy's heart gave a lurch and she turned away. West was dead! Had the bees killed him, or was it the fit, the thing Ben had warned him about? He had certainly been in a fine rage, just before the bees arrived and then he had panicked. But would Ben now be blamed for his death? It was a great relief, but she couldn't feel glad at the news; he was a tragic figure.

Thinking of the future, so much would change, especially for Sara. The people and animals that the man had bullied would be free; a long shadow was gone from the moor. Amy knew they would all feel safer, the Harlands and decent people like them who were always wondering what he would do next, while most folk, the ones who only saw his public face, thought he was an angel. Even Jake the dog was safer now that West was gone.

Ben looked grave at the news. 'I'm sorry to hear it. He was badly affected by bee stings, he told us that, one day on the moor. There was nothing any of us could have done.'

The doctor went on, 'His man Dickens told me he was going to report the matter to the police. He said that you actually set the bees on to Mr West, after you had an argument with him.' Amy held her breath; trouble was coming. West had gone, but Dickens and the rest of the gang were still up there on the moorland and they would be bound to cause more trouble.

Ben raised dark eyebrows. 'Nonsense. You'll know, Andrews, that nobody can control insects, tell them what to do! The hive was an aggressive one – I was stung myself.' He rolled up a sleeve to show the swollen arm. 'Those bees swarmed off today and I hope they'll go into the woods where they won't hurt anybody else. I'll destroy any that are left. You see, we'd been extracting honey and that upset them ... it was unfortunate that the man came here just at the wrong time.'

'Quite so, quite so. I didn't imagine that it could be deliberate. What a terrible death!' The doctor winced. 'I've seen some dreadful sights in my time, and that was one of them.'

Abruptly Ben said, 'We drink tea at this time of day, would you like to join us?'

He led the way into the kitchen and Amy pulled the kettle over the fire. 'I'd better tell you the story, doctor.' They sat at the table and Amy wondered how much he would say. 'We have here a dog belonging to Mr West and he came to collect it yesterday. It had been badly mistreated and I offered to buy it, but he lost his temper. He and the man both had whips in their hands and Dickens caught me once ... and then the bees arrived.'

'Dear me, that was a difficult situation for you. I always found Mr West most pleasant and of course he gave generously to charitable causes.' Dr Andrews thought for awhile. 'But I believe he drank heavily at times and that can lead to instability of character. In fact his liver was affected, although I shouldn't say so and I suppose that could have increased the effect of the stings.'

Amy arranged cups and saucers and made the tea, trying to get used to the news.

It was strange how West's charitable work made people think he was a decent man.

But he was violent and if the bees hadn't attacked, it might have been Ben that died. The man Dickens had an ugly look and she remembered West's savage attack on the

217

dog. She shuddered to think of Ben coming to harm.

As the doctor took his cup he said to Ben, 'There's one other thing you should know. Dickens also said that you attacked Mr West and tried to smother him. He said you took off your shirt to do it. Now I find that hard to believe.'

Ben sighed; he was in his patient mood. 'I was trying to save him, as it happens. The shirt was intended to protect him from more stings, but he fought me as well as the bees. And of course without a shirt, I was stung much more. You can't imagine I'd take it off to fight him with!'

'Well, Dickens is not what you would call a credible witness after all, if you take his former life into account,' Dr Andrews admitted. 'I believe he has a criminal record and was rescued from a life of vice by Mr West, who was turning him into an honest citizen. I suppose the charities will miss him, Mr West did a great deal of good. He had other workers who were being reformed.'

Dickens had been hired for his criminal skills, surely. His size and brute strength had been useful and he hadn't cared whether Amy lived or died when he threw her into the river. The whole gang must have been desperate men!

Amy could see Ben's mouth twitching at the doctor's information, although he said nothing. What a hypocrite West must have been. How clever of him to recruit these men on the pretext of reforming them, get the credit for good deeds and then use them for criminal activities. Maybe that was how he'd made his fortune in the first place. Five or six sheep at a time were not much, but they would add up – and then there was the wool ... and they probably stole other things as well. Didn't Mr Brown say something about losing a good horse once?

The doctor seemed to be enjoying himself; it was not often that such drama took place in Masham. He went on, 'Did you hear that Mr West's wife has been missing for some months? The poor lady disappeared, in early summer it was, and has never been found. He had given up hope of finding her alive, I believe and I suppose that was another burden for him.'

'Dear me, how strange,' Ben murmured and Amy did not dare look at him.

'Yes, I read a report in the papers that suggested she had been walking on the moor and had possibly fallen down an old mine shaft. There are some dangerous places on the moor.' Dr Andrews accepted a piece of seed cake complacently. 'Of course, she had her own problems.' He looked wise, as though he knew more than he could tell.

Amy kept her head down. Sara's biggest problem had been Saul West and the most dangerous place on the moor had been her own home, poor lass. Her husband must have told everybody that she was mad and Sara would now have to live it down. Perhaps she never would.

Yardley changed the subject. 'Do you expect many cases of influenza this winter, doctor?' Andrews eagerly started on a list of recipes for avoiding the influenza if you didn't have it and treating it, if you did. Ben listened with a faraway expression as though his mind was on something else. The mustard plasters and possets seemed to go right over his head.

Of course, there was an enquiry about the death of an important man like Saul West. The police decided to have a discussion to decide whether the coroner needed to be told, in view of conflicting reports. The doctor, Ben Yardley and Amy, who was a witness, met the police in their office a few days later, to explain what happened on that fateful afternoon.

Dr Andrews spoke first and said that he was satisfied there had been no foul play. The cause of death was asphyxiation, most probably a reaction to bee venom. He explained that some people cannot tolerate even one sting and the unfortunate Mr West had accidentally received many stings. He added that he believed the farmer had not known that Mr West was going to visit him that day.

The police sergeant asked why the bees had attacked Mr West in preference to the other people present and wanted to know what Mr Yardley had been doing with his shirt, as reported by Dickens. They seemed satisfied with the answers.

Amy thought that was the end of it, but then Ben, as beekeeper, was called upon to explain the nature of bee stings and did so at some length. She winced as Ben described how the barbed sting lodged in the victim's skin and continued to pump poison after the bee has gone. 'When it stings in this way the bee dies, part of its body is left behind, but that's not much comfort,' Ben said. 'I took some stings out of Mr West's arms, but he was fighting me, so I wasn't very effective.'

'So you could say that Mr West was poisoned?' The policeman made another note.

Ben continued, 'As Dr Andrews has pointed out, the poison in bee stings has a strong effect on some people. The body reacts by swelling and if the throat or mouth is stung, this can impede the airways and the victim chokes to death. Then there is the effect of the shock. A person with an aversion to insects might have an acute nervous reaction to something like this.'

'Do you agree?' the sergeant asked the

doctor, who nodded.

'Yardley puts it very well.' He sounded surprised.

'Of course I know that bee stings can be fatal, but I'd never seen a case before.' Ben spoke with quiet confidence. 'I expected that Dr Andrews would apply ice to the swellings and then some salve, we use lavender oil. I sent Mr West to the doctor with Dickens because the man would not allow me to help him.' He paused. 'Dickens drove fast, they would have reached the surgery only a few minutes after they left my farm. He may have choked, but on the other hand he was stung more times than I have ever experienced. The quantity of venom could well have been lethal, especially to a susceptible person. In either case this death could not have been prevented by Dr Andrews, or anyone else for that matter.'

Sergeant Taylor looked over his rimless glasses at the tenant farmer. 'What would you know about it?'

'I know a little. I'm not an expert on poisons, but...' Ben stopped and then seemed to make up his mind. 'I am a doctor. I have a degree in medicine.'

There was a shocked pause. Mr Yardley was a doctor! All eyes turned to him, looking for signs of medical knowledge. Amy realized her mouth was slightly open.

'I'm very sorry, Dr Yardley,' the policeman

222

said with a new respect. 'I never knew that. You must know a lot about it.' Dr Andrews looked shocked, as though he couldn't imagine the farmer as a doctor.

'I've not practised for some time,' Ben acknowledged with a tired smile. 'As you know, I'm now the tenant of Banks Farm.'

That explained a lot, Amy thought as she watched Ben. He had a confidence about him and under the grimness he was a very gentle man. And he always thought he knew best... He must be very clever, so in some things he did know best. So this was what he'd been doing in York. But why had he turned his back on doctoring? It was a mystery.

As soon as the meeting was over, Amy slipped into the old bakery to visit Sara while Ben went to buy some oats. Sara and Molly were both working in the now spotless bakery kitchen and Molly was taking a tray of bread loaves from one of the ovens. 'The first batch,' she said proudly. 'I reckon we could do well here, you know. We could open the bakery again.' The fragrance of fresh bread floated through the room.

Sara shook her head. 'Not much chance of that! But it's good to know that the ovens still work – and cleaning the place up has been something for me to do.' She sighed. 'I can't stay here much longer, I'll have to go somewhere else. You've all been so good to me, but I've got to go where he can't find me.'

Amy looked at them both. 'Sit down, Sara, please, and you too, Mother. I've something to tell you.' They were all attention and she went straight to the point. 'I've come to tell you that Saul West died yesterday. I know it's true, we've been talking to the doctor.'

The atmosphere in the kitchen was suddenly tense. Sara was white. 'I can't believe it! He was fit and healthy, apart from his drinking. Are you quite sure?'

Amy explained what had happened and Sara hid her face in her hands. 'Such a horrible death! Oh Saul, why did you have to go the way you did? I thought once that we could have been happy, but he wasn't capable of it. He had to take risks, he had to drink...' she looked up at Amy. 'I'm sorry. It's a great shock.'

Molly patted her hand. 'Well, you don't need to stay here any more, lass. It's grand that you can do as you want now, love. It changes everything.' She looked round the kitchen. 'Well, our first batch of bread was likely our last!' She sounded disappointed. 'Never mind, let's try a slice, straight from the oven.'

Sara would need some time to grasp the situation. She could walk out on the square and get on with her life, although some explanations would be called for. Most folks had heard she was missing. Drying her tears, she tried to smile. 'I was thinking of getting a job in service. I think I'll go home tonight, see Ma and Pa. It's not too far to walk. I've only seen them a few times since … it happened.'

Amy was working on her butter stall on the day of the funeral and she watched the solemn procession wending its slow way round the outside of the square to the church. Naturally enough for so important a man it was a big affair with black horses, nodding plumes and all the trappings of grief except genuine sadness, Amy thought.

All the prominent people thronged the square, swamping the Wednesday market with mourners in top hats. There were snatches of conversation as they passed, mainly about how much Saul West was worth and who would inherit the estate.

Several paupers had been brought along, children from the orphanage in Ripon with grey suits and pale faces. Mr West had been their benefactor. What a strange man, Amy thought as she wrapped butter, charming and raging as it suited him, kind to the poor and cruel to people and animals.

'Sheep may safely graze now, I presume,' said Ben when he collected Amy and her baskets from the market. 'We can only hope that the farms will be sold and the workers turned off. I would hate to think that the villains who stole the sheep would continue with their tricks – West may not have been the only organizer.' He seemed rather lighter in mood, but nothing more had been said about his doctoring. Maybe it was a relief to have his secret known, but why had it been such a secret?

'The autumn sheep sales will be on soon, we'll have to look out for yours among the rest,' Amy suggested. 'Maybe buy them back, if you want to keep them?' Ben snorted, but he didn't disagree.

A few weeks later Sara called at Banks Farm, driving her father's trap. She jumped down, full of energy, when she saw Amy in the yard. 'I've come to thank you all for saving my life. I'm going to see your mother, Amy. Now we can start up the bakery again.' Sara was wearing new clothes and her hair was curled, making her look years younger than the prisoner in the bakery.

'But Sara – you were going to be a teacher! And in any case, won't you – won't Saul have left you some money?' Amy pushed the fair hair out of her eyes, embarrassed. 'Not that I want to know your private affairs, but I thought you'd be provided for.'

Sara laughed, a carefree sound. 'Saul left the land to his dear mother – I think he hated her, actually – and quite a lot of money to his charities. He was a benefactor, you know! He took pleasure in telling me that, and he said

226

he'd leave me nothing, after I lost the baby ... but my father's going to help me until I can earn some money. I'd rather be quite free of him, I don't want his money.'

Jake the dog came across the yard and his tail started to wag when he recognized Sara. He sat down and held up a paw to be shaken. Ben came out of the stables and smiled at Amy. 'Take him home,' he said gruffly to Sara. 'He's obviously your dog.'

Sara bent down to pat the dog, her eyes full of tears. 'I taught him that, and he's remembered! Good boy!' Jake's white teeth showed in a grin and the missing part of his ear gave him a rakish look. 'What a shiny coat you have!'

Amy went to see her mother the next week, after selling butter. She had not been home for some time to face Gran's freezing silence. It was a relief this time that Gran spoke to her, but with a disapproving look at Amy's expanding waistline. 'Disgusting, I call it, flaunting yourself on a market stall when you're expecting. Decent women hide themselves away.'

'Oh Gran, it hardly shows in this dress,' Amy protested, pulling the shawl across the bulge protectively. A baby wasn't something to be ashamed of, but she knew it wasn't supposed to be decent to be seen in public like this, not until you'd been 'churched' after the birth and made pure again. Amy

227

had read the prayer book service for the Churching of Women. Why were things so hard for women? They would be easier, perhaps if she were docile and obedient and always did as she was told. 'Well, and how are the bakery plans, Ma?' she asked, to change the subject.

'We've ordered some fat and flour from Percy's father, and a load of coal,' Molly said happily. Amy was glad the bakery would get her away from Gran, who always felt bound to disapprove ... and here it came.

'Nobody round here wants to buy cakes and such, they bake their own,' Gran sniffed. 'You're not in York here so you needn't get fancy ideas. And that lass of Lawson's that you think so much of won't stop here long, she'll be off somewhere and you'll be left with a loss on your hands. A daft idea, I say, to start summat new at your time of life.'

Molly looked rather subdued, so Amy whispered to her, 'Just the time to start something new, I'd say. You needn't be old before your time, Ma!' Molly was fifty, an age when a widow could go either way: decide to be old, or start something new.

The next day the three women met at the bakery to talk about what could be done. 'You could help as well, Amy, it would be easier than farm work,' Sara suggested.

Amy disagreed; she couldn't leave Ben after all they'd been through. 'I've never done much baking, Sara, Ma did most of it,' she said quickly. 'But Ma's very good. Very good indeed. Her sponge cakes are sheer heaven!'

'Well, you can supply the cream for them, then,' Molly said placidly. 'But I think we'll have to make cake that's not too expensive, or folks won't buy it. Now, what about Fat Rascals? Nice rich scones with plenty of currants. And parkin?'

Sara nodded. 'We need to make some items that will keep for a week or so, if they're not sold straight away. Yorkshire parkin will keep – it's made of treacle and oatmeal. I've been looking up recipes.' She looked over at Amy. 'You want to stay on the farm, then? It would be grand to have you here with us.'

It was good to feel wanted, but baking was indoor work. 'I love farming, being outdoors,' Amy admitted. 'It's been a strange time, but Banks Farm is going well. I'd like to know what is happening on Saul West's farms and whether we still have to watch out for sheep stealing. You haven't heard anything, Sara?'

Sara looked serious. 'The only thing I know is that Saul's mother is still alive. That could be something to watch.'

SIXTEEN

The Masham folk were surprised one morning to find that the old, neglected bakery had come suddenly to life, although one or two had wondered about the comings and goings lately. Doors and windows had been given a fresh coat of paint, the little window panes sparkled and the shop was scrubbed and polished. 'Patrick would have liked to see this,' Amy said sadly, but in the main it was an exciting new beginning and many neighbours called in to wish them well.

Ben Yardley was impressed by Sara's energy. 'I wonder what we can do to help them at the bakery?' he asked at breakfast one morning. 'The girl deserves to succeed, after all her troubles.'

Mrs Shaw smiled at Amy. 'I was wondering what to do with all the apples and plums in the orchard – they're ready for picking now. Your mother could make apple pies to sell, Amy. And perhaps they'd like to make plum jam? It would be quite useful for jam rolls and tarts. They could make some for us, as well.'

The autumn sheep fair brought many

people into Masham from the neighbouring villages and from the high moorland; it was like a festival. Amy and Ben scanned the pens of sheep, but found no animals from their farm. Cold autumn winds whipped the golden leaves across the cobbles of the square and Amy drew her shawl more tightly round her. What would happen if the baby got cold? Her feet hurt with standing for so long. 'Let's go to the bakery for a cup of tea,' she said to Ben. Amy had advised, and Ben had later suggested that they wouldn't buy any sheep, just in case there was still a chance of losing them. All seemed to be quiet on the moor, but that meant nothing. The gang would still be there and they might decide to make some money for themselves.

When they stepped in out of the wind, the warm smell of baking surrounded them. Molly led them from the shop to the kitchen and gave them tea and scones, while Sara did a brisk trade in the shop. It was a perfect time to sell good fresh food and Molly's meat pies were popular with the farmers. Both Molly and Sara looked neat and professional in white aprons over their dark dresses and white caps, their smiles reflecting the success of the day. Money was coming in and the customers were happy. The brief chats with neighbours must be doing both of them good; Amy thought. Molly was beginning to enjoy herself.

In the kitchen Ben Yardley leaned back in his chair, his dark face thoughtful. 'Word soon gets round, you know. When people come in to town they'll be sure to take some of your bread or cakes home with them. But will it be enough for a living for you, I wonder?'

Molly refilled his teacup. 'We've had a good order from the King's Head across the square, Mr Yardley. They're to put on a dinner for the show committee and the cook's given notice. We've been asked to make them a dozen apple pies and there'll be more orders if they like them.'

Amy got up and went into the store room. Looking around she said, 'Ma, you could put a few tables in here, to give folks a cup of tea on market day!' The others had a look and Ben worked out how many tables it would hold. The business was off to a good start.

As the days shortened, the cows gave less milk and so butter making stopped for the winter. Amy was thankful; the effort of churning was tiring her as she grew heavier. But the cattle now stayed in the shed at night and there was much cleaning out and bedding down every day. One or two cows would be milked over the winter months, but most of them would have a rest and calve again in spring.

One day as Amy fed the calves, Ben leaned over the pen. 'It's time we found a good man to work for us. And to look after Sheepcote. I don't want to leave the house up there empty for too long, but how am I going to find a worker, or a man and wife? I could advertise I suppose, but somehow I don't want to take on a stranger.'

'You took that risk with me,' Amy reminded him boldly.

Ben handed her another pail of milk for the next calf. 'So I did, and look at the trouble it brought me. Nothing but nagging and advice.'

As the calf sucked noisily Amy looked up at Ben, struck with a new idea. 'You could ask Tom Harland from up on the moor. He wants to get married and he's looking for a farm to rent, but it might suit him to work for you for a few years and save some money. He could have the Sheepcote house, couldn't he?' The house that she had so hoped she and Patrick were going to live in. She swallowed and went on, 'It might work quite well. I would recommend the lad.'

Ben sighed. 'There you go again, telling me what's good for me. Should I take any notice of a woman's recommendation?'

Of course Ben took no notice of Amy, but she smiled when he rode up to the moor the next day. He came back for milking in a good mood and when the horse was stabled he helped Amy to tie up the cows. 'I happened to see young Tom,' he said casually. 'He's delighted with the idea of working at Sheepcote; he's going to see his girl tonight to talk about it, see if she agrees.'

Amy kept her face straight. 'That's good, Ben.' Tom would marry Sally and they would live happily ever after. She would be pleased for them, not bitter ... she would try never to be bitter because she had lost Patrick. 'His father will be pleased, there's a younger brother who left school this year – Will can take Tom's place on the farm.'

Ben laughed. 'I know them fairly well, as it happens. I've been taking hives up to the heather there for years, and seen the boys grow up. So Tom won't need a character from you, Amy. Tom's going to start straight away, and live in the house, get some furniture together. The sooner the better, you're doing too much for a woman in your condition, my girl.'

It was no use thinking of furniture; Tom and Sally would get the linen press and the good old four-poster bed that had been meant for Amy. Casting round for another subject she said quickly, 'I wonder if there's any brambles at Sheepcote? But I suppose a man wouldn't notice. Mrs Shaw wants me to make some jam.' Mrs Shaw came from York and was new to making bramble jam.

'I don't know about brambles, but I've seen crab apples in our hedges and the odd mushroom. You should keep a look out for mushrooms, I love them.' Ben was giving each cow an armful of hay as he talked and the animals looked round at him with large eyes shining in the lamplight. The shed was full of the sound of contented munching and fragrant with the scent of the hay, a good place to be on an autumn evening. Would the baby love farming as much as Amy did, she wondered as they went into the house for supper.

The next morning, Amy decided to look for mushrooms when she went to check the sheep. After milking she took a basket and wandered down to the river with the dog Bess, slower now than before. Under her feet the earth was soft after recent rain. The water was placid, streaked with orange and yellow reflections of the trees and dewdrops in the grass sparkled like diamonds. There was a faint smell of autumn in the air, a mixture of wood smoke and decaying leaves. Peace had come back to the river, but here there was always a sense of permanence; whatever happened, the river still flowed gently between its banks, carrying water from the moors to the sea.

Amy saw a kingfisher as a brief flash of colour as he went downstream, reminding her of Patrick. He had come and gone as swiftly, leaving a bright memory. In spite of the heartache, she was at peace. There was consolation in the lovely morning.

Pushing open the gate to the Five Acre, Amy thought that the sheep would also be enjoying the morning. The lambs were weaned and about forty of the older ewes were here with the ram by the river, away from the main flock. There was utter silence as she went along the track, not even the odd bleat of a sheep to her neighbour. They were lying down, none of them grazing.

Amy went over to look at the sheep and was surprised they didn't move as she approached. She spoke to them gently as she always did, but there was no reply. Coming nearer, she saw that the ewes were not sitting in a group and chewing the cud – they were lying sprawled in the grass.

The sheep were all dead, including the prize ram and the trampled grass was red with blood.

Amy felt her head spinning with the shock Every single sheep was lying in a pool of blood, their bellies torn, ripped out and one or two had been partly chewed. They were fairly close together and must have been rounded up before the killing. There was a buzz of flies above the carcases. Amy felt sick. She took a deep breath and closed her eyes, but the hum of the flies was still loud. How could she tell Ben that his best sheep, his pedigree ewes and the fine ram, were dead?

The sheepdog was running round and sniffing the ground. Telling Bess to sit and stay, Amy made herself go up to the nearest sheep and touch it; the body was still slightly warm. Was this the work of a pack of dogs from the town? Such a thing had never happened before. Over the years, the Appletons had seen very few dogs in their fields. The town folk understood that a stray dog was soon a dead dog in a field of sheep; the farmers shot strays to protect their stock. When the town folks walked by the river, dogs were put on a lead. Farmers usually kept their working dogs chained up when they were not being supervised. Ben's dogs were always in the yard when they were not being worked.

The feeling of nausea persisted as Amy stood in the pasture, listening to the silence; her body was reacting to another shock. How could her baby be born calm and happy? The poor little thing must have felt so many jolts to his mother's system, beginning with falling in the river. Amy realized that now he was a person in her mind, a little boy who must be protected – or even a little girl, that was possible. 'Jonathan,' she whispered. Almost as if he heard her, for the first time she felt the baby move. Her hand on her belly, she could feel a slight kick. 'You'll soon be free,' she promised him. 'I'll try to look after you, bairn.'

It was important that before Jonathan was born, peace must be restored to the river and the farm. Another thought slipped into Amy's mind and made her feel cold in spite of the sunshine. Could this be a deliberate act? Could someone who wished Ben Yardley ill have brought a savage dog or dogs to do this killing? If so, it must have happened during the night. She looked around carefully, but there was no sign of a dog, no tracks in the dew, nothing except trampling round the sheep. The river bank had a slight clue; next to a tree stump there was an area of bare earth and on it, the imprint of a huge dog's paw, bigger than any paw that Amy had seen. The poor ewes must have met their dreadful death in terror.

Either the dog had swum across the river to attack the sheep, or it had been brought there in a boat. The tree stump could have been used to tie up a boat and the water under it was deep; if a dog had come ashore there it would have struggled, but a few yards down river there was a shallow gravelly beach it could have used more easily. But could one dog kill so many sheep? You would think that some could have got away. It must have been a pack of dogs that herded them into such a tight group.

As best she could Amy walked back to the

farm, the mushrooms forgotten. Ben Yardley was grim when he heard her story, but he said little. He loaded the shotgun and hurried down to the river, but of course there was nothing to be seen. 'I will shoot any dog that shows itself on this farm,' he promised.

Tom Harland jogged into the yard on his pony, looking very pleased with his new job. He had moved in to the house at Sheepcote overnight, wasting no time at all. 'I thought I'd better come over and see if you want a hand with owt,' he said. His face fell when they told him what had happened and he was quiet for a while.

Ben told Tom to stable the pony. 'You'll have to help me to bury the sheep, the sooner the better. We can't leave them lying there. Everything all right at Sheepcote, I hope?'

'Yes, sir, all the stock are fine. But this – savaging... I wonder if it has anything to do with Saul West. I know he's dead, but – he had a lot of influence, and–' Tom looked round the yard and dropped his voice, 'so has his mother. The old lady will know how he died.'

Amy shuddered. She could see now that Ben could be in danger, they might all be in danger. Thank goodness the Harlands knew what West had been like; there were probably other people on the moor who didn't believe in the landowner's kindly public face and knew how savage he could be.

A cloud passed over the sun. Ben shook his head and went off to find two spades and Tom turned to Amy with the shock still in his eyes. 'They say his mother influenced him, made him worse. Saul West wanted a knighthood, he was helping charities with that in mind.'

'I wonder if West's men could have killed the sheep? Do you think his mother might have told them to take revenge?' Amy felt cold. There were still shadows over them ... how long would it be before they were gone? Sara had also mentioned the mother.

Tom shrugged. 'He was trying to be a good community man, but his mother ... some folks on the moor are scared of her, they call her the witch of Carlsmoor.'

'You can't blame his mother for a grown man's crimes,' Ben growled, coming back with the spades. 'Surely you don't think she has magic powers? I thought all that nonsense died out long ago.'

Tom blushed. 'No, Mr Yardley. That's daft of course, we know there's no witches, but – d'you remember we used to scare each other at school with tales of the witch, Amy?'

'I remember the witch of Carlsmoor!' Amy nodded. 'The talk at school, that is – I don't think we ever saw her ... and you say she's Saul West's mother?'

'She is that, and no mistake.' Tom was

240

earnest. 'And trouble is, everybody over the moor thinks they know what happened. That Bert Dickens has been telling anybody that will listen how Mr Yardley murdered his boss–' Tom stopped abruptly, but his employer had heard and the dark face clouded over.

'You think they will believe this?' Ben barked and Tom looked nervous. He was not yet used to Mr Yardley's abrupt manner. 'West was not murdered, as I'm sure you realize. He could not tolerate bee stings and he came here at the wrong time. Please do not talk about murder. I tried to help him, but he fought me off.' He frowned for a moment. 'The sheep first, we'll get that job over. And then it's time I went over to West's place to explain things, to whichever of his relations is still there. It's the right thing to do, in the circumstances. They have the right to know what happened here on that day.'

'Be careful, Mr Yardley, if you go up to the moor,' Tom said quietly.

'It was an unfortunate accident, Tom. My conscience is clear. But to think that someone might have set dogs on to my sheep deliberately ... well, it's bizarre. I never heard of such a thing.'

Ben was going up to confront this witch of Carlsmoor; anything might happen. The woman must be ugly and spiteful; as children they had been deliciously frightened of a being that nobody had actually seen, a sort of moorland myth. But now she was real, and would be dangerous if she was bent on revenge. Amy realized that Tom was worried about the whole thing. Could Ben talk her into being reasonable? Would he be able to get the true story of what had happened to the sheep? Amy put a hand on his arm as he was turning away. 'Please Ben, take me and Tom with you when you go to Carlsmoor. Don't go alone.' Ben shrugged and after a moment Amy said, 'Let's talk to Sara first, she might know something. Let's start at the bakery.'

SEVENTEEN

It was not until the next day that Ben and Amy went to Masham in the trap, Ben in a morose mood. Amy kept very quiet; the sheep slaughter had affected her too. It was a pleasant change to go into the bakery and sniff the warm smells of baking. Molly was serving in the shop and Sara was working behind the scenes, putting icing on buns. She seemed pleased to see them.

'I realise that to talk about your time at Carlsmoor will be painful for you,' Ben began when they had accepted a cup of tea. They were both cold after a ride in the trap in a biting wind and Amy curled her hands round the cup gratefully. 'But we thought you might be able to help us.' He spared her the details of the sheep massacre, but said that they'd lost more sheep and feared that somebody still wished them ill. Anything she remembered about Saul West could be useful.

Amy had carefully avoided talking about Saul when she was with Sara, knowing that the terror was still there under the surface. Perhaps now that the danger was over, she might even want to talk about her ordeal. Now she sat still, waiting.

Sara decorated some buns with pink icing and frowned in thought. 'I've told you he gave to charity, he wanted to be popular,' she began. 'He was hoping for a title or to be a leader, a mayor or high sheriff or something like that. He would have been good at it,' she added with a bitter smile. 'I think he wanted ... recognition, you might call it, because he was a nobody. Saul was born on the moor but sent away to County Durham when he was a baby. That's why when he was success-ful, after he made a fortune, he bought the Carlsmoor estate and built a posh house on the moor, to show people what he's achieved. He was an important man, Saul West, Esquire of Carlsmoor Hall. But all the time, he was a criminal.'

'And his mother?' Amy asked gently.

Sara shook her head. 'I only met her a few times, she took against me. That was the first of my problems,' she admitted. 'His mother had sent him away, got rid of him as a baby and he never forgave her, but he came back. She was an influence on him, a bad influence as far as I could tell. He was different when he came back from seeing his mother. He used to drink a lot of whisky and then beat me, when he'd been there... I really think he hated her.' Sara switched to white icing. 'But she must have known about his illegal dealings that made money, the things he never talked about.' She reached for another bun. 'The moorland's a fine place if you want to keep your doings quiet, of course. I never realized how different it is, until I went to live up there.'

Now she had started, Sara seemed to want to talk about the past and perhaps it would be good for her. 'What sort of doings were they up to, do you think?' Amy asked.

'Well, his mother always had a house at Slapestones, one of the more remote farms he bought and when he came back, Saul spent a lot of time there. He had cattle there, a whole lot of bulls. And cocks, for cock fighting. They still do it up at the Moortop Inn, you know, in the yard at the back. A lot of gambling goes on. Well, I think Saul's mother looks after that farm, but I've never been there. I only know about the fighting cocks because one of the men joked with him about it and I overheard them.' She sighed. 'Not a normal family, I'm afraid. Saul's mother was really Alison Dent, I don't know where Saul got the name West. And I've no idea who his father was.'

'Did you know she was the witch of Carlsmoor, that we used to talk about?' Amy looked up at Sara.

The girl's face registered shock. 'I'd no idea! I remember we used to scare each other with stories of the witch ... they said she could fly on a broomstick. She wasn't there in the winter time, she went off somewhere else. That was strange, wasn't it? But I never thought to connect the witch with Saul's mother.'

Molly bustled in from the shop. 'Are those buns ready, love? Mrs Brown wants a dozen.' She took a tray of buns and Amy noticed how much quicker her movements were, how much happier she seemed than when they were stuck together in that little house of Gran's.

When her mother had gone Amy picked up the empty trays and took them to the sink. 'I may as well help you while we're here, lass. Now, do you think that this witch woman would want to do us harm? Or be able to, now her son is gone?'

'She wished me plenty of harm, I do know. Saul's man, Bert Dickens tried to warn me about her. He was sorry for me, he said. But Saul saw him talking to me and he said no more. He could have lost his house and his job, just because he tried to warn me about Alison... I don't like Dickens, but I was grateful.' Sara looked at the clock and took a batch of pies from the oven. 'Thank goodness Saul didn't hear what he was saying.'

Ben had listened in silence and now he said, 'What sort of harm did the woman intend, do you know?'

Sara's face was flushed from the heat of the oven. 'She wanted Saul to marry money, and marry into the gentry. I met him at a charity concert when he was looking for a wife, that was my bad luck. Saul was much older than I am of course, but he was charming at first. He decided to marry me and it all happened very quickly. And his mother was annoyed.' Sara managed a laugh. 'Bert had been working at Slapestones, that's where Alison lives. He heard her in the stable one day, telling Saul she could get rid of me easy. She said, "Those dogs would make a meal of her, it would all be over in a few minutes and you could be twenty miles away. Dreadful accident, it would be. Then you'd be free to marry".' She paused. 'The next week Saul beat me again and I knew I had to get away. He would kill me, or she would. That was

246

when – when you found me.'

'Dogs?' Ben and Amy spoke together.

'Why yes, Saul bred mastiffs. Huge, slavering things, always tied up, Bert said. I never saw them, thank goodness ... although I sometimes heard them barking from over the moor, when the wind came from that way. Bert thought he got a lot of money for them. As guard dogs and for blood sports...' She shuddered. 'He would have told me more, but Saul came and stopped him.'

Ben stood up. 'It's time we were off, Sara. Thank you for talking to us. Those sheep we lost this week were actually killed by dogs. It seems possible that the witch was responsible.' The cold air came to meet them as he opened the door.

Sara looked scared. 'Take care, all of you,' she said quietly.

On the way home Ben looked across at his passenger, wrapped in a shawl with only the tip of her nose showing. 'I think those dogs might be bred for bull baiting, Amy. Sara said there were a lot of bulls at the farm. That's been illegal for over thirty years, but perhaps it still goes on. It's the sort of thing that West would enjoy.'

Amy shuddered. 'I can't bear to think of it ... setting dogs on to a bull, to see which gets killed first.'

'And the bull is tethered...' Ben's tone was ferocious. 'We're dealing with very unpleasant people, you know.'

Amy summoned her energy; the baby was not due for months yet; she couldn't afford to make him an excuse and although she was feeling tired, the heaviness was beginning to wear off. 'Right, Ben, we'll move all the sheep to the field behind the house and get Tom to do the same at Sheepcote. We'll keep loaded guns handy – and you should tell the police, too.'

'I will, but I'll also go to see this Mrs Dent.'

The next day there was a light powdering of snow, the first of the winter. In the valley it soon melted, but the moors sparkled with frosting like one of Sara's cakes. Ben was thoughtful as his horse picked its way along a moorland track. He fingered the pistol in his belt, an old weapon that had belonged to his father. At least he would have some defence if the dogs were set upon him. The moors were dark and forbidding; views of the valley were hidden by mist and snow.

It had been hard work to persuade Katherine that he was doing the right thing in going up to the moor, and even harder to insist that Amy stay behind. The poor girl was getting into the later stages of her pregnancy and she often looked white and tired, but she was as keen as he was to confront whoever it was that had murdered his sheep.

Before setting out on Mary, the steady mare, Ben had visited the police station and reported the crime. He asked whether there had been any reports of stray or wild dogs about the area. This place was much less civilized than his little farm near York. Tom had said that sometimes stray dogs could form packs and inflict much damage on stock before they were killed, although Amy didn't remember such a thing happening. Banks Farm was part of a well-managed estate employing several gamekeepers. That should be some sort of protection, after all; he would speak to the agent.

'No sir, no reports at all,' the policeman assured him. 'But we'll keep a watch.'

Ben had wondered whether Slapestones would be hard to find, but he could hear the ominous, deep-throated baying of dogs rolling over the heather from a distance and the sounds guided him to the farm. It was well hidden on the sheltered side of a ridge, quite safe from the curious eyes of anyone who might be crossing the moor. Young men from the West Riding towns sometimes came on walking tours up here in the summer, keeping to the main tracks. The dogs might have given the location of the farm away, but they were more of a deterrent to visitors. Just to hear them made you wish you had stayed at home. The horse slowed and seemed reluctant to follow the rough track to the farm.

249

As they drew nearer Ben was surprised to see well maintained stone walls surrounding a garden, behind which was a solidly built old farmhouse with clean windows and fresh paint. There was a yard and farm buildings clustered round it. He thought the mullioned windows and long chimneys were in the Tudor style; this house had been here for centuries. Of course West had been wealthy; he must have made sure that his mother was comfortable. Sara said she had lived here before Saul came back to the moor, so perhaps he'd renovated the old house recently.

Very cautiously, Yardley rode down the track and dismounted, tying Mary up under an open shed which would shelter her from the worst of the weather. The mare rolled her eyes and tossed her head as the dogs increased their clamour. 'Steady girl, they can't reach you,' he said soothingly as he loosened the girth, to ease the mare while she was waiting. Then he wondered whether this was wise; he might have to make a quick getaway. In spite of the fresh paint, Slapestones was not a hospitable place. He quickly tightened the girth again.

To get to the house, he had to walk through the yard. Three enormous dogs leaped towards him at the ends of their long chains, mouths wide and drooling saliva. Ben flattened himself against the garden wall, prepared to jump over it if needed. How far did those chains extend? When standing on their hind legs, the dogs were taller than he was. The massive bodies had great depth. The animals had prick ears like a wolf, fierce, ugly faces, more bandog than mastiff, yellow teeth and protruding ribs. These dogs were undernourished and in spite of his revulsion, Ben felt sorry for them. Starving dogs would be much more dangerous. They would need no urging to kill if they were really hungry and bandogs, he knew, were always keen to kill. They were a breed of ancient English hunting dog, feared all over the world.

To his surprise, when he reached the house Ben was still intact and he realized that the end of the chains were just short of where he stood. The dogs would be a sure deterrent to any except the most determined visitor. When his presence was known, would they be slipped from their chains? In spite of the pistol, Ben knew he was in danger. It would not be possible to shoot all three at once – and there could be more; there were other kennels across the yard.

What would happen next? What would a woman do, a wild moorlander, confronted with the man she thought was her son's killer? She might not give him a chance to tell her the truth – or she might not believe it.

The dogs' frantic barking increased and

Ben could hardly hear his knock on the door, but surely the dogs made his presence obvious. He waited, then knocked again.

The door opened soundlessly and Ben found himself looking down at a very small but upright figure, neat and trim, with bright blue eyes and a fierce expression. The woman frowned. 'What do you want?'

'To talk to you about my sheep. Stolen sheep, and dead sheep. You must know that your dogs raided Banks Farm.' Attack was supposed to be the best form of defence and Ben felt in great need of defence. If the dogs were let loose, he was finished. He had intended to come here to explain West's death, but the dogs had changed his mind. They were obviously the culprits.

A strange look came into the woman's face. 'I know you! It's Dr Yardley. Ben Yardley. Oh dear, what have we done?'

Ben himself was just as shocked. 'Alison ... Mrs West. I had no idea you–' He stopped himself. A patient from his former life, something he had hoped to avoid, was the last thing he had expected. Up here on the moor you didn't expect to meet citizens of York.

'*I had no idea you were the witch of Carlsmoor*. That's what you were going to say. How could you? I go by the name of Dent, on the moor.' He could hardly hear her for the noise of the dogs, barking and

252

howling. The woman put a hand on his arm and drew him into the house. 'Come in, it's too noisy and too cold to talk out here.'

It was a relief to get inside, out of the dreadful yard. She led the way to a room with cushioned chairs, set round a huge log fire. The books and pictures made it very unlike a typical moorland farmhouse. 'What a pickle! I now find that the surly tenant farmer Dickens describes – he tells me has caused the death of my son – is also Dr Ben Yardley, who once saved my life.' The intelligent eyes looked straight into his. 'That, I do not forget. And also, we became friends.'

Ben needed a few moments to recover; the change from dire peril to a friendly reception was too sudden. The dogs were still barking, but the sound was now distant, muted by the thick stone walls of the house. It looked as though he would get away with his life, after all. Unless ... could he trust her? She was taking West's death very calmly – perhaps too calmly; there might be an outburst soon. But it was hard to associate the Alison he had known in York with a son like Saul West. That was the biggest shock of all. Tom had said that West had been sent away as a baby ... so he could have had a difficult upbringing.

The woman went to a cupboard and drew out a bottle and two glasses. 'We must drink together, Ben Yardley. I have some bochet here, made on the moor.' She glanced out of the window. 'Just the thing for snowy weather. You've had a cold ride and an uneasy one I fear, coming up here to see me.'

Ben nodded and accepted the glass of mead, holding it up to the light. 'You're not trying to poison me, are you?' It could be a witch's brew. He sniffed it and the fragrance was of heather. 'You drink first, Alison.'

The woman laughed and took a sip from her drink, motioning him to sit by the fire. Her eyes were without guile.

Ben hesitated, then drank. The mead was potent, sweet and strong, heart-warming stuff on a snowy day, but not poison – or so he hoped.

'Are you here to confess, or to deny your guilt?' Alison smiled and Ben felt himself relax a little. Her composure in the face of horror was amazing ... she was not an emotional woman, he remembered. 'You said you've come to tell me about the sheep. That was Dickens' idea for revenge, of course. But I certainly wished you ill. Poor Saul! He had his faults, but it was a dreadful way to die. Perhaps you can tell me the truth about Saul's death. I know you respect the truth, Dr Yardley.' She sat back, composed, glass in hand, showing no emotion when she spoke of her son beyond a sort of impersonal sympathy. A big black cat sat on the hearthrug, a real witch's cat with slanting green eyes.

Ben looked into the fire. 'You'll know that bee stings affected him?' he began.

'I suppose he told me... I don't know a great deal about Saul, I'm afraid. I never was close to him.'

EIGHTEEN

There was a silence and then the woman went on, 'Saul came back here last year, but before then I had not seen him for many years.' Alison shook her head. 'I'm afraid I was born with little maternal feeling, which was just as well, as it turned out. I soon realized that I could never rear the child, so I sent him away to be cared for, to give him better care than mine. He was too difficult; Saul was not – not normal. He could be charming and agreeable, but his rages were terrible, he was cruel and he loved no one – not even himself.' Half to herself she added, 'He took after my husband ... his father was violent. I came here to get away from him, before Saul was born.' She looked into the fire. 'Of course, Saul resented the fact that he'd been sent away. His adult life was spent trying to prove how successful he was.'

It was a relief that she knew Saul's true nature. 'Well, my bees were in an aggressive

255

state when he came into the yard and he stood no chance of avoiding them. It's true we had argued about the dog I had taken from him after he'd beaten it within an inch of its life, and about my stolen sheep. You probably don't know that his sheep stealing gang caused the death of my worker, who was newly married and about to become a father. Saul had a lot to answer for.' Ben paused to see what effect this had on the woman, but she didn't react. 'I tried to wrap my shirt round him to protect him, but he thought I was attacking him and he fought me. Naturally after all that had happened, he saw me as an enemy.'

'But you are a doctor, Ben. Could you do nothing for him?' Alison's voice shook just a little; she was affected by this death, after all.

'He didn't know that. In Masham I started a new life as a farmer, left medicine behind me. To him I was a peasant, someone to patronize. Of course I was trying to help him – if he'd let me. But the stings were fatal and I think nobody could have saved him. The poison affects some people that way. There is nothing anyone can do ... we have no antidote. Bees can be dangerous sometimes.'

'So you were not to blame,' Alison said thoughtfully. 'I had a suspicion that Dickens was not telling the truth, although it's fair to say that he might not have understood what you were trying to do. He's a man who always expects the worst of everybody. Who can control a hive of bees, tell them who to sting? He has probably told me other lies.' She refilled his glass and through the window, Ben could see the snow was now whirling down in large flakes from a leaden sky. 'For example, Dickens says he feeds the dogs well, but I know they are much thinner since Saul died – and more dangerous.' She sat quietly for a while; the only sound was the ticking of an old clock. 'Dickens will have to go. I will get rid of all the questionable elements of Saul's business. I inherited it from him; he never told me what was going on, but I don't intend to continue. Saul organized blood sports, he said that men were naturally bloodthirsty and he could turn a profit from it. He was cruel, Ben. I sometimes wondered whether he would some day turn on me. He never forgot the fact that I didn't mother him.'

There was so much this woman could tell him. 'I certainly hope you don't continue his activities. What do you know about the sheep stealing? Saul was the instigator, I suppose?' Ben sat back in his chair and looked into the fire.

'He was – I have found out more about it since he died, from Dickens of course. Now I realize why he was so angry when I tried to tell him to behave honestly! It was regrettable, of course but he must have made a lot of money from stealing livestock and he was good at covering his tracks.' The precise voice was firm. 'From riverside farms they floated sheep out on a sort of barge and on the edge of the moor, they rounded them up at dusk and took them over to a deserted farm somewhere. Dickens said the sheep were sold in markets all over the north and some were sent straight to butchers. Saul had special carts built that could move fast and concealed the load.' She laughed. 'I believe there was a thin layer of turnips or hay, sitting on a roof under which were the sheep.'

The witch of Carlsmoor seemed to be living up to her name; detached, not concerned for the victims of Saul's depredations, indifferent to his ethics. 'My sheep are safe, now?' Ben gave her a serious look. 'This business cost a young man his life. I've still to get to the bottom of that.'

Alison looked at him. 'So you said... I didn't know anything about a death. What a waste. Your sheep would always have been safe if I'd known who you were, Ben. No other doctor would have made such efforts to save me... But why are you not still a doctor in York? What brought you to this outlandish spot?'

Ben had never told anyone outside York why he had given up medicine, but the mead had relaxed him. Tension had drained from him and sitting by the fire in that pleasant room he felt very tired; they had all been on edge for so long, ever since he took the farm. 'It's a long story. Not all my patients were as grateful as you are, Alison. One man reported me because he said I had killed his wife. It was not true, but the woman – she was stubborn and refused to take my advice – died after she had been my patient. Her condition – I told her so bluntly – was self-inflicted, brought on by a highly unsuitable diet and a lack of exercise. They were wealthy people and they were influential. I was accused of negligence, but the case was not proved.'

'You could have lived it down, in time,' Alison said gently.

Ben shook his head. 'Even so, some of my patients went elsewhere and after a while I decided to sell the practice. To be honest, I'd lost my confidence – a doctor needs to be confident, to reassure the sick.' He sighed. 'Farming has its appeal, you see. Animals don't lodge formal complaints, they just bite you or tread on your toe.' Ben was surprised to find that the memory was still painful; this was why he'd been so furious to hear he was accused of killing West.

Alison was indignant. 'You were the best doctor that York ever had. Several people told me so! Perhaps not the most charming, but you were truthful and kind. You see, I'm being honest with you! Some people value flattery above honesty, I'm afraid.'

Ben smiled ruefully. 'Charm has never been my strong point, as my worker points out.' It was a pity that Amy wasn't there to hear a testimonial from a grateful patient.

'And what happened to the lovely Sylvia? Did you marry and live happily ever after?'

It was still a shock to hear Sylvia's name mentioned, although the heartache had faded. 'She didn't want to marry a farmer.' His fiancée had worked at the surgery, receiving the patients, who had all thought she was wonderful. It was a black day when he realized that Sylvia loved the successful practice and the social standing of a doctor's wife much more than she loved Ben Yardley. She told him that she wasn't going to bury herself in the country and if he persisted in going farming, then he could have back his ring.

Ben smiled and then said, 'Will you tell me why you are called a witch?' It must be his turn to ask the questions by now.

'Confession time.' There was a grim smile on the handsome old face. 'I live in York in the winter months, the moor is dead then, as you'll find out for yourself. I shall go to York as soon as Saul's affairs are organized to my satisfaction. However many barrels of gin or bottles of mead there are in the cellar, you freeze to the bone, up here in the snow; you can feel it starting today. In summer I do see something of the older neighbours, but they don't visit in the winter.'

Ben nodded but said nothing, not wanting to interrupt her story.

'My house in York – you may remember – looks over the river; I have other friends there, a more normal life. But I say nothing to the moorlanders about where I go and the story grew up that I fly off on a broomstick and come back with the spring. The only summer I spent in York was after the pneumonia that nearly carried me away... You stayed with me for three days and nights, Ben. And visited many times after the worst was over. I became – fond of you. I wished that you were my son, instead of Saul.'

'And your lungs, Alison? Did they recover completely?' Ben realized he was thinking like a doctor again. She looked very healthy, sitting there in the firelight with a straight back.

'Fairly well, but I'm careful. That's one reason to go back to York soon, to avoid the worst weather. Do you know, I'm so glad to see you. When your practice was sold no one could tell me where you'd gone, although I did ask. Sylvia was gone too. I wouldn't be here now, enjoying my old age, if it wasn't for Dr Yardley. I'll make damned sure that Dickens doesn't annoy you again. In any case, he'll be finding a new job soon.'

The snow was still falling and Ben knew he had to get home before dark. As he stood up to leave, he looked through to the kitchen where shelves held shining rows of bottles and jars. It looked like a still room. 'What do you concoct in there?' he asked.

Alison laughed. 'I'm a witch, remember. Spells and brews ... that's what the children think. Do you believe me? I thought you wouldn't. Well then, there are bilberries in plenty here and I make jam, and wine, mead, of course, and crab apple jelly. Blackberry jelly too. I take the stuff back to York in the autumn. I supply several shops.'

As she opened the door for him Ben looked out to where the dogs were once more straining at the chains. 'I'd be careful of those brutes, if I were you, they might eat you if they're hungry. By the way, did you tell Saul to let the dogs kill his wife?'

Alison closed the door again, to shut out the dogs' barking. 'Of course not! What a shocking suggestion. I thought she was rather spineless, but that was probably because he kept her down. Didn't she die out on the moor, poor thing? That was what he told me.' The blue eyes were clear and innocent. Dickens must have made up the story to frighten Sara.

'You'll be pleased to know that Sara survived.'

Ben detected a real, human smile on Alison's face, and heard something like a sigh of relief. 'Yes, I am pleased. I was so afraid that Saul had driven her – to her death. He married her quickly and then fell out of love.' She opened the door to let him out and a cold blast of air hit them. 'You take care too, Ben. The moor's a dangerous place.'

The bleak landscape was unfamiliar in its blanket of snow, but Ben was able to find his way with the help of the standing stones that guarded sections of the track Nobody knew how old they were or what they were there for, but now it seemed to him that they were tall way markers, to guide travellers in bad weather. If you wandered off the track on Carlsmoor in a snow storm, you might not be found for months. There was a case, he remembered grimly, of a body found preserved in the peat up here ... a traveller who had lost his way in Roman times. He had been there for about two thousand years before he was found.

'Come on, Mary,' he said to the horse. 'We'll soon be home.' Once he could see the lights of Masham Ben was able to relax and his mind went back to Alison West. He had known her as a middle class, respectable widow with a comfortable income, inherited from her family, West Riding woollen manufacturers. She was well educated and sensible, never wasting his time with imaginary ailments. To think that all these years she had lived a second life on the moor and had been labelled a witch... Saul had probably kept his wife and his mother apart deliberately. If they had got together, life might have been better for both of them and they might have been able to curb some of his excesses. But once the drink took hold of a man, it was hard to help him.

Did Dr Yardley miss the life of a medical man? He'd had very little time to think about it, but it had been good to use his skill to save a life, as he had with Alison.

Yes, he did miss medicine, but not the city life in York. He loved York's history, but he never wanted to live in town again. For one thing, Amy wouldn't be there... Ben shut that thought down abruptly.

The horse was tiring in the snow and Ben patted her neck. 'You're doing well, girl.' There had been little satisfaction in being a farmer so far, but they had been through troubled times. Perhaps this was the end of them, perhaps things would go well through the winter, Amy's baby would be born... Poor Amy might have trouble still to come; childbirth could be a dangerous time and she was not a big woman, the sort that popped out babies as easily as shelling peas. Amy needed taking care of, he thought with a thump of the heart at the idea of anything going wrong. He'd made a mistake when he allowed her near the bees in her condition, but he hadn't thought of it at the time.

Ben was shocked at Amy's appearance when the horse stumbled into the farmyard, just on dark. She was carrying milk into the dairy, pails half full as Ben had suggested for one in her condition, but she looked worried and exhausted, with huge eyes in a white face. 'What's the matter, girl?' he asked gently, but she shook her head and went on to the dairy. He thought she had been crying.

Some time later they met at the supper table and Ben moved the lamp so that he could see Amy more clearly. 'Had a bad day, Amy?' he asked gently. Mrs Shaw was in the kitchen and Amy stood up to go to her, but Ben stopped her with a hand on her shoulder. 'You don't feel ill?' Heavens, she had about four months to go before the birth.

'Nothing's wrong, Ben, I'm well. I was just – worried, that's all. When the snow came and it was dark and you were out there... I thought you were eaten by the dogs, or lost on the moor. I though the worst, it was silly of me. But I was that glad to see you...' Amy gave him a watery smile and vanished into the kitchen.

Ben frowned and poured himself a glass of water. Amy was bound to fear the worst, it had happened to her, twice. First her father had gone and then her world had fallen apart once more when Patrick died, and, well, she wasn't likely to be all that fond of himself, but her world would change again if he failed to come home. Without Ben, Amy would have no job and no home. Was that it? Or did she have some sort of affection for the surly tenant farmer she had learned to work with? They hadn't had a real argument for a long time; Amy had toned down the advice and Ben himself had tried to be civil. Maybe it wouldn't last, but he rather hoped it would.

For a few weeks, it seemed as though peace would prevail. There were no more sheep losses and nothing was heard of West's men. There was less work as the cows went dry and all the surplus sheep were sold. The builders got on with the conversion of the apple loft into what was to be a separate cottage for Amy.

Amy had found it hard at first to believe that the dreaded old woman behind Saul West had turned out to be a friend of Ben's and even better, would make sure that they lost no more sheep. It was hard to forget the past, but she decided to focus on practical things that should be done. 'Tom and Sally are getting married after Christmas,' she told Sara on a visit to the bakery. 'I'd like to make them something.' Cushions would be good, but she had no feathers.

'Why not a patchwork quilt?' Sara suggested. 'And if you tell me you don't sit down long enough to make one, well it's time you did. That Ben Yardley shouldn't be working you too hard, think of the baby!'

A patchwork quilt would take hours and hours of sewing and a great deal of material. 'I don't know where to start, Sara and I'd need a lot of stuff.' Amy wasn't sure whether she could manage to finish a quilt. 'But don't worry, Ben won't let me do very much on the farm these days.'

'It's easy, it just takes time, that's all. You cut out a pattern from paper, square or a honeycomb shape if you like. Then work out colours that go well together and cut them to the pattern. Do the top first. Cut the stuff a bit bigger than your pattern and then sew it over the shape. There's three layers, a sort of filling and then the backing. Look, I'll show you mine.' Sara lived behind the shop most of the time and her bed was covered by a pretty quilt in pastel colours. 'My mother made it.'

They went back to the shop and Sara served a customer. 'Yes, a quilt's the thing,' she decided when the shop was empty again. 'You can have my old dresses, for a start. I don't want to wear them ever again, the clothes I had ... before. Saul wanted a well dressed wife ... there's some good fabric in them, too good to waste.' Sara thought for a moment. 'I've been back to the house, to get my things. If I make some squares and your

267

mother and maybe even your Gran can help, we can get it done in time, I think.'

Amy shuddered at the thought of asking Gran to help with a quilt for Tom Harland and his bride, but Sara looked at it from the outside. 'Your Gran probably needs something to do, she'll often be lonely when your mother's with me.' Perhaps Gran deserved to be lonely, but Amy decided to try treating her like the Gran she ought to be. There was nothing to lose.

The idea of making a quilt seemed much more possible when Sara's clever fingers had cut up many squares of rich deep colours, shining silks and brocades. It was going to be a very special quilt, not just a cotton one. 'Ball gowns,' she explained briefly, 'for charity balls. Saul used to go to them all. Now, Molly's keen to help, so you go home with a few of these and show them to your Gran. She can still see quite well, can't she?'

'Only too well,' Amy muttered. Gran could pick out a missing button on Amy's dress at fifty paces, or so it seemed. Rather reluctantly she went to see her grandmother, while her mother was working at the shop, knowing it was a risky thing to do.

NINETEEN

'Shut door lass, anybody would think you were born in a field,' was Gran's greeting as Amy walked through the door.

'How are you today, Gran?' Resisting the temptation to bang the door, Amy knelt down humbly beside Gran's chair. 'Now, do you remember the Harlands from up on the moor? I thought you might. Well, Tom's getting married soon – he works for Mr Yardley now. We'd like to make a patchwork quilt for them. Do you know how to do it?' She held out some of the bright cloth pieces.

Gran perched her spectacles on her nose and looked at the material. 'Trust you not to know how to sew. That's good stuff you've got though, nice to work with. Don't go spoiling it, now... The best way to do it is like this.' She picked up the pieces and reached into her work basket for a box of pins. 'I used to know the Harlands, good folks they were. I think you're going to need my help, I can't see you getting it right on your own. For one thing, to look at your dresses you've no idea of colours.' The project was under way.

Amy made her way back to Banks Farm

feeling that she had learned some kind of lesson. Gran's rudeness had always made her reply in kind, but if you took no notice, it might be possible to get along with the old girl, especially if there was something to talk about apart from Amy's shortcomings. They'd had a conversation that was almost normal before she left. Maybe there were some things that Gran could teach her, now that they didn't have to live together.

When Amy told Mrs Shaw about the quilt that evening, she was offered more material and also help with the sewing. 'I haven't done quilting for years,' Ben's aunt said happily. 'Now, how much time have we got?'

Even Ben took an interest in the forthcoming wedding. 'Tom's working so hard,' he said from behind his newspaper. 'I think we should offer to have a wedding breakfast for the guests here at the farm, after the service. We're not too far out of town.' Sally's parents should have traditionally provided a 'ham tea', but her mother had been very ill. Tom had told him they'd manage without a party.

Amy stared at Ben in amazement. Was he sickening for something? 'But you don't like people, you said so,' she accused him.

'Tom and Sally are not just "people", Amy. Tom's a good young man and I've been talking to Sally, she wants to work for us too. She can milk cows.' Ben looked pleased.

270

I will not feel jealous, Amy told herself. Sally was taking over her house – the house she'd dreamed of living in with Patrick – and now, she would probably take Amy's job. Sally was pretty and plump, well made and tall, with great big muscles on her arms. She was everything that Amy was not, and she would take over.

As the world turned, the solstice passed and 1868 drew nearer, Amy's anxiety gave way to a pleasant feeling of anticipation. The baby would be born in a few weeks, the bakery business was thriving and Gran was too busy sewing for the quilt to cause much grief. Amy was kept busy plucking geese to sell at the market and helping to make puddings and pies.

Ben gave Amy her wages the week before Christmas and he was generous. She planned to go to Ripon with the Thursday carrier, but Mrs Shaw took the trap one day to the market and Amy went with her to buy a few small extra things for Christmas. She had made a pincushion for Gran and one for Mrs Shaw. It would be good to find some little gift for Ben, but what could you buy for a grumpy farmer?

After much thought, Amy bought him a big notebook for writing down everything that happened on the farm, so Ben could keep a diary. She would give him a little talk about how useful it was to make a note of

271

dates of cutting hay, sowing corn, cows calving and the like. Behind the cowshed door, Amy had chalked up the date on which each cow calved, but they needed something better than that. For an educated man, Ben had very few records. She would tell him– Amy sighed. Perhaps not. She would just give him the book and leave it to him.

The winter was mild and on Christmas Day, they drove to church in pale sunshine.

Amy spent the rest of the day at home and slept that night in the lumpy little bed in the attic. She was older and maybe a little wiser than when she had last slept there, and not so restless. It was even possible to imagine that some of her problems had been avoidable. It must have been hard for Gran, when her peace was invaded by an untidy young woman who seemed to have no direction in life. Perhaps after her father died she and Ma should have taken a house of their own.

The mild weather continued and one day it brought a visitor to Masham. Amy was helping in the bakery when a trap drew up and a small elderly woman came into the shop. She quietly bought some buns, but when Sara looked at her over the counter she gave a gasp. 'Mrs West!' She blushed and said to Amy, 'This is Saul's mother.' The witch of Carlsmoor looked at them both with sharp blue eyes. 'And Amy is my friend, she works for Mr Yardley.'

'Good day Amy, I know your employer well. I've come to see Sara...' Amy tactfully went into the kitchen, wondering what was to happen, but she was called back 'There's nothing private about this,' the witch said. Amy looked at her curiously; the woman who had scared them as children was certainly old; she was straight backed and handsome, but not in the least like Saul West.

There was a short silence and then the woman smiled at Sara. 'We should have got together before he died, but he told me you didn't want to see me.'

Sara's eyes widened. 'He told me that about you!'

Mrs West nodded. 'I thought as much. I often wondered how you managed to cope with him. However, that's all over now. I want you to know, Sara, that I have left Saul's estate to you in my will, and I'm arranging with my lawyers to transfer half of it to you straight away. They will get in touch with you soon.'

'There's no need, I can manage quite well,' Sara stammered.

'No, don't argue, Sara. It's the least I can do, my dear, after the dreadful time you must have had. I feel guilty that I didn't try to get to know you before, or to help you. But we were all kept in the dark by Saul and I had no influence on him at all.' She gave a sigh. 'I feel better now. Here's my address in

York. Call to see me if you visit the city, won't you?'

'Oh, my goodness. Won't you have a cup of tea?' Sara said weakly, obviously shocked. Amy went off to put the kettle on, but when she came back with the tray, the witch had gone.

'She wouldn't stay to be thanked,' Sara said faintly, as pale as her apron.

Amy passed her a cup of tea and laughed. 'You won't need the bakery now, my lass. You're a woman of property!'

Sara straightened up and set her cap level. 'Yes, I will. I'll keep the bakery and make a success of it, with Molly. That's what we want to do.'

It was such a mild winter that everyone was looking forward to an early spring. But in February the snow came back.

The old farmers knew it would because the sun shone on Candlemas Day, always a bad sign. Amy couldn't resist telling Ben that if the badger looked out of his sett on the second of February and saw the sun, he would go back to sleep because there was half of winter yet to come. 'Thank goodness you told us,' Ben said sarcastically. 'We'd better get some supplies if we're to be snowed in. Have you enough flour to last for a month, Kate?'

Mrs Shaw laughed and Amy blushed. 'Just

you wait and see,' she warned. And later in the month it started to snow and went on snowing for three days: deceptively gentle, deceptively beautiful large flakes, falling out of a leaden sky.

Sheep tended to shelter under the lee of the stone walls, but that was where the drifts were deepest. Ben had to dig them out, at all hours of the day and night. This had happened before, Amy told Ben, and her father had worked out which were the safest fields for the ewes in bad conditions. 'We brought them into the barn for lambing, some years. Maybe we could do that?' she suggested.

'I'm hoping the weather will improve before lambing,' Ben said with a wry smile.

One night the wind got up and drifted the lying snow; it was a piercing blast, straight from the North Pole. Deep drifts were swept up and dumped down in new places. Ben went out to check the ewes with a lantern, heavily swathed in scarves and gloves. Amy was thankful she was not allowed to help; they agreed it was not the work for a heavily pregnant woman. Mrs Shaw had a cold and went to bed early, but Amy stayed by the fire, listening to the wind howling in the chimney. She kept the fire high and pulled the kettle over, then poured some elderberry cordial ready to give Ben a hot drink when he came in.

Ben was away for an hour, and then another hour. What could he be doing? Amy felt alarm rising, the dread that he might have come to harm. You could freeze to death outside on such a night. She walked up and down the room, and eventually put on a shawl and went to stand at the open door. 'Where are you, Ben?' she called, but her voice was lost in the force of the wind.

The yard was black where they had cleared the snow, an island in a sea of white.

At the far side of the yard she could see a faint light ... was it Ben's lantern? But it was low, as if it stood on the ground. Wrapping the shawl tightly round her, Amy set off across the yard towards the light. As her eyes got used to the darkness she saw that Ben was slumped over the stone water trough, clinging to it for support, his coat trailing in the water. His face was covered in something dark that looked like blood.

'Ben! What happened?' Amy shook him gently, but Ben was only half conscious. Blood still trickled from a cut on his head. The wind howled with renewed force and Amy nearly lost her shawl. Had he been attacked?

'Fell over a wall,' Ben mumbled, clinging to the water trough.

'We've got to get inside. It's dangerous out here,' Amy said as firmly as she could between chattering teeth. 'Come on Ben, lean on me and we'll get to the house. It's not far!' Snow was whirling round them in all directions and she could only see a faint glimmer of light from the kitchen window.

It seemed very far to get to safety across the yard and Ben didn't seem to care very much whether he got there or not. He wanted to lie down. Amy pulled and tugged until he struggled to his feet and when he leaned on her, he was very heavy. But it was a matter of life and death and somehow, she edged him over the yard, inch by painful inch. 'Leave me alone!' he said at one point and Amy almost despaired.

'Come on, you know how dangerous it is. Don't make things any harder for me!'

That seemed to rouse him a little, but when they got to the kitchen he lay on the floor and refused to move. Ben was breathing heavily and he was very cold.

Amy was putting a cushion under his head when Mrs Shaw appeared in her nightgown. Her glance swept over them both and she gave a little gasp. 'We've got to get those wet clothes off,' she said to Amy quietly. She disappeared and came back with blankets, which she put before the fire to warm.

Amy rubbed the icy hands and feet and Ben stirred in pain as the circulation started to come back. She sponged the blood from his face with warm water Together the women undressed him and wrapped the blankets round him. Amy felt shy, but it was

277

no time for prudery.

'Why was he out there in the dark for so long?' Mrs Shaw asked.

'Digging sheep out is heavy work, and slow. I found him by the water trough but I don't know how long he'd been there. When my dad was here, we always went out in twos in the snow. He reckoned it was safer...' Amy tailed off. She should have been out there with Ben, helping him, but for the baby.

'Benjamin needs more workers. More men to do the heavy work. I have thought for some time that you and he were doing too much, and in weather like this he needs help.' Mrs Shaw looked across at Amy. 'You must look after the baby, too, Amy. I don't expect you to do this kind of thing.'

The kettle was boiling and Mrs Shaw made a cup of hot, milky tea. She put her arm under Ben's head to raise him up a little. 'Here, drink this, my dear.'

With difficulty, Ben roused himself and took a few sips from the cup. 'You're a good aunt,' he mumbled, and went to sleep.

Amy knew that the snow had that effect; you were cold, you wanted to lie down and sleep and if nobody found you in time, you froze to death. It had happened to a lad she knew at school and her father had always warned her about it. But Ben was getting warmer, she had found him in time. Except that pneumonia and fevers could follow,

278

when you had been exposed to such wet and cold.

Eventually they helped Ben to his bed, with hot bricks at his feet and a heavy eiderdown over him as well as sheets and blankets. They left him to sleep. Amy peeped in at him once through the night and heard rough, uneven breathing, but he still slept.

The next morning, Tom Harland appeared on his pony and helped Amy with feeding the cows. Mrs Shaw prepared breakfast and when Amy came in from the yard she saw that the older woman was looking worried. 'Ben's rather weak,' she said. 'I'll try to get him to eat some porridge.'

The sun was shining on the snow and all the world was sparkling; robins hopped about the farm yard, picking up what they could. Out in the garden there were several moorland birds, feathers fluffed out against the cold, shyly looking for food. Amy went out to throw them some crumbs, her breath hanging in clouds on the frosty air. Through the cruel but beautiful winter, they had to be strong to survive, all of them: birds, animals, people. She clenched her fists, willing Ben to get better, but she knew that he was in danger.

Was she needlessly worrying? She wished she could be sure. But two winters ago, Amy's father had died after working all day in the cold and wet. If Ben got pneumonia...

He was younger than Jon Appleton, but not as used to the harsh conditions. The world would be bleak indeed if Ben died.

Back at the house, Mrs Shaw was taking action. 'We'll do everything in our power to help him,' she told Amy fiercely. 'Just as I thought he was getting back to normal, this happens!' She bustled out into the yard to ask Tom to fetch Dr Andrews and then set about making home remedies.

Ben had taken a little porridge, but not much and was lying with his eyes closed, coughing from time to time. Directed by his aunt, Amy dipped a piece of flannel in boiling water, sprinkled it with turpentine and then laid it on Ben's chest. He shook his head and smiled weakly, but said nothing. When she straightened up, he caught her fingers in his and she felt how hot he was. 'Don't worry about me, little Amy,' he whispered hoarsely. 'Just look after that baby.'

Amy did worry, more so as Ben slowly worsened. By the time the doctor arrived he was burning and delirious, muttering about people and things from the past. He called out the name Sylvia several times. Amy sponged his face and hands with cold water and put salve on the cuts.

'If only we had some drug to lower temperature!' Dr Andrews said. There was little he could actually do. 'Bring in some ice from the yard, we might cool him down that way.'

He lowered his voice. 'The high temperature is what kills, the body can't stand it.'

Mrs Shaw and Amy sat with Ben in turn, trying to cool him with icy water. The cloths they applied to his burning skin were soon hot again. His dark hair lay lankly on his brow and Amy moved it away with gentle hands. From time to time she brought in a bucket full of snow and a succession of cloths were kept cold.

Late in the evening he fell into a light sleep and Amy stayed beside him, changing the cloths at intervals, watching and thinking. Face the worst, she told herself, it's happened before. If the worst happened and Ben died, the farm would pass to another tenant, possibly young Tom Harland. Mrs Shaw would go back to York and Amy herself would go to the bakery, where a job awaited her. Molly and Sara were building up the business and needed her help, they said. Life would go on, if they lost Ben. But a light would go out. Sitting there watching the haggard dark face with its growth of stubble, Amy realized that she loved this man. But he loved Sylvia ... whoever she had been.

Was it a reaction, after losing Patrick, just pent-up emotion? Was she just grateful for his kindness, surprising as it had been after their unpromising start? Ben would have been kind to anyone who worked for him. Amy sat quietly through the long night, feel-

281

ing and thinking. Gradually she realized that Ben was dear to her as no other person had been; the months of working together had made them friends and companions. A deep love had quietly developed and she hadn't known it was there, hidden among the gruff words.

Ben woke and she gave him a drink of water. His smile was so sweet as she took back the glass that Amy felt like swooning. She brushed his cheek gently, but he drew her down to him and kissed her on the mouth. 'Strange how life turns out,' he said quietly. 'You are here, and now I have to leave.'

Amy tried not to let him see the fear on her face. He must think she was Sylvia, the woman whose name he had been calling. 'Don't talk of leaving, I won't let you. You're staying right here with us...' But he had drifted off again into his own world.

For two days Ben hovered on the edge of delirium. Tom Harland took on the farm chores and Amy did most of the nursing. Then one morning of cold and bitter rain he woke and he was lucid. 'How about breakfast?' he asked, tried to sit up and fell back again. Amy panicked and ran to him... Was this a sudden rally before the end, as sometimes happened? Oh Ben, are you slipping away from us? She put her arms round him and raised him up with pillows at his back, and found he was laughing weakly. 'Don't be alarmed. It is my professional opinion that the patient will survive,' he said. Ben had turned the corner, but he was very weak.

Mrs Shaw had made some strong beef tea, simmering beef for hours, and she gave him a small cup of the tea. This was followed an hour later with lemon and honey. She talked of possets and caudles, reminding Amy of Gran. The patient took everything without complaint, which was not like him.

In a day or two Ben was able to take a bath and shave. 'I feel more human now,' he said, sitting by the fire in an enormous shawl and grinning over at Amy. 'I can't think why you took so much care of me, Amy. I know I'm a misery.'

It was such a relief to realize that Ben would survive. 'It's my job, sir. I do the same with the cows and calves,' she reminded him flatly. 'In fact, a dose of linseed might be the very thing for your cough.' She often gave linseed to the calves in the winter, to put a shine on their coats. Keep to the everyday; it was dangerous to think about feelings.

TWENTY

'I suppose women shouldn't talk to men about ... having babies. Gran would say it's not ladylike. But you are a doctor, Ben, so...' Amy tailed off in embarrassment. 'I didn't have brothers or sisters, so I don't know much at all about it. Only, I'll be glad when it's over!' She was clearing away the breakfast dishes while Mrs Shaw was upstairs. This baby weighed heavily on her mind as well as her body.

Ben looked up from the newspaper he was reading. 'I've told you what I used to say to my patients; just get plenty of good food, sleep, fresh air and exercise and leave the rest to nature. Pregnancy isn't an illness, although some of them wanted it treating as such.'

'Well, I've helped a lot of calves and lambs into the world, but humans are different, I think. A great many women die, I know of a few myself. It must be more dangerous for humans.' Amy went to take the teapot but Ben grabbed it and poured himself another cup of tea.

'Don't worry too much, Amy. From what I learned when I was at York, things are improving. Miss Nightingale was nursing sol-

284

diers of course, but her influence has spread and she insists on absolute cleanliness for all forms of nursing. The fever that follows an infection is one of the major causes of death after childbirth. So these days, enlightened people scrub to keep away the germs.'

Amy took the plates into the scullery and piled them in the sink. When she came back Ben was gazing into the fire. 'Just like we had to scrub to keep away the cattle plague?'

'The same principle. If germs can get in, they will – I believe some doctors have actually caused the fever by carrying germs from one patient to another.' Ben folded the newspaper and stood up. 'The other cause of trouble for women, apart from the very poor who can't afford to eat properly, is lack of exercise. They are flabby and weak, you see, often too fat. Some of my patients had servants to do their housework and they didn't move enough. Once they were pregnant, they lay on a sofa all day. And then, the fashionable ones were trapped in those hideous, huge dresses, laced and corseted – you've no idea how unhealthy it can be.' The thin face broke into a grin as he looked over at his helper. 'There's no danger of any of that for you, Amy. You're always on the move and your idea of a rest is to go for a long walk.'

'Thank you, doctor.' Amy dropped a shallow curtsy. Going for walks had got her into trouble with Gran, but Ben approved of it. She looked at him carefully. 'Do you miss doctoring at all?'

Ben thought for a moment. 'At first I was glad to get away from it ... there was trouble, you see. I was blamed for someone's death and it affected me very much. Coming here – well, it's a different world and we're beginning to make a success of the farm. You've helped me, lass, made me laugh when I needed it. But sometimes lately I've thought that it's a waste of all that training, to give up medicine entirely.'

'You won't go back to York, will you?' This was alarming. If he went back to doctoring, their world would disappear.

'Not to York. Dr Andrews asked me the other day if I'd act as locum in Masham when he goes on holiday. That would be good, to keep my hand in. As Katherine says, we need more help on the farm and if we employ a man, I'll be able to help Dr Andrews from time to time. The fellow hasn't had a day off for years.' Ben put on his boots and went out.

It was good to hear that Ben thought she was healthy, but there were other things to worry about, although she must try not to be a constant worrier like Gran, always looking on the black side. Amy washed the dishes thoughtfully, facing her fears. The snow had gone, but by the following week

286

when the baby was due, it could come back again. Deep snow would cut them off from Masham, from Dr Andrews. And then, what if the baby was sick, or ... died?

Mrs Shaw came in, they talked about the day's meals and gradually Amy's fears subsided. 'I'm taking the trap to Masham, you could come with me and go to see your mother,' Mrs Shaw offered. She, too was treating Amy as if she were normal.

By this time, getting her bulk into and out of the high trap was a struggle, but it was worth the effort. Wrapped up warmly against the cold, Amy enjoyed the ride, looking out as they went for signs of spring. She saw snowdrops in gardens and one or two early lambs in sheltered fields; spring would soon be on the way and their own ewes, what was left of them, would be lambing soon. But after a while the motion of the trap made her feel uneasy, and she wondered whether she should have stayed at the farm.

They called at the bakery and Mrs Shaw bought some bread. 'Your Ma's just gone home,' Sara said, so Mrs Shaw dropped Amy at the cottage – which meant that she would have to face Gran. She walked up the little path to the front door and wondered whether she would ever have to live there again.

At that moment the pains started and Amy got into the house quickly and sat down, panting. The baby was on its way; this was the moment she'd dreaded. 'I think it's here,' she said.

Molly looked flustered, but Gran knew what to do. 'Put kettle on, we'll need plenty of hot water. We'll get everything ready and then your mother can go for the doctor. Now lass, there's nowt to be afraid of. Babies happen every day.' This was a new Gran, full of purpose. 'You're in best place here, right among your own folks. We'll look after you.' She shook her head. 'There's many a lass goes for a ride in a trap to persuade baby to come.'

Afterwards, Amy found it hard to remember what happened. Mrs Shaw had gone home without her, Amy had been settled in the best bedroom, towels and cloths had been brought and water was boiling. She looked round at the spotless room; Ben would approve, she thought, there's no room for germs here. Then there was a haze of pain for several hours, Dr Andrews was there ... Gran was helping him.

Another interval, and Molly was washing a crying little scrap of humanity that looked more like a monkey than a baby, and at last, she held her son in her arms. He looked much more normal now, Patrick's son, dressed in baby clothes that Molly had made for him. It was over, the baby was alive and well, he had all his little fingers and toes ...

and a good appetite for milk.

It was best left to nature, after all, Amy thought as she looked down at the little head with its downy fair hair, more like hers than Patrick's. Her body had responded, she'd been able to give birth with no complications. Ben had been right.

'Well done, my dear,' the doctor said before he left. 'Your grandmother will give you all the advice you need.' Was he being sarcastic? Evidently not. 'She's a very capable woman.'

Gran came in with a cup of tea for the new mother. 'Here, get this down you and I've got some soup for you later,' she said briskly. 'Think on, lass, you'll have to do as I tell you for a while!' But the eyes were soft and the smile was a real one; Gran had changed somehow. 'You'll maybe not know, but I was a midwife once, a long time ago.'

Amy looked up, wide eyed. 'I suppose I must have known, but I'd forgotten.' She'd never thought of Gran as a young woman, or even as a person with a point of view.

'Eh, but it's grand to have a bairn in the house again! I always hoped your mother would have more than one, but it was not to be.' Gran put a gentle finger under the baby's chin. 'He's like you, Amy – that fair look he has. What will you call him?'

Amy put down her cup and lay back; she wanted to sleep. 'I'd like to call him Jona-

289

than, after my father. Jonathan Seaton ... it sounds quite well.' How wonderful, to have a real Granny after all these years! 'Thank you Gran, for everything. It's good to be here.'

Gran paused on her way to the door. 'You just do as I tell you, lass, and you and me will get on well. I was proud of you today, you got on with the job and had that bairn with no fuss at all.' She hesitated. 'You've turned out better than I thought.' How long had it been since Gran had said anything like that?

Molly was very happy. 'Your Gran's that pleased with you, I can't believe it!'

Late in the evening Ben called in for only a few minutes. 'Just checking up,' he said and he examined the baby minutely. 'He'll grow up to be a good looking lad,' was the verdict. 'And you, Amy...?' He took her hand gently and she clung to him. 'Thank you for coming to see us, Ben.'

Little Jonathan Seaton turned out to be a model baby, eating and sleeping just when he should. Amy studied him for hours, trying to trace Patrick's likeness in the baby face. How Patrick would have loved him! She knew instinctively that he would have wanted several children. Perhaps she should let his mother know that she had a grandson. She would write to her. 'Invite the poor woman to come to see him,' Molly sug-

290

gested. It had been agreed that Amy would stay at home for a few weeks, after which the new cottage at Banks Farm would be ready for her.

Ben came to collect Amy and the baby three weeks later. 'You'll have had enough coddling by now,' he said with a grin. 'Back to reality for you, my girl.' The little house was waiting for her, warmed by a log fire, freshly painted and furnished with some pieces that Gran had stored in the old workshop. 'But not too much hard work at first. I've got a man, Jim Healey, coming in every day to work on the farm.'

Patrick's mother arrived on a blustery spring day, driven by an elderly man who stayed outside with the horse. 'Sampson is my gardener,' she explained. 'He will not need any refreshment.' She sat uneasily on the edge of a chair, holding little Jonathan, who was blowing bubbles. Amy was sorry for her; she had lost her boy and life would not be the same for her since Patrick died. Ben had invited her into the parlour and Amy hoped that he wouldn't leave them alone together; it was hard to know what to say. But Amy was staggered by Mrs Seaton's suggestion. She came straight to the point.

'I am here today for a purpose. I have been thinking about the baby's future, and now I realize that it's my duty to look after Patrick's son,' she began. 'And so I will bring him to

Ripon as soon as he's weaned, and hire a nanny to look after him.'

'Take him away?' Amy gasped and thought she would faint. The woman wanted to take her baby. Ben was frowning and he put his hand protectively over Amy's; it calmed her.

'Yes, that is my plan.' Mrs Seaton handed the little boy back as he'd started to dribble over her coat.

Amy wiped his mouth and then held him to her. 'But – why? I'm his mother, I can look after him!' She looked fiercely over the top of Jonathan's head at this woman who was now the enemy.

'It is for the best. He will go to a good school and have all the benefits of a respectable household. He will be much better off, I'm sure you'll agree, than with a maidservant who has to work for a living, and on a tenanted farm, too.' Mrs Seaton was evidently weighing up their social position as she looked round the room. 'He would probably end up as a farm labourer, or the like.' She evidently thought that farming lay on the bottom of the social scale; Amy remembered that she'd tried to keep Patrick away from farms.

But ... Patrick would have wanted his child to have a farm upbringing, that was what he'd planned. He himself had got away from Ripon and his mother.

There was a horrified silence. Ben had his

dark, grim look. Seeing the shock on Amy's face, Mrs Seaton added, 'Of course it's natural that you will feel the parting at first. But you can visit him from time to time. And you will be much more free to go on with your life than if you were encumbered by a small child.' Here Jonathan gave a small gasp as though he too was shocked at the idea.

It was time to fight and the next few minutes would be crucial; they would decide the baby's future. What could she say? Was there any way they could take the child from her legally? 'No, I will not give up my son,' Amy said quietly. 'It may be hard, but I'll give him the best education I can, and my Gran will help to pay for it.' Good old Gran had promised to help Amy as much as she could with Jonathan's schooling. Gran was a changed woman and now – Amy could do no wrong – and Jonathan was the apple of her eye.

Mrs Seaton turned her beady eyes on Amy. 'But how can you be so selfish? The child will be living in poverty, in a low class of society! Not at all the thing for a Seaton. Most of the Seatons are clergymen, you know and one of them has an estate in Northumberland.' The woman's pinched face was sour and Amy lost all sympathy for her.

Amy did know about the relations, because Patrick had told her. For Patrick's sake as well as for Jonathan's, she had to think of a good reason to keep him away from them. She had to say something that would keep the woman away for ever.

'But–' Amy began, and then she stopped. These people were more powerful than she was, they could take her baby away and there was nothing she could do – except hide, as Sara had done. She would have to go away if she wanted to keep him.

'So it's settled, then,' Mrs Seaton said, with a smug look.

Ben held up his hand. 'May I say a few words?'

Mrs Seaton turned her frosty gaze on the tenant farmer. Her eyes were blue like Patrick's, but cold, icy cold where his had been warm and humorous. 'What has it got to do with you, may I ask? I hardly think that you should have a say, Mr Yardley. I have come here to deal with Amy and to advise a young and ignorant girl to her advantage.'

'Leaving aside your disparaging remarks about our social standing, it has a lot to do with me, as it happens, ma'am. I have to tell you that Jonathan will be very well cared for at Banks Farm. He will be my stepson.' There was utter silence in the room.

Mrs Seaton's eyes were wide with horror. Amy looked at the floor. Ben was telling a story that would get her out of trouble.

Ben smiled and continued with his bomb-

294

shell. 'Amy is to be my wife. Amy and I will be married in a few months and I intend to bring up the child as my own. In case you are concerned about my low class origins, I am a professional man, a doctor and I will encourage Jonathan to study medicine, or any other profession he chooses. Including, if he so wishes, the Church!' He took Amy's hand protectively again and silenced her with a look 'My fiancée and I will welcome you at any time to visit Jonathan, but we will keep him here with us.'

It was embarrassing, but Amy blushed and kept quiet. Ben knew what he was doing and he was a good actor, most convincing. The deception worked; Mrs Seaton changed immediately. She stood up and dusted down her coat as though it had been dirtied by sitting in their chair, looking more disgusted than ever.

'It is surprising that Amy is to marry again so soon. It shocks me, I must say, to find such a lack of decency in my grandson's mother. In fact, the question arises as to whether the child is Patrick's, or … not.' She raised her eyebrows. 'I had no idea that Amy had another … suitor. Perhaps it is for the best that I leave him here with you, if there is the least doubt about his paternity.' She dusted her gloved hands together in a symbol of dismissal.

'There is no doubt at all,' Ben said through

clenched teeth. He stood up and opened the door and Mrs Seaton sailed out without another word.

Amy stood up shakily. The interview was over and the danger retreated; she let out her breath slowly in a long sigh. How dare the woman...? But it was over. What she thought didn't matter, and Jonathan had been saved from her clutches. 'Oh dear Ben, there goes your reputation,' she said.

'Rubbish!' said the grumpy farmer irritably.

Mrs Seaton's vehicle creaked off down the drive with her gardener holding the reins and the horse wandering erratically. They watched it go and then Amy turned to Ben with the baby in her arms. He chuckled and smiled at the farmer as though he knew what had happened and Ben gradually seemed to relax. Jonathan seemed to have his father's happy temperament, thank goodness. 'I just don't know how to thank you, Ben. I'll never forget your saving him from that woman! But I'm sorry you had to tell lies to do it.'

Ben's dark eyes looked into Amy's. 'I told no lies, Amy. At least, I hope not. I know it was the wrong way to do it, but – it had the desired effect. Will you marry me, my little Miss Know-all? Then you can always tell me what to do.'

Amy was speechless with shock.

'Let's go for a walk.' Ben steered her away from the house, down the track to the river and carried Jonathan himself. Was he just being very kind? It was like him to consider her needs before his own. But what about Sylvia, the woman he had called for when he was ill?

'You don't have to – to marry me, just because you said that,' Amy ventured.

The wind had dropped and it was a perfect spring day. May blossom showered them from the hedges and the grassy fields were green with the first grass. I've been here a year, and what a year it has been, she thought. 'You don't have to feel responsible for me,' Amy managed after a while.

'Why ever not? You seem to feel that you have to look after me!' Ben was laughing at her.

When they got to the river bank she sat on an old seat and looked into the flowing water. So much had happened, so much water had flowed on down to the sea in the last few months. Last spring she had been in love with Patrick, and now... 'It's like you to be kind, Ben, but think of your own future.'

'That's what we'll do.' Ben sat down beside her and drew Amy with Jonathan into his arms. 'I think of our future, believe me. I'm a bit older than you, but it doesn't matter, does it? Perhaps I should admit that I love you, Amy, that has something to do with it. I realized that I loved you the day–'

'Not the day I started work here!' Amy felt

like laughing hysterically. The world was turning upside down ... again.

'Certainly not, you were most annoying. You were nearly always right! No, it was the day I marched you down the aisle to marry Patrick. All I could do was to wish you all the good fortune in the world, the pair of you. I'd have prayed for you if I'd been godly. There in the church I decided to help you both as much as I could. And then – Patrick died. I mourned the lad with you... I was fond of him too. And then there was the baby. Given time, I thought you might agree to marry me – maybe next year. But when that woman intervened, I spoke on impulse, to save the situation from descending into a quarrel. I realized it might surprise you ... did it?' Ben's arms tightened round her and Amy felt a surge of joy.

'I've never been so shocked in my life. Grumpy old Ben Yardley offering to marry me! But I thought it was just to send her away.'

'And ... is it too soon for you?' Ben's voice was almost a whisper. He was evidently wondering whether she would feel disloyal to Patrick.

Amy told him about seeing the kingfisher on the river. 'Patrick was like that, a flash of gold and he was gone. I loved him for such a short time ... and now, we have Jonathan ... and ourselves. We have to think of the future.'

She put a hand up to his face. 'But what about you, Ben? When you were ill, you called out for someone named Sylvia.'

Ben looked surprised. 'Did I? A name from long ago. Sylvia was going to marry me, but didn't fancy farming. And I'm so glad!' His smile was warming. His deep voice dropped as he said, 'We can wait a while, if you'd rather not make up your mind now. I've no right to expect you to love me. You keep reminding me how grumpy I can be, but I'm much worse when you are not there!'

Amy decided not to keep him waiting. 'I found out that I couldn't live without you when you were ill, during the snow. I just wanted to look after you for ever. That's why I was worried that you might go back to York. I love you, Ben, but are you sure you want to take on a widow with a child?'

'Quite sure.' Ben kissed her and no more was said for a while. Then he went on, 'I won't go back to the old life, but we will set off on a new one together. We could buy more land, employ staff so we could be managers. You'd enjoy that.'

'Jonathan might want to be a farmer,' Amy murmured. And the baby waved his fists as though he agreed.

The publishers hope that this book has given you enjoyable reading. Large Print Books are especially designed to be as easy to see and hold as possible. If you wish a complete list of our books please ask at your local library or write directly to:

Magna Large Print Books
Magna House, Long Preston,
Skipton, North Yorkshire.
BD23 4ND

This Large Print Book, for people
who cannot read normal print,
is published under the auspices of

THE ULVERSCROFT FOUNDATION